P9-DNY-568

"YOU DON'T NEED THE PISTOL, LONGARM," LEOTA WHISPERED.

"If you don't want me to visit you, I'll go back to my own bed..."

Longarm took her in his arms as their kiss began, and was surprised to find that she was naked. He rubbed his calloused hands down her sides to the swell of her hips, her skin smooth and yielding to his firm caress...

TABOR EVANS

ON THE
PAINTED DESERT

A JOVE BOOK

LONGARM ON THE PAINTED DESERT

A Jove Book/published by arrangement with
the author

PRINTING HISTORY
Jove edition/September 1984

All rights reserved.
Copyright © 1984 by Jove Publications, Inc.
This book may not be reproduced in whole or in part,
by mimeograph or any other means, without permission.
For information address: The Berkley Publishing Group,
200 Madison Avenue, New York, N.Y. 10016.

ISBN: 0-515-06270-7

Jove books are published by The Berkley Publishing Group,
200 Madison Avenue, New York, N.Y. 10016. The words
"A JOVE BOOK" and the "J" with sunburst are trademarks
belonging to Jove Publications, Inc.

PRINTED IN THE UNITED STATES OF AMERICA

Chapter 1

"Now, you just stand real still, Packer," Longarm said. "I don't want to have to shoot you."

"I don't know who you are, mister," the man holding the shotgun replied. "But my name ain't Packer, and I ain't got any hankering to shoot you either. So why don't you just lower that Colt you got aimed at me."

"Not so fast, Packer," Longarm told him. "I'm a deputy U. S. marshal. We got a tip downtown that you were hiding out here, and I'm calling on you now to surrender peaceful."

Except for the emphasis given his words by the blue-steel Colt revolver in his hand, Longarm might have been commenting on the weather. He did not raise his voice, but kept it casually conversational.

Holding the Colt rock-steady, Longarm kept its muzzle trained on the man who stood facing him on the opposite side of the room, a bare wooden table between them. He hadn't gotten a clear look at the man's face, except to note that it was thin and full-bearded. The other stood with his back to the low-turned kerosene lamp that was held in a bracket high on the wall, and his face and torso were in deep black shadows.

Longarm paid no attention to the twin muzzles of the double-barrelled shotgun in the man's hands, though his keen eyes and quick mind were noting the gun's details. He could tell it was an old weapon, for the faint light that trickled from the wall lamp outlined every slight irregularity in the gun's Damascus barrels. Longarm assumed it had side-hammers, perhaps converted from caps to factory-loaded shells, but that did not make the shotgun any less deadly. Its muzzles were like wicked little black mouths, yawning menacingly only a yard or so away from Longarm's gunmetal-blue eyes, but the deputy continued to behave as though the menacing weapon did not exist.

1

"Damned if you don't act like you're the only one that's got a gun," the man said, frowning. "You ever see what a load of number three buck out of a twelve-gauge double does to a man's head at this range?"

"I've seen my share of men shot," Longarm replied coolly. There was a shrug in his voice, as though the question held no real interest for him. In spite of his easy manner and casual words, Longarm's mind was busy calculating his chances, playing for the moment when the attention of the man holding the shotgun would waver and give him the split second of time he needed.

Longarm's survey of the room in which he stood facing his adversary gave him little encouragement. It was the kitchen of a small frame house on the southwest side of Denver. Longarm and Henry, the little pink-cheeked clerk, had been the only ones left in the U. S. Marshal's office just before closing time when the excited informant rushed in and told of spotting the long-wanted Alfred Packer in a downtown saloon, and following the fugitive to this house.

By the time Longarm had questioned the informant thoroughly and had made up his mind that the tip wasn't just a figment of the tipster's imagination, darkness had fallen. Longarm had found the house without any trouble after he'd done a bit of hiking around the sparsely settled neighborhood from the end of the horsecar line that had been built from downtown to the new suburb. The house stood a bit apart from the other dwellings in the newly settled area, and had the earmarks of the kind of location a fugitive would choose.

Moving with practiced silence, Longarm had gone around the house. He'd found all the windows shuttered, their shades drawn. The back door, outlined by a thin line of lamplight, had drawn his attention. Moving as stealthily as an Indian in moccasins, Longarm had gone up the two steps to the tiny back porch and tried the doorknob.

It had opened with only the slightest squeak of protest. He'd pushed it open a crack, enough to peer through and see a kitchen range on one side of the room, a square table in its center, a kerosene lamp turned low in a bracket on the wall opposite the door, and a head-high cabinet in the corner.

Drawing his Colt, Longarm had swung the door wide. He'd stepped into the kitchen just as a door that had been hidden by the cabinet opened and the shotgun-carrying man emerged. The

2

two had seen each other at almost the same instant, and the Mexican standoff in which they were now locked had been the result.

Longarm said, "Now listen to me, Packer. You're in a game you can't win. If you—"

"Hold on!" the man interrupted. "I told you before, my name ain't Packer!"

"Well, now, I wouldn't expect you to admit it all that easy, Packer," Longarm said soothingly. "You've got away with dodging the law for five or six years, now, so I guess you figure you can go on dodging the rest of your life."

"I wish you'd quit calling me Packer," the man insisted.

"Makes you nervous, does it?" Longarm smiled. The smile did not extend to his eyes. He kept them fixed on the shotgun muzzle, which did not waver by a fraction of an inch.

"If we're talking about the same Packer, it does."

"Let's just stop this beating around the bush," Longarm suggested. "You know damned well which Packer I mean, because you're him. Alfred Packer. Some folks call him the Man Eater."

"I figured that's who you meant," the shotgun wielder said. "Oh, I've heard about him. Who hasn't, here in Colorado? But I'll give you a bit of gospel truth, mister. I never ate a bite of human flesh in my life. Damn it, just the *idea* of it turns my stomach!"

"I'd expect you to say that, Packer." Longarm continued to carry out his idea, playing for time. "Was I in your boots, I'd deny it, too. The thing that sticks in my craw is that you sure know an awful lot about what Packer done, if you ain't him."

"Damn it! There's not anybody in the country who don't know about the Man Eater! He killed six men who got snowbound with him on a prospecting trip up in the San Juan Mountains back in seventy-five or seventy-six. Killed 'em and ate most of two of 'em, before a thaw come along and somebody found him with what was left of the bodies."

Longarm nodded slowly. "Yep. That's the way it happened, all right. I guess you know the rest of the story, too?"

"Sure! The sheriff down in Ouray County arrested Packer, but he got away. And nobody's seen hide nor hair of him since."

"Until right now, that is," Longarm said. "And it was more luck than anything else that somebody saw you downtown in Denver today and followed you out here to your hideout. After

3

that, they tipped us off to where we could find you."

"Then they made a mistake."

"Like I said a minute ago, I wouldn't expect you'd admit to being Packer," Longarm went on quietly. "But you got to agree you sure fit his description. You're tall and skinny, thin-faced, high cheeks, dark eyes. And you got that full set of long black whiskers. Was I to see you on the street, I wouldn't have a bit of trouble picking you out from that description, even if I only read it on a wanted flyer."

"How in hell does anybody know what Packer's got hisself up to look like now?" the shotgun holder challenged. "If I was really Alfred Packer, I'd've shaved off my beard a long time ago and dyed my hair red or blonded it and stuffed my gut till I put on a load of fat."

"Sounds like you know a lot of answers. Now, I'll admit I got a suspicious mind," Longarm said. "Being a law officer, I hear a lot of stories, and some of 'em are wilder than the maybe I just put up to you."

"What're you driving at?" the man asked, frowning. "If you're trying to tell me something, it got lost in all the words you threw at me."

"Oh, I don't mind explaining," Longarm said, still playing for time. "What I was getting at, the way you rattled off what you'd've done if you was in Packer's place sorta makes me figure you just might've done it at one time or other."

"Now, that's just damn foolishness!"

"Is it? A man that ain't afraid of something don't come in carrying a gun the way you did. Looks to me like you was sorta expecting trouble."

"There's been a lot of houses broken into lately in this part of Denver. It's out so far from town, and there ain't enough policemen out here—"

Longarm broke in, "Now, that makes it a pretty good neighborhood for a man to keep from being noticed, don't it? A man that's wanted by the law'd be likely to pick out a place just like this one, I've found."

"I live out here because it's cheap," the man said curtly.

"Cheap and private, too," Longarm said thoughtfully. He waited, and when the other man made no comment, went on, "Now, let me do a little maybeing, sorta clear the air. Let's suppose you're Alfred Packer—"

"Which I'm not!" the other snapped.

4

"Never mind that. I'm just supposing right now," Longarm told him. "We'll put it the other way around if it'll make you feel any better. Let's suppose you really *ain't* Packer, but here I come, a U. S. marshal, and say you are. Now, the easiest way you can prove you ain't is to put that scattergun down and go to the office with me, quiet and peaceful. Because if you ain't Alfred Packer, I'll see you get every chance in the world to prove you ain't, and to prove who you really are."

For several moments the man stood silent, though he did not allow the shotgun's muzzle to waver or take his eyes off Longarm. At last he shook his head.

"I don't like your maybe a damn bit, Marshal," he said. "I've got a hunch that if word got out around Denver that you had Alfred Packer, the Man Eater, in your office, there'd be a lynch mob get together before you could snap your fingers. I don't like the idea of getting hauled up on the closest lamppost by a rope around my neck."

"I'd guarantee to have enough men from our office and from the Denver police to keep a mob from getting to you," Longarm promised. "And I'll see you get a fair trial when your case comes to court."

"Alfred Packer couldn't get a fair trial anyplace in Colorado, Marshal. You know that."

"I guess I'd have to agree with you," Longarm said. "But there's such a thing as moving a trial to another state. My chief could get your case switched to someplace else."

Once more the man shook his head. "You know, Marshal, it don't matter a bit to a man whether he's strung up by a mob or by a paid hangman. He's just as dead. Anyhow, even if somebody who'd done what Packer did was just put in prison for a term, I wouldn't give him much chance to serve his term out. The other convicts would take care of him before he'd been there very long."

"You seem to know a hell of a lot about what it's like in prison for a man who's never been locked up," Longarm observed.

"Only what I've heard, Marshal. But anyhow, I'm not Packer, so I don't plan to give up to you."

While he was speaking the man raised the butt of his shotgun to his shoulder and shifted his position slightly, turning his body so that the shouldered gun was still aimed at Longarm's head. Longarm did not move or speak. When the intensification

5

of his weapon's threat brought no reaction, he spoke again.

"I don't see we've got much more to talk about, Marshal," he said. His voice was harsh now. "Killing's not my way, but if you don't put your gun on the table and walk backward out that door, I'm going to blow your head to pieces."

Longarm's poker face did not betray what he'd seen when the man across the table changed his posture. He said quietly, "I don't think you're ready to shoot just yet, and I don't want to have to kill you."

"You got it twisted, Marshal. *You'll* be the one to die if I pull down on my trigger."

"If you'll take a look at your gun, you'll see you ain't cocked either barrel yet."

"You're lying," the man replied, his voice tightening and going up to a higher pitch. "Trying to trick me to look away from you. I won't take your bait, Marshal! Back off, now!"

"If you knew anything about me, you'd know I don't lie," Longarm said, still keeping his voice level. "Now, this Colt of mine is double-action, and I can trigger off two shots while you're raising your thumb to cock your shotgun."

"That old trick don't fool me a bit! Go on, now! Lay your gun on the table before I change my mind and kill you anyhow!"

"If you're ready to die, I guess we might as well settle it right now," Longarm said quietly.

"I don't plan to die." Without moving or taking his eyes off Longarm, he raised his voice and shouted, "Annie! Come on in, now, and let the marshal get a look at you!"

Longarm had not seen the door in the dark corner to his right, where it had been partly hidden by the kitchen range. The door opened and he flicked his eyes away from the man with the shotgun for a fraction of a second. He was not overjoyed by what he saw. A woman came through the door, preceded by the barrel of a rifle. Like the shotgun, the rifle was aimed directly at him and the range in the little room was so short that even a novice could not possibly miss the target he made.

"Sort of changes things a bit, don't it, Marshal?" the man asked.

"Not a whole lot. The only difference is that now I got to shoot twice instead of once," Longarm replied.

He forced into his voice a confidence that he no longer felt, and his confidence did not increase when the man holding the

6

shotgun glanced down and exclaimed with surprise.

"I'll be damned! You weren't lying or bluffing, were you, Marshal?"

"If you knew me a little better, Packer, you'd know I don't lie or bluff."

"I can't believe I really didn't have this old scattergun cocked," the man said, half to himself, half to Longarm. "Well, thanks for warning me. Now, just lay your Colt down on the table real careful, and there won't be any more need for us to worry which one of us is going to get killed."

Longarm saw that he had no choice but to obey. The man went on, "It's a good thing I had Annie standing ready. And I still don't like for you to call me Packer. I'm not lying about that, either."

As he laid his revolver on the table, Longarm swore inwardly at his conscience. It inconvenienced him at times such as this, but he still knew he'd never change, never be able to shoot down an unarmed man, or to kill in anything except a fair gunfight.

"I guess maybe you ain't been lying about not being Packer," Longarm said as he put his pistol down.

"You finally decided I wasn't, did you? What made you change your mind, Marshal?"

"If you was Packer, you'd've shot me in cold blood the minute I took my hand off my Colt," Longarm answered. "But whoever you are, I know you're on the wrong side of the law. I can tell that from the way you been talking."

"Who I am and which side of the law I'm on's neither here nor there," the man replied. "What's bothering me now is what I'm going to do with you while Annie and I get out of here."

"Don't kill him, Jase!" Annie said quickly. "You and me've got enough trouble the way it is. Don't go making things worse!"

"You know I'm not a killer, Annie," the man replied. "Just give me a minute to think. I'll figure out what to do."

"Tie him up and leave him here," she suggested. "That'll give us enough time to get down to the depot and catch a train someplace else. We've still got enough money left to pay our fares."

"Sure. That's what I'm thinking about. But we've got to tie him up and make sure he'll stay put long enough for us to get clear." He turned to Longarm and said, "I guess you carry handcuffs with you on the job?" Longarm had no choice but

7

to nod. Jase extended one hand and went on, "Give me your cuffs, then. If I fasten you up to that cast-iron stove over there, I don't imagine you'll get loose soon enough to stop me and Annie from getting away."

Longarm saw the first and perhaps the only chance he was going to have. He reached under his coat and took his handcuffs from his belt.

Holding one of the steel circlets, he extended his hand as though to pass them to Jase, and as the other man took one hand away from the shotgun stock to reach for the cuff that dangled below Longarm's hand, Longarm brought the cuffs up in a quick, circling swipe that knocked the barrel of Annie's rifle to one side.

Annie was taken by surprise. She triggered the rifle. The slug narrowly missed Jase and tore through the chinaware on the shelves across the room.

At the same time that Longarm whipped the cuffs through the air, he used his knee to send the table crashing into Jase.

In the instant when both Annie and Jase were off balance, Longarm slid his derringer from his vest pocket. By the time the pair had recovered from their surprise, he was covering them with the stubby little weapon.

"I got two shots here," Longarm said harshly. "And there's no way I can miss, you're so close. Now, let them guns drop and get your hands up! Looks like the two of you are going to see what Denver's jail looks like from the inside."

Chapter 2

With the swift moves acquired through long experience, Longarm snapped one cuff on Jase's right wrist, the other on Annie's left. Neither of them protested. They were still in a state of mild shock from the speed with which they'd been transformed from whip-hand holders to helpless prisoners.

Longarm let the pair stand in the center of the kitchen, staring down at the steel circles on their wrists, while he slid a long slim cigar from his vest pocket, flicked a match into flame with an ivory-hard thumbnail, and puffed the cheroot until its end glowed red. Then he took a good, close look at his prisoners—the first opportunity he'd had to do so.

Jase—Longarm supposed the man had more name than that, but didn't know what it was—stood an inch or so shorter than Longarm's six feet two and was quite thin. With his full beard he fitted the descriptions of Packer on the wanted flyers that had been circulating among lawmen for the past five years or more.

Annie was a dark blonde, her hair done up in a loose bun at the back of her neck. Her face was full and just missed being chubby. Her nose was pugged, uptilted, with broad nostrils, and her mouth was large in relationship to her short, rounded chin. She was no beauty, but if she smiled her face would be attractive. Longarm could tell little about her figure in the full-cut, rather shapeless dress she was wearing.

Jase looked up from the handcuffs after a moment and asked, "Now that you've got us, what're you going to do with us?"

"There's not but one thing I can do," Longarm replied. "I got to take you to jail."

"But we haven't done anything!" Annie protested. "At least, I haven't!"

"Not unless you count holding that rifle on me," Longarm reminded her.

9

"I did that because Jase made me do it!" she snapped.

"If you can make the judge believe that, he might not hold you," Longarm said. "At least, not any longer'n it'll take me to find out what your real name is. If you'll stop and think a minute, the only names I got for you two are Annie and Jase."

"My full name's Jason Chambers," the man volunteered. "You'll dig it up sooner or later, so I might as well tell you."

"How about you?" Longarm asked, turning to the woman.

"Annie Evans," she said, then, after a moment's hesitation, added, "I guess you've already figured out we're not married."

"I had a hunch that was the way of it. Anything else you feel like telling me?" When neither of them spoke, Longarm went on, "I got a pretty good idea you're wanted someplace, or you wouldn't've been trying to get away from me. Now, down at the U. S. marshal's office, we've got a great big stack of wanted flyers. It won't take me very long to find out all I need to know about you."

Chambers said, "Hell, you'll dig it up anyway, so I might as well come clean. I'm wanted for robbing a trading post about six months ago on the Flathead Reservation up in Montana. But I didn't hurt anybody or kill anybody."

"You won't find any of those wanted flyers on me," Annie said quickly. "I haven't done anything but go along with Jase."

"She's telling the truth, Marshal," Chambers said quickly. "Annie didn't even know I was running from the law until I had to leave Montana in a hurry."

"That's right." Annie nodded. "But I started thinking about leaving Jase a month ago, when we got so hard up for cash that he started talking about pulling another robbery so we'd have money to move."

"I always talked her into staying, though," Jason said. "And I talked her into backing me up tonight when I spotted you prowling around outside. It wasn't any of it her idea."

"Well, that's a pretty good start," Longarm told them. "As long as neither one of you's lying to me. But, for all I know, you two could be wanted all the way from Canada to Mexico. That's the first thing I'll have to make sure of."

"You mean you don't believe us?" Chambers asked.

"Would you, if you was me?"

Slowly, Chambers shook his head. "No, I guess not. But, remember, you didn't believe me when I told you I wasn't

Packer. I've got a lot less reason for lying to you now than I had then."

"If you've both come clean, I don't imagine the judge will be real hard on either one of you," Longarm said thoughtfully. "But he's the one you'll have to convince, not me."

"Where are you going to find a judge at this time of night?" Chambers frowned. "They all close up court about the middle of the afternoon."

"They do that," Longarm agreed. "Except I can't put you in jail without a judge orders it, so here in Denver we got a deal set up to take new prisoners to a judge's house for him to sign a jail commitment order. That keeps you in jail up to a month, while we find out where all you're wanted."

"You sure don't give a fellow much leeway around here," the prisoner grumbled.

"Don't worry, it's all straight and legal," Longarm assured him. "Come on, now. The sooner we go, the quicker we'll get things settled."

Longarm's prediction as to the judge's reaction proved to be accurate. He ordered Jason Chambers to jail until a reply could be received from the authorities in Montana. After listening to Annie's story and questioning Longarm about her actions in helping Chambers, the judge told her she was free to go.

"But where can I go?" she asked Longarm when he'd delivered Chambers to jail and they were in the hackney cab he'd hired to take her back to the house where she and Chambers had lived. "The house rent's due in a week, and I haven't got the money to pay to stay there another month."

"Ain't you got some kinfolks somewhere that you can stay with till you figure out what to do?" he asked.

Annie shook her head. "No. Oh, sure, I've got a few aunts and uncles and cousins someplace back in Ohio, but I wouldn't know how to go about finding them."

"How about your parents?"

"They're both dead. They got killed when the wagon turned over after the team run away while we were moving out West."

"What were you doing when you ran into that Jason fellow?"

"I was a housemaid in a hotel up in Billings."

"Well, now, there's plenty of hotels here in Denver," Long-arm told her. "It just happens that I got a few friends in the

11

hotel business. So maybe I can give you a hand finding a job."

"Would you, Marshal Long? I'd surely appreciate it."

"I'll see what I can do in the morning," Longarm promised as the hackman reined up his nag in front of the dark house. "Suppose you come into town later tomorrow—about five o'clock. That's the time I get off. I'll be at the U. S. marshal's office in the federal building."

For a moment Annie said nothing, but sat staring at the dark house. Then she said, "Marshal Long, would it put you out too much if I asked you to come in with me? I . . . well, I'm sort of nervous, going into the house by myself."

"Why, there's nothing inside there that'll bother you."

"I know that, but I'm still nervous. You wouldn't have to stay but a minute, just until I get some lamps lighted up. And maybe you'd look around the place to see that nobody's come in while we was away."

"Well, I don't see it'd hurt me none to oblige you," Longarm said after a moment's thought. "Come on. I'll get your lamps lit up and see you're settled in, then I'll go on back to town."

After lighting the lamps in the kitchen and sitting room of the little house, Longarm took the precaution of unloading the rifle and shotgun and dropping their ammunition into his coat pocket. Then, while Annie cleaned up the china that had fallen to the floor and broken when her wild shot hit the shelves, he moved the table and chairs back to their proper places. The job took only a few minutes, and when the room was back in its original condition Longarm dusted off his coat sleeves and picked up his hat from the chair where he'd placed it.

"I'll be getting on back to town now," he told Annie. "I won't forget to ask around about a job for you, like I promised to do. Unless you've changed your mind and want to move on."

"I'll need more money than I've got now before I can move," she said. "And almost any kind of job sure would look good to me right now." Then, after a moment's hesitation, she added, "But you don't have to run off, do you, Marshal Long? There's a nice big piece of round steak and plenty of potatoes in the pantry, more than enough for the two of us."

"You mean you'd cook supper for me, after I've arrested you and put your . . . well, put Jason Chambers in jail?"

"Sure I would. I'd be right glad to. You've been as nice to

me as you could be, the way things are, Marshal Long. Will you stay and eat with me?"

"It takes more willpower than I got to turn down steak and potatoes," Longarm smiled. "Besides, I haven't had any more supper than you have."

"Then take off your coat, Marshal, and get comfortable."

"I don't mind if I do. But if we're going to have supper together, you might as well quit calling me Marshal."

"That's all I know to call you. What's your first name?"

"I don't answer to it so good, but I got a sorta nickname my friends use. It's Longarm."

"Well, if we're having a meal together, I guess we're going to be friends, Longarm. Now, you can sit down in the easy chair in the parlor and stretch your legs out and smoke a cigar, or you can sit here in the kitchen and keep me company while I cook," Annie said. "It'll only take a few minutes for me to get supper on the table."

"It ain't often I get a chance to set in a kitchen," Longarm told her. "I'll just settle in and watch, if it's all the same to you."

While Longarm leaned back in one of the kitchen chairs and puffed a cheroot, Annie bustled about, peeling potatoes, pounding the steak and dredging it in flour, then setting the table while the food sizzled on the coal-oil burner of the kitchen range. She chattered away as she worked, content for Longarm to answer her with an occasional word or nod. When everything was ready and all that remained was for them to wait until the steak finished cooking, she sat down across the table from Longarm.

"It's nice to have a man to talk to while I fix supper," she said. "I'm real glad you could stay."

"It ain't often I get a home-cooked meal, Annie. That steak smells real good, now it's started sizzling."

"I'm a pretty good cook, Longarm, if I do say so myself."

"And I'm getting hungrier by the minute."

They talked little during supper. Longarm did full justice to the meal, and when he pushed his chair away, Annie refilled his coffee cup and sat down again.

"This is nice," she said. "Jase never did like to keep me company in the kitchen when he was here."

"Sounds to me like he was just sorta leaning on you to do

for him," Longarm suggested.

"Oh, me and him haven't hit it off real good for quite a while. I guess both of us have just been waiting for something to happen that'd give us a reason to go our own way."

"And you figure this is a good time to do so?"

"I know it is. Even if Jase don't go to jail, we won't be travelling together any more."

"Have you and him talked about splitting up before? Because I didn't notice you saying anything about it to him tonight."

"We didn't have to talk, Longarm. A couple that's been going together as long as me and Jase, we know when it's time to go our own ways. Besides, Jase will likely go to jail, won't he, for robbing that place up in Montana?"

"I'd imagine he'll be put away for a year or two," Longarm agreed. "But, look here, Annie, if you're figuring on me and you taking up together—"

"No," Annie interrupted, "I know better than to count on anything like that. I'm not your style, and I don't suppose you'd be mine for very long. But being by myself again is going to take a little getting used to."

"I'd imagine you'll manage." Longarm stood up and reached for his hat. "Well, I do thank you for supper, Annie, but I got to be getting along if I want to catch the last horsecar back to town. If I miss it, it's a pretty good hike, and I'm too full for a long walk right now."

"You don't have to go, you know," Annie said.

Her voice was soft and pleading, and Longarm could read in her eyes that she meant her invitation. He waited for a moment before answering.

"You don't owe me nothing, Annie," he said. "It ain't that I don't appreciate being asked—"

Annie broke in, "I'm not trying to pay you for being decent to me, Longarm. And I'm not afraid to stay here by myself. But there's something about you that draws me to you. Please stay."

Longarm hesitated for only a moment, reading the plea in her eyes. "Well, if you really want me to . . ."

"I do. I'm not any simpering virgin, Longarm. I'm old enough and I've had enough experience to know what I want."

"Then I will."

Annie sighed and smiled at the same time. She took the

lamp off its wall bracket and blew it out. She'd lighted a lamp in the sitting room earlier, and its glow trickled through the half-open kitchen door. For a moment she and Longarm stood apart in the intimacy of the dusky glow. Then Annie pulled Longarm's head down and their lips met. Her lips were alive under his, writhing and drawing Longarm's tongue into her mouth. They held the kiss for a long while, and both were breathless when Annie finally pulled away.

"Come on to the bedroom," she whispered. "I don't want to waste time cleaning up the kitchen. I can do that tomorrow."

Longarm followed her through the door behind the stove and down a short narrow hall into the bedroom. Like the kitchen, it joined the sitting room, and was dimly lighted through a half-open door. Annie stopped inside the bedroom door and turned to face Longarm, her arms extended.

"Just thinking about being with you has got me all excited," she whispered as Longarm moved into her embrace. "I think I knew from the first minute I saw you that we were going to get to know each other this way."

Longarm bent to kiss her upraised lips. Annie shuddered as the kiss was prolonged and began rubbing her breasts against Longarm's chest. Her hand crept down to his crotch and she began exploring, squeezing and stroking. Longarm responded, and her hand tightened on him when she felt him beginning to swell. She broke their kiss and pulled away from him.

"I don't believe what I was feeling," she whispered. "Hurry, Longarm! I can't wait to get in bed with you!"

Longarm was as ready as Annie was to get to bed, but he took the precautions that he always followed when in strange surroundings. Pulling a chair up beside the bed, he hung his gunbelt on the back, where the butt of his Colt would be ready to his hand. He folded his vest carefully, placing it on the chair's seat with the pocket that contained the derringer uppermost.

He glanced at Annie and saw that she'd already taken off her dress and camisole and was untying the drawstring of her pantalettes. Her breasts were much fuller than Longarm had thought they'd be, and as Annie leaned forward to step out of the pantaletters they swayed invitingly, their dark buds drawing his eyes. He wasted no time levering out of his boots and shedding his underwear and trousers at the same time. Annie was standing in the little heap of clothing she'd discarded, watching him. When he turned to face her she gasped and stepped up beside him.

"I thought you'd be big, but I didn't expect anything like this," she said, closing her soft hand around his jutting shaft. "Stand still, Longarm, and let me ride you."

Longarm spread his feet apart and braced his legs while Annie clasped her hands behind his neck and levered herself off the floor. She wrapped her legs around his waist and dangled for a moment while Longarm guided himself into her. Then she locked her legs and pulled him to her with a gasping sigh.

"Oh!" she groaned. "I don't think I've ever been filled this way before! Don't move for a minute, Longarm! Just let me hang onto you until I get used to having you in me!"

"You do just what you want to," Longarm told her. "I sorta like the way this feels, too."

Annie clung motionless for a few moments, her head on Longarm's shoulder, her hands still locked around his neck. Then she stirred and began rotating her hips slowly while still suspended in midair. Gradually she began moving faster, and her body began to quiver. Then suddenly she gasped and threw her head back, her dark gold hair falling free to sway in midair as she tightened her legs around Longarm's waist and quivered for a few frantic moments. Finally she sighed and her taut muscles relaxed.

"Oh, my!" she whispered. "I wasn't expecting that! You don't know what you're doing to me, Longarm!"

Longarm did not reply. He spanned the distance between them and the bed with a single step and lowered Annie to the sheets, keeping intact the bond of flesh.

They lay quietly for a moment. Then Annie stirred. She began shifting her shoulders from side to side, and Longarm felt the tips of her budded rosettes rasping on the dark bronze curls that covered his broad chest.

Raising his head, Longarm peered through the dim light at Annie's face. Her lips were a bit apart, curled in a smile of satisfied pleasure. Her eyes were closed, her hair spread in rippling waves across the pillow on which her head rested. He lunged, burying himself deeper than he had been, and a small happy cry burst from Annie's lips.

"Oh, yes!" she whispered. "Do that again, Longarm! And again! Don't stop!"

16

Longarm began thrusting with slow, measured strokes. He was in no hurry. The long night stretched ahead. Annie's languor soon vanished. She stirred and brought her head up, seeking his lips. Longarm met her kiss without breaking the rhythm of his stroking, and soon Annie's tongue thrust into his mouth to twine with his. She rubbed her upper lip against the bristles of his moustache and her round chin against the bristles of his jaw, and a bubbling murmur of pleasure rose from her throat.

Short of breath, they broke their kiss by unspoken mutual consent. After she'd taken a few deep breaths, Annie whispered, "Oh, Longarm, this is wonderful! I don't know how long you can keep going, but I hope you won't stop soon!"

"Don't worry, Annie," Longarm assured her. "I ain't got no ideas about stopping. I'm enjoying it as much as you are."

Annie shifted under the weight of Longarm's body, spreading her legs wider, opening herself to take in his long slow strokes. She clamped her legs around him, forcing him to shorten the length of his lunges, but not their depth.

After a long while had passed Annie began to moan again, soft throaty cries lost in the dimness of the room. Beneath him, Longarm could feel her muscles growing taut once more. He began thrusting faster, his own climax building now. Annie's body began quivering rhythmically. Longarm stroked faster. He, too, was building to the point of no return.

Annie's soft moans flowed into sobs, and Longarm felt quick tremors rippling through her body. When she began to cry out and the tremors grew to uninterrupted writhings and her sobs shrilled through the night, Longarm speeded up, hurrying his own climax to meet hers.

They reached the peak together. Longarm's rasping breath softened and Annie's cries died away. They lay quietly, letting their trembling die as sensation faded away.

Annie was the first to speak. She whispered, "I guess I knew you were somebody special the first time I saw you, Longarm. But I didn't know *how* special. You're not going to leave me yet, are you?"

"Not for a long time, Annie. We'll sleep a while, but the night's not done with yet. It'll be a while before the horsecars start running agin, and I don't aim to go until they do."

Chapter 3

Chief Marshal Billy Vail looked across his paper-littered desk at Longarm and shook his head. "You mind telling me where you went after you left the barbershop?" he asked.

Longarm passed a callused palm over the long dark bristles on his chin before replying, "Now, don't worry, Billy. I won't let nobody get a close look at me till I've had a shave."

"Fine," the chief marshal said. "You'll have to tell the barber to shave you fast, though, because I want you to be on the southbound D&RG that pulls out in about two hours."

"I take it that you're sending me down to Pueblo or Trinidad on a new case?"

"It'll be a little bit more of a trip than that. The reason I want you on that morning train is to make connections with the westbound Santa Fe limited at Trinidad. There's an urgent case waiting for you in Flagstaff."

"Arizona Territory again, Billy?" Longarm grimaced. "Damn it, seems to me like I been spending an awful lot of time there lately. If I got to be there so much, maybe you better just put me out there permanent."

"If you really mean that, you can ask for a transfer," Vail said coldly.

Longarm saw he'd gone a bit too far. He said hastily, "Now you know I don't like the hot weather they got there, Billy."

"And you know I wouldn't be sending you to Arizona again if the Army and the Indian Bureau hadn't asked for you by name."

Longarm grunted. "That's the first time I ever got a feeling anybody back in Washington even knew my name. Well, what is it now, Billy? Another hoof-and-mouth panic, or has somebody been killing off the Indian chiefs again?"

"Neither one. But the way you handled both of those cases is why they asked for you," Vail replied. "The Army liked the way you managed to get that British professor out of trouble and avoided what might've been a nasty fight between the Hopis and the Navajos, and Justice was pretty well pleased with what you did to stop the hoof-and-mouth panic from spreading."

"If you read my reports, you'd've seen that I had a lot of pretty good luck on both of them cases, Billy."

"I read the reports, but I'm still not sure just how you pulled things off. Anyhow, the Army got a letter of thanks from the British Embassy, and the Indian Bureau passed on a good word about your work in getting rid of that bad apple they had in charge of their office in Winslow."

"How come I never heard about them nice letters, Billy?"

"Because I didn't hear about them myself until I got this new case on the direct wire from Washington last night. It seems the big brass from both the Indian Bureau and the Army asked for you to be assigned to it."

"Well, if I got to go, I guess I got to," said Longarm. "What am I going to run into this time?"

"Something that's a little more in our line than those two fancy jobs we've been talking about. This new case is just a straightforward matter of robbery at the Navajo Ordnance Depot."

"Ordnance means cannon." Longarm frowned thoughtfully. "You don't mean to tell me somebody's been stealing cannons?"

"Now, what thief in his right mind would steal a cannon?" Vail asked. "No, this is just a case of somebody robbing the depot of a big bunch of money."

"Just where is this Navajo Ordnance Depot, Billy? I can't recall that I ever heard of it before."

"It's the Army's main ammunition and gun supply depot, just a little way south of Flagstaff."

"Flagstaff's a pretty good-sized town," Longarm said with a frown. "Don't the department have a deputy stationed there?"

Vail nodded. "Yes, they do. His name's Ferguson, and he's been there quite a while. As I remember, his appointment was strictly political, so I don't suppose they trust him to handle something like this."

Longarm pulled over the red morocco-upholstered chair that

he claimed was the only one in Vail's office that was comfortable and settled into it.

Lighting a cheroot, he leaned back and said, "Well, suppose you lay it out for me, and we'll talk about it a little bit. It'll help if I know what kinda wasp's nest I'm going to be poking my nose into."

Vail picked up a stack of flimsies that Longarm recognized as having come from the private telegraph wire to Washington in the federal building's basement. The chief marshal ruffled the sheets of thin paper and laid them out in sequence on his desk.

"It looks to me like this isn't more than an open-and-shut case of payroll robbery," he told Longarm. "It just happened the day before yesterday, and the Army's still not sure exactly how much money was stolen."

"I see the Army ain't changed its ways a damn bit," Longarm commented through a cloud of blue cigar smoke. "Handling the taxpayers' money like it was just bales of plain paper."

"It wasn't paper money the robbers got," Vail said. "In case you don't remember, the Army likes to pay off the soldiers in silver cartwheels."

"I guess I'd forgot that. But how come they can't tell us how much was stolen?"

"It seems they've got a legitimate excuse this time," Vail answered. "There was a sizeable amount of operating funds for the depot included in the money chest. They'll let me know when they've figured out how much."

"What'd the outlaws do? Hold up the quartermaster's wagon between the railroad station and the post?"

"According to this message, they marched right into the paymaster's office in broad daylight and walked out with the money chest."

"You mean they raided the depot headquarters? Damn it, Billy, don't the Army post sentries anyplace these days?"

"That's a question you'll have to ask when you get there, Long," Vail said. "It doesn't give any more details here."

"Well, does it give you any idea why the high-muckety-mucks back in Washington pointed a finger at me to handle this damn case?" Longarm frowned.

"Yes. The Army's not supposed to send any kind of armed force onto the Navajo Reservation unless it's got permission

20

from the Indian Bureau. The bureau didn't give them permission because . . . well, you know why. It's the same thing that got you sent there before. They're afraid the Navajos and the soldiers will get into a fracas and set off another Indian war."

"Hell's bells, Billy! The Army's full of nervous nellies today. When Kit Carson whipped the Navajos so bad, back in the Sixties, they promised him they'd never fight no more, and I can't recall that they've ever gone back on their sworn word."

"Just the same, they're not letting any soldiers go onto the Navajo Reservation. That's one of the things you can't do, by the way: take even a single soldier with you if you have to go on Navajo lands."

"Which means I got to do the whole job single-handed, I guess?"

"I don't recall many times when you've asked for help," Vail said, trying to hide the grin twitching at the corners of his mouth. "If you need any this time, get it from the deputy in Flagstaff, not the Army."

"From what you said about him, I'd be better off getting any help I need from the Navajo Police."

"That's up to you, after you get there and look over the situation. And, speaking of getting there, you'd better be ready to catch that D&RG train. You've got just a little less than two hours to make it to the depot."

"Oh, I'll be on the train, Billy. Don't worry about that. I'll even have a clean shave on my face when I get on the coach."

"That'll be a big improvement," Vail said. "The clerk ought to have your papers and travel vouchers ready by now. I had him start on them as soon as I saw this message."

"Fine. Oh, yes, one more thing before I pull out. You know anything about the deputy in Flagstaff or the commander of that ordnance depot? Anything that might help me?"

"All I know about the commander of the depot is his name. Lieutenant Colonel R. W. Brady, and I don't know what the R. and W. stand for. You'll have to find that out yourself."

"How about that deputy marshal in the Flagstaff office?" Longarm asked. "You got any idea what he's like?"

"I've run into him just once, and that was five or six years ago, when I was still in the field. His name's Paul Ferguson and, like I mentioned, he's an old-timer. I'd guess he's pushing retirement time by now. That's about all I can tell you, except

21

that he's got a reputation in the department of passing on as much work as he can to his deputies."

"Well, I'll find out what I need to know soon enough, I guess." Longarm stood up and stretched. "All right, Billy, I'll be on my way. You'll hear from me when the case is closed."

In keeping his promise to Vail, Longarm also managed to keep his promise to Annie. Instead of going to his regular barber, he strolled from the federal building to the Windsor Hotel. After getting out of the chair, freshly shaved and trimmed, he spent a few minutes talking to the manager of that luxurious hostelry. Then he sent a bellhop to Annie with a note assuring her she'd find a job at the Windsor. Only then did he hail a cab, pick up his gear from his rooming house on the wrong side of Cherry Creek, and head for the Denver & Rio Grande depot.

Unlike so many of Longarm's train trips, this one proved to be uneventful. On the early evening of the second day after he'd left Denver, he stepped off the westbound Santa Fe limited at the depot in Flagstaff. As he'd expected, there was a Harvey House just across the street from the depot. Claiming his saddle gear and Winchester from the baggage master, Longarm started across the street to register.

Since late afternoon, when the blazing sun had dropped behind the towering peaks of the San Francisco Mountains, the town had been shaded from its blistering rays. Even now, though, two hours after sundown, Longarm's feet got uncomfortably warm from heat retained in the hard-baked ground sizzling up through his boot soles in the short distance he had to walk from the depot to the Harvey House. He sighed with relief when he stepped into the hotel's cool lobby and went to the registration desk.

"I'll likely be here for a few days," he told the clerk. "And I figured I'd best make sure you still take government vouchers for room rent before I sign the register."

"We certainly do," the clerk replied. "We value the custom you government people give us."

"Then I'll just cash this one now," Longarm said, digging into his wallet for one of the vouchers given him in Denver.

After glancing at the voucher, the clerk whirled the registration ledger around and waited while Longarm scrawled his signature. "Oh," he said after looking at the name. "A deputy

22

U. S. marshal. I hope that whatever brings you to our city isn't a serious case."

"It ain't got much to do with your city," Longarm replied. "I guess you heard about the robbery out at the ordnance depot a few days ago?"

"Yes, yes, of course! Terrible!" The desk clerk turned from the till and counted out the change from the voucher. He went on, "But at least no one from Flagstaff is suspected, as far as I've heard."

"I wouldn't know about that till I start digging into it," Longarm replied, pocketing his change. He glanced around the lobby. "I don't see a sign for your saloon," he told the clerk. "Which one of them doors is it?"

For a moment the clerk did not reply. Then he said somewhat apologetically, "I'm afraid we don't have a saloon in the hotel, Marshal Long. Mr. Harvey is a strict temperance man."

"I recall now, I couldn't buy a drink at the Harvey House in Gallup when I stopped there a while back. But I'd plumb forgot about that," Longarm replied.

"I hope that won't keep you from favoring us with your business," the clerk went on. "There's a saloon on almost every corner here in Flagstaff, so you won't have any trouble finding a drink if that's what you're after."

"I feel like I need one right now, to wash the dust outa my throat after that dry train trip. Tell you what. You have the bellboy take my gear up to my room. I'll find the closest saloon and have my drink, then come on back and settle in."

Longarm had no trouble finding a saloon. There was one on the corner across the street from the Harvey House. Pushing through the batwings, he surveyed the array of bottles on the backbar, looking for Tom Moore, but nowhere did he see a label bearing the distiller's familiar face. Every one of the half-dozen bottles of rye on the backbar bore a Pennsylvania label.

"I hope you got a bottle of decent Maryland rye on hand," he told the aproned barkeep who ambled down the bar to serve him. "All the rye you got up there is distilled up in the north, and bourbon's a mite too sweet for my taste."

"Well, now," the barkeep said. "No matter how persnickety a man's taste is, we always try to oblige our customers. If you'll stay right where you are for a minute, I think I can find just exactly what you're looking for."

Longarm watched the barkeep disappear into a door at the end of the bar. He took out a cheroot, and had just touched a match to its end when the man came back through the door carrying a quart bottle of Tom Moore. He placed the bottle on the bar in front of Longarm.

"This suit you all right?" he asked.

Longarm nodded and laid a half eagle on the mahogany. "I'll pay you for the bottle and take it with me after I've had a swallow or two here."

"I'll have to charge you two dollars for that bottle," the barkeep said, frowning. "It's expensive whiskey."

"And worth every penny it costs," Longarm told him. He slapped the bottom of the bottle against the heel of his left hand and the cork popped out a fraction of an inch. "Just put me out a glass, if you don't mind."

"Glad to oblige." The barkeep put a glass and a pitcher of water on the bar in front of Longarm, who'd already clamped his strong teeth on the protruding cork and pulled it from the bottle. Picking up the gold piece, the barkeep turned to the till to make change.

Longarm pushed the water aside and filled the glass with Tom Moore. After he'd taken a sip, he asked the barkeep, "You mind telling me why you hide this liquor where a man who wants a shot of good rye whiskey can't see it?"

"It's this way, friend," the barkeep replied. "Flagstaff's a nickel beer and dime shot town, and a man that buys two drinks looks to get the next one on the house. We'd lose money serving that expensive rye across the bar."

"Not that it's any of my business, but you got me curious. If you don't serve Tom Moore across the bar, why do you keep it on hand?"

"Why, we order it special for one of our customers who's got the same taste you seem to have. There just happened to be a few bottles in the storeroom that he hasn't picked up yet."

"I get the idea," Longarm said. He drained his glass and picked up the bottle of Tom Moore. "I don't know how long I'm going to be in town, but you might set back another one of these bottles in case I need it."

"Like I told you, we try to oblige our customers," the barkeep replied. "We'll get another shipment next week. Drop in any time, or if you just want us to keep that bottle you got and have it handy to serve you, we'll do that, too."

"Why, that's right friendly, and I'll take you up on it right now." Longarm handed the bottle to the barkeep, then said, "Maybe you can tell me where I'd be likely to find the local U. S. marshal at this time of day. His name's Ferguson, but I'd guess you already know that."

"Oh, everybody in Flag knows Paul," the barkeep said. "At this time of day he's most apt to be at the Silver Star, because it's the nearest saloon to his office."

"And I reckon his office'd be someplace along Main Street?"

"Yep. Just turn right when you go outside and follow the street on down about four squares. You can't miss it. You'll see the Silver Star on the corner, and I'd guess old Paul will be at his regular table back in the corner."

When Longarm pushed through the batwings of the Silver Star he had no difficulty in picking out the man he was looking for. Billy Vail had described Ferguson as a lawman gone to seed, and the man sprawled in a chair at the back corner table looked the part. Even if he hadn't seen the silver rim of a badge like his own in the gap between his shirt and leather vest, Longarm could have identified Paul Ferguson. He walked across the saloon and stopped beside the table.

"I'm betting you're Paul Ferguson," he said.

Ferguson looked up. His wrinkle-pouched grey eyes were bloodshot and he squinted when the light from the lantern that hung on the wall beside the table struck them. He had a straggle of untrimmed grey moustache and his puffy, heavily tanned creased cheeks needed shaving. His flat-brimmed crown-peaked Stetson was shoved far back on his head, which was bald except for tufts of grey above each ear. There were stains on his checked flannel shirt and the curve of his potbelly that protruded under his covert cloth trousers.

"You'd win," he said gruffly. "What if I am?"

"My name's Long. Deputy outa the Denver office. I just got to town, and thought I better look you up and say howdy."

Ferguson grunted, then said raspingly, "You're the one they call Longarm, I guess?"

"Some folks do."

"Well, sit down. I had a wire from the chief marshal up in Prescott saying you'd be in to take over that Army robbery case."

"I guess you know I didn't ask for the job," Longarm said, pulling a chair around so that he could sit facing Ferguson.

"Sure. You're like me—like all of us deputies. A damn flunky for the pen-pushers back in Washington."

"I'm doing just what you'd be if you was in my boots," Longarm said.

"I guess you'll be looking for me to help you."

"Not especially. I got the idea from what Chief Vail said that they wanted you to keep the office going while I take care of the work out in the field."

"Don't try to make it sound good, Long. I been slapped in the face, and I don't like it a damn bit."

"Now, I'm sorry you feel that way," Longarm said. He kept his voice carefully neutral. "From what Billy Vail told me when he laid out the case, it's going to take a lot of hard travel."

"Well, damn it, I ain't too old to fork a horse!"

"That's neither here nor there, the way they look at things back East. Anyways, I'm here and I'd like to work with you as much as possible."

"I don't see as I'd be much help, the way things stand. All I know is what I found out the day the robbery was pulled off. You'll get the same story I'd tell you when you talk to the brass out at the depot."

"It's your territory, Ferguson," Longarm said. "You know it better'n I do. I'm sure there's things you can tell me that'd help out when I start digging."

For the first time since Longarm had joined him, Ferguson straightened up in his chair and sat erect. His rheumy grey eyes were cold as he stared at Longarm.

"Let's get things straight right now," he said. "You got your way of working, I got mine. I wouldn't want you poking your nose into a case I was handling, and I don't aim to poke my nose into yours. Do you get what I'm telling you, Long?"

"I sure do." Longarm saw that he'd be doing more harm than good by being persistent. He stood up. "Like you said, you got your ways, I got mine. If I get in a real bind, I'll come to see you. Aside from that, I'll stay outa your way as much as I can."

"Good," Ferguson snapped. "We'll leave it that way, then. Goodbye, Long."

Walking down Flagstaff's almost deserted Main Street on

his way back to the Harvey House, Longarm reviewed his brief conversation with Ferguson and shook his head thoughtfully.

Now, there's one damned unhappy man, old son, he told himself. *It's easy to see he must've been a real good man when he was in his prime, and he knows that he ain't one no longer. There's got to be a lesson there for you. Question is, are you smart enough to learn what it is?*

Chapter 4

Although the bright orange sun had just cleared the ragged mountaintops on the eastern horizon, the air was already warm when Longarm reined in his livery-stable nag at the sentry box of the Navajo Ordnance Depot. He'd watched the depot take shape through the windless morning air as he approached it from Flagstaff. The heat haze that would blur distant vision a few hours later had not yet begun to form, and he'd been able to see the depot clearly while he was still several miles away.

Sections of the original cedar-post stockade which had enclosed the fort from which the weapons and munitions supply depot evolved were still intact. The posts stood in a line across the front of the installation, broken only by a gateless gap in the center, and along the sides there were also long areas where the posts remained in place.

However, at several points outside the fence line on both sides there were sprawling adobe buildings with narrow slitted windows, and the stockade walls had been removed in front of these. In the rear a two-story adobe barracks building rose above the enclosed area. The depot looked exactly like what it was: a former stockaded fort that had expanded willy-nilly without any thought of its appearance and with no provision for protection once its usefulness as a fortification had ended.

There was a sentry box outside the gap in the front of the stockade, but the sentry did not come out until Longarm had ridden past the box and was entering the gaping opening.

"Hey, mister!" the soldier called, trailing his rifle butt on the ground as he emerged from the box. "You're supposed to stop and tell me who you are and what your business is before you go inside the gate."

Longarm reined in and looked back at the young soldier. He said, "My name's Long. I'm a deputy U. S. marshal outa Denver, and I got business with Colonel Brady."

"Oh. Well, I guess it's all right for you to go ahead, if you're going to see the colonel," the youth said. There was still a strain of doubt in his voice.

"You don't want to look at my badge or anything like that?"

"All the sergeant told me I had to do was find out who comes in," the soldier frowned. "He didn't say to do anything else."

"Is this the first time you've been on sentry-go?"

"Yes, sir. I only signed up three weeks ago."

"Well, you'll learn the ropes as you go along," Longarm told him. "Now, if it's all right for me to go on in, maybe you can tell me where to find Colonel Brady."

"He's likely still in his quarters, mister. Officers' row, that is. It's on the right-hand side of the big barracks."

"I'll find him without any trouble, then," Longarm said. He toed his horse into motion and headed for the tall rectangle of the barracks building at the rear of the depot.

There was a surprising amount of activity for such an early hour of the day. Wagons rumbled across the enclosure, and the flare of forges and ringing of hammers on anvils came from the buildings outside the stockade's perimeter, where field-pieces stood in various stages of disassembly from their carriages. Through the open door of one of the sheds Longarm could see cases of rifles stacked inside, and humped sections of the ground with masonry steps leading down to subterranean entrances revealed the location of powder storage bunkers.

As Longarm approached the rear of the stockade the bustling atmosphere lessened. Here there was a minimum of activity: a few soldiers in dungarees were raking the corrals that stood outside the back stockade walls, others were carrying buckets of water from the well to the stables, a few lounged outside the two-story barracks building. A small parade ground, barely big enough to accommodate two companies in formation, separated the working area from the barracks and officers' quarters.

There was little difference between the half-dozen adobe houses that stood along one side of the parade ground, but one was a bit bigger than the others, and Longarm decided that it must be the one assigned to the depot commander. He reined up in front of it, swung out of the saddle, and rapped at the front door. A soldier in fatigues opened it and looked questioningly at the early visitor.

"Is this Colonel Brady's quarters?" Longarm asked.

29

"Yes, sir. But the colonel can't be disturbed right now. He's having breakfast, and he's got a rule that nobody at all can bother him when he's at the table. If you want to see him you can come back later, or go wait for him at headquarters."

"Maybe if you'll tell him what I want to talk to him about he'll break the rule this time," Longarm suggested.

"Oh, I couldn't do that, mister. When the colonel makes a rule, nobody on the depot dasts to break it. Why, if I was to—"

From somewhere inside a voice broke into the orderly's words with a gruff shout. "Halloran! Where the devil did you get off to? I'm ready for more coffee, damn it!"

"Coming, Colonel!" the orderly at replied. He turned back to Longarm. "You better catch the colonel at headquarters, mister. You'll get along with him a lot better there, after his breakfast's settled." The orderly started to close the door but found Longarm's booted foot blocking the threshold.

"You tell the colonel that Deputy U. S. Marshal Custis Long's here from Denver and needs to see him," he told the orderly. "I got to get busy trying to run down the gang that stole the depot payroll, and I ain't got time to waste waiting around."

"Halloran!" the colonel's voice was raised to a higher pitch this time. "Get that coffee for me, on the double!"

"Just a second, Colonel," Halloran called. "I'll be—"

Footsteps stamping toward the door interrupted him. Longarm looked over Halloran's shoulder and saw a short, stocky man marching up the hall toward the door. He could only have been the depot commanding officer, for the silver oak leaves of a lieutenant colonel adorned the shoulder straps of his duty uniform, a grey flannel shirt worn with blue serge trousers. The trousers were tucked into boots that had been buffed to a gleaming polish that would put a mirror to shame.

Colonel Brady was a small man. Longarm wondered how he'd gotten past the Army's regulation on minimum height. His face was tanned to a deep brown, but his hands were white, indicating that he wore gloves outdoors. His hair was grey, and he sported an imposing set of official cavalry whiskers, puffed-out sideburns that extended to the jawline and blended into a full, bushy moustache while his chin was clean-shaven.

"Just who in the hell are you wasting your time with?" the colonel demanded as he strode toward the door. "Damn it,

Halloran, you know my standing orders! Nobody interrupts me at breakfast!"

Longarm spoke before Halloran could turn to reply. "Don't blame your orderly, Colonel. I come out here early because I got to talk to you before I can start on my job."

"And who the devil might you be?" Brady demanded.

"Name's Long. Deputy U. S. marshal outa Denver. I'm here to handle that robbery you had at the depot, and every minute I waste in starting the trail I need to pick up is getting colder."

For a moment Brady was silent, studying Longarm. Then he compressed his lips into a thin line, grunted, and said, "Since you're here, you might as well come in." He turned to the orderly. "Halloran, when you bring that fresh coffee, bring a cup for Marshal Long. But first, step over and tell Major Craven that I want him to come join me while I'm talking with the marshal."

Longarm followed Brady down a short hall and into a cheerfully sunlit dining room. A table beside a double window held a plate and an empty coffee cup. On the plate there was a half-eaten slice of toast and the remains of an egg. Brady motioned for Longarm to sit down, then took his place where the plate rested. He pushed it aside distastefully.

"Hell of a note when a man can't eat breakfast in peace," he said, adding hastily, "No offense, Marshal. I don't blame you a bit for coming out early. In fact, it does you credit. I'm sure you're anxious to get on the trail of that outlaw gang."

"I figure you and me are both in about the same situation, Colonel," Longarm said quietly. "Even if we have got a bunch of government rules and red tape tying us up when it comes down to how we do our jobs, there ain't nobody standing over us to tell us when to go to work and when to knock off for the day."

"Well, that's one way of looking at it, I suppose," Brady nodded. "And I suppose it could be carried a little further. We might not like the red tape that ties us down, but we've learned how to get along with it."

"I guess by that you mean you figure you ought've sent out a detachment to run down them fellows that robbed the depot here, instead of waiting for me to come all the way from Denver?"

"I wasn't going to say that in so many words, Long, but

I'm glad you understand how I feel. It's a job we ought to be doing ourselves, but GHQ in Washington ordered us to turn it over to you. They didn't ask us to like doing that, of course."

"Oh, I understand how you feel, Colonel. Fact is, I ain't no gladder to be here than you are to have me," Longarm said.

"Perhaps understanding each other will make it a little bit easier for us to get along together." Brady frowned.

"I don't aim to get in your way, Colonel, or anything like that. Soon as I find out how many men I'm looking for and what they look like, I'll be trailing out after 'em."

Before the colonel could say anything, Halloran came in with a coffee pot in one hand, a cup and saucer in the other. He poured coffee into the colonel's cup, then put the cup and saucer down in front of Longarm and filled the cup.

"Major Craven will be here any minute, sir," the orderly said. "Will you want me to get him a cup, too?"

"If Henry wants coffee, let him ask for it," Brady snapped. "Leave the pot on the table and clear away these dirty dishes."

Before Halloran could get the table cleared, Major Craven arrived. He was the opposite of Brady in every respect except that of age. Where Brady was short and slight in stature, Craven was a bulky man with a protuberant belly, who moved slowly and deliberately. He was clean-shaven and his cheeks were flushed with the tracery of fine crisscrossed veins that were usually the sign of a heavy drinker. Looking at the two men closely while Brady introduced him to Craven, Longarm judged both of the officers to be in their late fifties.

"Now that I'm here, Bob, let's get started," Craven said as he pulled out a chair and sat down between Brady and Longarm. "I don't know what we can tell Marshal Long that he doesn't already know, but we'll have to try."

"I ain't had time to tell the colonel this yet," Longarm said, "but I don't know one thing about this robbery except that some kind of gang pulled it off. You men will have to start at the beginning and tell me what happened."

Brady turned to Craven. "That's pretty much up to you, then. I imagine the marshal wants an eyewitness account, and I wasn't in your office when it happened. Go ahead, Henry."

"There's not much to tell," Craven said. "In posts and forts, payroll money's delivered every three months. This time the routine was the same as it always is. The money was counted and locked in chests at corps headquarters in Fort Sam Houston.

There was a chest for each post in the Territory, and they were all shipped by rail to El Paso. From Fort Bliss the chests moved by wagons with cavalry escorts. The wagon that had the chest for the depot here stopped at Bowie, Apache, Verdi, and then went up to Mojave. On its way back to Bliss it stopped to drop off our shipment."

"I know the Army's got its own way of doing things, but ain't that a sorta roundabout way of getting your payroll here?" Longarm frowned. "Seems to me it'd've been easier to ship it on the railroad."

"It would be, of course," Brady said. "I suppose it's like so many routines we have at these Western forts, Marshal. We're still following regulations and procedures that were established fifty years ago, when the Territories were being settled."

"And I don't guess there's any way you can get the high-muckety-mucks back East to change things?"

"If you know the Army, you know the answer." Brady smiled thinly. "Every day I do things here that I'd like to change, but we field officers don't have anything to say about them."

Longarm nodded sympathetically. He took out a cheroot and lighted it, then went on, "It's the same thing in the Justice Department, I'd expect. But if I was bossing a bunch of outlaws I'd've stuck up that money wagon before most of them chests was delivered instead of waiting till there was just one left."

"I can give you three good reasons why they picked us out, Marshal," Craven volunteered. "One is that we're right at the edge of the Navajo Reservation, which made their getaway easy. Another is that we're not a fighting outfit here. The only combat cadre we've got is two cavalry platoons. To me, that means the brass in Washington didn't think we're important enough to justify stationing a full company here."

"Both of them reasons makes sense," Longarm agreed after waiting a moment for Craven to add the third. "You said you had three reasons, Major. What's the other one?"

"Two enlisted men from the depot here who helped the outlaws carry out the robbery," Craven said, tight-lipped.

"Hold on now!" Longarm exclaimed, his jaw dropping. "This is the first time I heard anything about it being an inside job!"

"You must've known about it!" Brady snapped. "I certainly

33

included it in my report to corps headquarters!"

"Oh, I ain't questioning that, Colonel," Longarm said. "I guess maybe it got left out from the message my chief got in Denver, or else he'd've told me about it. Damn it, it seems like I don't know from Adam's off ox about what happened. Maybe you better tell me from the beginning what took place."

"There's not a great deal to tell," Craven said before the colonel could speak. "Two men rode up to the gate. Each one was leading a spare horse. When the sentry asked them what their business was, one held a gun on him and forced him into his box. The other led both horses into the depot and stopped at the quartermaster's office." When Longarm raised his eyebrows questioningly, the major added quickly, "That's my command. We've got our own building about fifty yards from headquarters."

"That's clear enough, Major," Longarm said. "I'm following you all right. If there's anything I need to ask you, I'll take the liberty of interrupting you."

"Lieutenant Fletcher hadn't opened the money chest, he'd left the key in his quarters and the clerk had gone after it," Craven continued. "Fletcher and the staff sergeant, Riley, were the only two in the office. The man from outside held a gun on them and told Fletcher to open the chest. When he found out about the missing key, he stuck his head out the door and called and two of our enlisted men, Simms and Karp, came in. They—"

"Hold on a minute, Major," Longarm broke in. "These two soldiers—were they men who'd been here a long time, or fresh recruits?"

"They'd both been here less than three months."

"Long enough to know their way around, but not long enough to make any close friends." Longarm frowned. "From what you've said, it strikes me this scheme's been planned quite a spell."

Brady interrupted to say, "Henry and I came to the same conclusion. It's pretty obvious that the two men on the post had come here after the job was decided on and planned."

"Could they work it out so they'd be stationed here?"

Brady nodded. "That would be easy if they were smart. All they'd have to do is ask to be stationed here, or say they knew something about blacksmithing or machine work."

"That don't sound like the Army to me," Longarm frowned.

"It used to be you did what you were ordered, and went where you were sent, whether you liked it or not."

"You don't know what the Army's going through these days, Marshal," the colonel said. "With cattle ranches spreading so fast and so many big new outfits springing up, men who would've joined the army a few years ago are finding jobs on the ranches."

"Ranchers are so hard pressed for hands they're paying raw men twenty dollars, even twenty-five a month now," Craven put in. "An experienced cowhand can draw a dollar a day. The army's still paying buck privates thirteen dollars a month. I don't suppose you can blame a man for hiring out where he's going to get the best pay, but it's playing hell with our enlistments."

"We're not getting the young men, either," Brady added. "A few years back, youngsters we could train were enlisting. They did what they were told and went where we needed to station them. It's not that way any more. We're getting drifters and Tramps and veterans from the War. A lot of them are pretty hard-boiled, and plenty of them know something about Army regulations, so they turn into barracks lawyers and keep things stirred up."

"When I first came in your gate I sorta got the idea the Army's changed a lot," Longarm commented. "The young fellow on duty was awful green."

"Like most line soldiers these days," Brady said bitterly.

"You got some kind of service records on them two that was stationed here?" Longarm asked. "Used to be, a soldier had a service record that—"

"They still do," Brady interrupted. "I've got the records of both Simms and Karp in my office. I'll go over them with you later, whenever you're ready."

"Good," Longarm nodded. "Well, go on about the holdup, if you don't mind. The major'd said there wasn't no way to open the money chest."

"Yes," Craven nodded. "The outlaws argued a minute about shooting off the padlock, but they didn't want to risk rousing the post. Then Karp told them he could steal one of our light wagons, and that's exactly what he did. They hoisted the chest into the wagon and Karp drove it off while the others tied up the sergeant and me. Then they left. We managed to get the ropes off after about ten minutes, but by then they were out of sight, over the humps of the trail into town."

Brady picked up the story. "Henry alerted me, and I ordered B Platoon to follow them. It took the men about two hours and ready, so the robbers had a good lead on them."

"Your troopers didn't pick up their trail?" Longarm asked. He took out a fresh cheroot and waited for Brady's answer before striking a match to light it.

Brady shook his head. "B Platoon milled around all day, but they couldn't find the outlaws' trail."

"That strikes me as odd," Longarm commented, striking a match and puffing his cheroot into a glow. "That money chest must've made a pretty good load. There'd oughta been wheel tracks the men could've spotted."

"Did you notice what the ground's like around here while you were riding out from town, Marshal?" Craven asked.

"Baked hard as sin," Longarm nodded. "But you got a scout attached to your outfit, ain't you?"

"No," Brady replied. "I sent a wire to Fort Wingate, and they put one of their scouts on the next train, but he didn't get here until evening. Yesterday he found the wagon."

"But not the money, from the way you said that," Longarm commented.

"Not the money, of course not. The robbers had shot off the lock and emptied the chest."

"That was a ways from here, I suppose?"

"Of course," Brady answered. "Thirty miles or so. They circled around Flagstaff and headed due north, just as we expected them to do."

"Figures," Longarm nodded through a puff of cigar smoke. "I guess by then you'd got word back from Washington that you wasn't to send your men onto the Navajo Reservation?"

"I had that message a half-hour after I'd sent a telegram to corps headquarters notifying them of the robbery," Brady said, his voice grim. "They're so damned spooked up back in the East that they've stopped anybody wearing an Army uniform from going on the Navajos' land."

"Well, that don't apply to me," Longarm said. "I'd imagine you can send that scout along with me to the edge of the reservation? It'll save me a lot of time."

Craven answered before Brady could speak. "Oh, he's ready to go with you. When Halloran said I was wanted here, I had an idea you'd arrived, so I sent my orderly to tell the scout to

36

meet us in my office. But if you don't mind me asking, Marshal, are you enough of a tracker to pick up the trail of those outlaws across the Painted Desert?"

"I'll manage," Longarm said curtly. "If they split up them bags of silver dollars, their horses would be loaded so heavy that I won't have no trouble following 'em. You got any idea how many bags it takes to hold your payroll?"

"Our pay muster runs to just under three thousand dollars a month, and they send us money for three paydays. It's in bags, a hundred silver dollars to each bag."

Longarm nodded, his mind busy looking ahead. Then he said, "I forgot to ask, Colonel, did they take the wagon horse when they headed north?"

"Yes. For a packhorse, I'm sure."

"The bags would weigh close to ten pounds apiece, then." Longarm frowned. "And if they load too many on a horse, it'd bust up a critter before it got started good."

"They had five other horses," Craven pointed out.

"I'm allowing for that. A horse can maybe carry about sixty pounds besides a man and his gear. I guess the odd nag could handle the rest, but they'd all leave deep tracks."

"There's something we haven't gotten around to mentioning yet, Marshal," Brady said. "There was more than the payroll in that chest. There were ten bags with fifty double eagles in each one. That's our running expenses for the next six months."

"That figures to ten thousand dollars!" Longarm exclaimed.

Brady nodded. "So, you see, you're not just after the nine thousand in payroll money. You're looking for five men who're carrying enough stolen cash to make them put up a good fight when you catch up with them. A lone man who catches up with the gang wouldn't have a chance winning a fight at five-to-one odds!"

Chapter 5

For a moment following the colonel's statement the three men sat in silence. Then Longarm said, "I'll worry about being able to handle the bunch when I catch up with 'em, not before."

"Your sentiments do you credit, Marshal, but a fact's a fact," Brady snapped. "Now, I suggest that if you or your chief in Denver have any influence at all, you join me in requesting that a detachment from my command and one of my senior officers go with you in pursuit of those thieves."

"Excuse me if I wasn't right in catching something you said a minute ago," Longarm frowned. "Didn't I understand that you got orders from Army headquarters for your men to stay off the Navajo Reservation?"

"Yes, of course I did," Brady replied. "But that doesn't mean those orders can't be changed if enough influence is brought to bear from the proper quarters."

"And you think my chief is one of them proper quarters you're talking about?"

"Obviously, Marshal Long," Brady said. "The Army has several hundred officers who outrank me, but I understand that there are only twenty or thirty chief marshals in the Justice Department. In other words, your chief is a lot closer to the top of the command chain than I am. He'd have a great deal more influence with his superiors than I have with mine."

"I don't guess you ever met my chief," Longarm said.

"No. I don't recall that I have," Brady agreed.

"Maybe I better tell you something about him, then. Billy Vail's an old soldier and he used to be a Texas Ranger. When he gets an order, he don't start asking questions; he just goes ahead and does what he's ordered to do."

"But surely he wants your mission to succeed!" Craven said.

"Oh, there ain't no question about that, Major," Longarm

replied. "He didn't send me here to let that bunch get away."

"Then, if he's got that much confidence in you, he'd certainly act on your request to have a cavalry detachment go along as a backup unit," Brady argued.

Longarm thought about the colonel's words for a moment, then shook his head. "It wouldn't do a damned bit of good, Colonel. I know that because Billy Vail told me it was a one-man trailing job. The War Department ain't about to send no troops onto that Navajo Reservation."

Brady and Craven exchanged glances. Then Brady said, "Very well. I suppose you're right, but I don't envy you the job."

"Oh, I get jobs worse'n this one, Colonel," Longarm said soberly, taking out a fresh cheroot and lighting it. "And you got to remember, I got my orders, just like you have."

"It's your decision, Long." The colonel shrugged. "I've been ordered to put the case in your hands, so it looks like you'll be on your own from here out."

"I ain't running down your offer to help, Colonel," Longarm told the officer. "Now, if you'll just fix me up with a horse and see if your scout's ready to ride out a ways and show me where he found that wagon, I'm ready to be on my way." He turned to Craven. "While I'm waiting for the horse, maybe you'll give me a look at those men's records, Major."

"Of course. We'll step over to my office and I'll get them out for you. At least they'll give you a description and you might be able to tell something else about them after you've seen their records."

After he'd scanned the papers covering the enlistments of the men Longarm asked Craven, "Anything strike you funny about them two, Major?"

Craven shook his head. "No. I didn't notice anything out of the usual routine about them either at the time they enlisted or when the colonel and I were reviewing their records the other day after the robbery."

"Well, there's some gaps in there that sorta gives me the idea both of them fellows has done time. Which ain't all that strange, considering the slick way they handled this job here."

"Is that going to help you find them?" the major asked.

"Maybe. Maybe not. But they've had time to cover quite a bit of ground, the time it took me to get on the case. If it turns out that I don't catch up with 'em, seeing the head start they

39

got, knowing they've run up against the law before might help me track 'em."

"I suppose all we can do here is to give you that horse you need and wish you luck," Craven said.

"Looks like it," Longarm agreed. "So, just as quick as your men can cinch my saddle up on a horse, and your scout can get ready, I'll be leaving."

Having seen Colonel Brady accept defeat seemed to make it easier for Craven to follow his superior's example. He nodded and turned to the clerk who'd been quietly at work at a desk in one corner of the office.

"Take Marshal Long's saddle gear to the corral, Perkins," he said. "Tell the hostler the marshal and Fraser will want to ride out as soon as their mounts are saddled. And if you run into Fraser, tell him the marshal's waiting here." After the clerk had left, Craven said, "I don't know what the devil's wrong with the Army today! Damn it, Fraser ought've been here before now." When Longarm made no comment, the major asked, "I don't suppose you'd even feel able to have Fraser go along with you, Marshal?"

"I guess you know what I'll have to say to that," Longarm replied.

"Yes, I suppose I do. Damn shame; Buck Fraser's a good man. Excellent tracker, knows the country on the reservation, and he's a man you can count on to stand firm in a fight."

"Well, I can do a passable job of tracking myself, and I ain't too worried about getting lost. I been through that reservation before, you know. If it was up to me, Major, I don't guess I'd mind having some company, but all I got to go by is my orders. And you know what they say."

"Yes, of course. Too bad it has to be that way, but—"

Whatever Major Craven had in mind to say was lost as a knock sounded at the door, and when he'd called "Come in," a bronzed man almost as tall as Longarm entered. The new-comer wore a set of fringed buckskins and moccasins, but his headgear was the regulation black cavalry hat bearing a gilt cavalry insigne. He wore a well-rubbed pistol belt and holster in which nestled a Schofield Model Smith & Wesson .44.

"Fraser," Major Craven nodded, after he saw that the scout was not going to salute. "This is Deputy Marshal Long, from Denver. He's the man you'll be guiding to the pay wagon and then on the trail the outlaws left to the reservation boundary."

"Heard about you, Long," Fraser said, extending his hand. As he and Longarm shook, the scout added, "You're the one they call Longarm, ain't you?" When Longarm nodded, Fraser continued, "Well, I'll make you a proposition, and if it sets right with you, I don't imagine we'll have any trouble getting along."

"What's your proposition?"

"Let's you and me start out as Buck and Longarm and not have a lot of 'sirs' or 'misters' between us."

"You're on, Buck," Longarm agreed instantly. "That suits me fine. And if you're ready to ride, we might as well get moving." To Craven he said, "Thanks for your help, Major. Look for me to be back with your money as soon as I've caught up with it."

"Good luck, Long," Craven replied. "You'll need all of it you can get."

As Longarm and the scout left the office and started toward the stables, the scout observed, "You sound right sure of yourself. I don't reckon you've seen the country you'll be trying to track them rascals over or you might've coppered your bet."

"Oh, I'll catch the robbers, all right," Longarm said in a quiet voice, not boasting, just stating a fact.

"By God, I think you just might!"

They reached the stables just as one of the hostlers was tightening the cinch of Longarm's battered McClellan saddle on a handsome chestnut gelding. The horse had the deep, full chest and barrel and the broad haunches of a Morgan, but its legs and the downward set of its head were signs that somewhere in its breeding line there had been thoroughbreds. The animal's mane had not been cropped in cavalry style, but flowed in a rippling sheen of deep reddish-brown down its neck and shoulders.

Longarm blinked and then stared in surprise when he saw the gelding. He said to Fraser, "Now, that's about the best-looking cavalry horse I've run across for a long time!"

"It sure don't look like many cavalry nags I've seen," the scout agreed. He indicated his own rough-coated animal, standing already saddled at one side of the stable door. "Look at what they handed me."

Longarm went up to the hostler and asked, "Are you sure

you didn't put my saddle on the wrong horse?"

"You'd be the U. S. marshal from Denver, I guess?" the man said.

"Yep. And that sure don't look like no horse I'd draw for the kinda trip I'm setting out to make."

"Oh, it's yours, all right, Marshal. The remount sergeant said he had orders to give you..." The stableman hesitated momentarily, then went on, "To give you this one special."

"Well, I'd say that's pretty special, all right. Who gave the sergeant them orders?"

"I can't rightly say, Marshal. It could've been the officer of the day, or it could've been the colonel. I got it from my sergeant, and that's all I know about it."

Longarm walked around the chestnut and inspected it closely. As far as he could see, it was sound in the legs and body. He turned back to the hostler. "It ain't blowed, is it?"

"No, sir! It's got good wind and... well, it's in as good condition as any horse on the depot. Just looks a little fancy, compared to most of 'em."

"Well, if that's your choice for me, I ain't going to argue with you," Longarm told the hostler. He swung into the saddle and said to Fraser, "Come on, Buck. It ain't going to get no earlier. Let's ride!"

By the time the Army scout had led Longarm from the depot on a curving course that avoided Flagstaff and they'd ridden northeast to a low slope sparsely covered by scrub cedar, the morning was gone and the sun was well past its zenith. They rode diagonally up the rise to a spot where the beginning fissures of small canyons began to seam the slanting ground. Longarm reined in when Fraser pulled up his own horse. He looked around but saw no sign of the wagon.

"Them robbers must've scouted the country pretty good," Fraser said as he led the way around a clump of the stunted trees to a narrow crevasse. Over his shoulder, as he let his horse pick its way into the gash, he went on, "I had one hell of a time finding this place. Never would've found it if their wagon hadn't been so overloaded."

Looking closely at the baked soil, Longarm could just make out the faint ruts cut by wagon wheels. In a moment, as the little canyon widened, he saw the wagon ahead in the bottom of the cut. It sat askew, the wheels on one side on higher ground than on the other, its white canvas top gleaming in the afternoon sun.

"I guess the ground's too hard to take a boot print," he said as he swung out of the saddle.

"Oh, there's a few around," the scout said. "There's some hoofprints, too, but nothing that'd tell a fellow much."

"You searched around pretty good, did you, when you found this place the first time?"

Fraser waved a hand at the bare, sterile soil. "What in hell is there to search, Longarm? Anything on the ground around here'd stand out like a cockroach on a bald man's head."

"I guess you're right about that," Longarm agreed as he took a cigar from his pocket and fumbled out a match.

"Soon as you've poked around all you want to, we can start making tracks," Fraser went on. "It ain't all that far to the reservation boundary, so we oughta get there before sunset."

Longarm flicked the match into flame with his iron-hard thumbnail and bent his head down to light his cigar. Just as he moved, a rifle barked from the scrub and the slug whistled through the air where his head had been a split second earlier.

Both men dropped out of their saddles and hit the hard dirt with the instantaneous reflexes of those who'd been the target of a hidden sniper before.

"You see where that shot come from?" Fraser asked.

"No. I let my guard down, like a damn fool. If I hadn't been lighting my stogie, it'd have taken half my head off."

"We didn't see no muzzle smoke, so it must've come from behind us," the scout said. "And whoever triggered that shot wasn't very far off, either."

"Fifty or sixty yards," Longarm agreed.

He slid along the ground on his belly until he could reach his saddle scabbard. There was no way to lift the Winchester out of its scabbard without standing up. Longarm rolled between the legs of his horse, then stood up behind it, using the animal as a shield. Reaching across the horse's shoulder, he slid the rifle from its barrel.

They'd reined in at the center of a cleared area, and when Longarm looked around he saw no covering shrubs within a dozen feet of the horses. He braced his feet and leaped for the nearest, hitting the ground with his knees flexed. He was still a yard or two from the nearest cover when he landed. He dropped flat as his feet hit the dirt and rolled toward the closest of the stunted cedars.

As he began rolling the unseen rifle rang out again and the bullet plowed a furrow in the ground where Longarm's feet had hit. By then he was a foot or two away, almost behind the cedar he'd been making for. The concealed marksman triggered still another shot, but this time Buck Fraser had seen the wisp of muzzle-blast in the trees downslope, and fired at the thin thread of quickly dissipating smoke.

"Did you get him?" Longarm called, straining his eyes to peer through the trunks of the bushlike cedars in the direction from which the shots had come.

"Not likely," Fraser replied. "But I seen his muzzle smoke when he triggered that last shot. See if you can spot him from where you are. I got him figured to be real close to fifty yards ahead and a leetle bit to the right."

Squinting against the heat waves that were radiating from the ground at this late hour of the afternoon, Longarm peered in the direction the scout had indicated, but saw nothing, nor did his keen ears catch any sounds of movement.

"Whoever's doing that shooting knows what he's about," he told his companion. "If I was him, I'd've got the hell outa the way the minute I let off that last shot."

"Maybe you're right," Fraser agreed. "If he's still out there, he sure ain't giving no sign I can make out."

"Just in case he's still skulking around, let's see if we can't do some sneaking ourselves, Buck," Longarm suggested. "You circle right, I'll go left."

Inching forward on their bellies, their rifles ready for use if a target for a quick snapshot should appear, the two began their maneuver. They made no effort to move silently. Their quarry knew where they were and that they'd be looking for him.

Progress over the hard-baked, stone-studded soil was at best uncomfortable, and downright miserable when their knees encountered one of the occasional patches of sharp-edged rocks that surfaced at intervals in the almost flint-hard ground.

They had covered about half the arc of the circle in which they were moving when they heard the thudding of hooves ahead. Abandoning any further effor at concealment, they both leaped to their feet, their rifles at ready. For a few seconds they scanned the terrain ahead, their eyes swivelling as they

44

sought the rider of the horse whose hoofbeats were fading fast.

For a few moments neither Longarm nor the scout saw any movement, then, almost at the same time, they glimpsed the crown of a felt hat a hundred yards distant above the rim of a gulley that ran almost parallel to the one in which the wagon stood. Both men fired at the tricky target, but they saw the puffs of soil spring up at the edge of the gulley in which the hidden rider was moving. Then the tip of the hat vanished, though the hoofbeats of its wearer could still be heard faintly.

"You wanta take after him?" Buck asked.

His eyes still fixed on the spot where their momentary target had disappeared, Longarm asked, "You got any idea where he might be heading?"

Fraser shook his head. "Not unless he's making for town. I don't know the lay of the land hereabouts all that good."

"Same with me. And the way he set us up for targets, with his getaway all figured out, is a pretty good sign he does."

"I don't like the idea of letting the son of a bitch get away," Fraser said, tight-lipped. "I got about as much use for back-shooters as I have for rattlesnakes."

"Same here," Longarm nodded. He took out a match and scraped it across his thumbnail to light the cheroot that was still clamped between his teeth. "It wouldn't make much sense to try to follow him, Buck. By the time we'd get back to our horses and take after him, he'd likely have ducked outa that gulley he was riding up, and into another one."

"We'd have about as much chance as a snowball in hell of catching up to him in this cut-up country," the scout agreed. "You got any idea about who he was? It ain't likely he was one of the gang you're after."

"I figure the same way," Longarm replied. "They wouldn't have doubled back on their trail. At least, I don't figure they would."

"If they did, it was after I left their tracks at the edge of the Navajo Reservation," Fraser said. "Faint as their tracks was, I'd've noticed if one of 'em had cut away from the rest."

"Hell, it could've been almost anybody." Longarm shrugged. "In my business, I step on a lot of toes. There's plenty of men carrying a grudge against me. One of 'em might've seen me in Flagstaff and been trailing after me ever since."

"Or it could just've been a stray outlaw, figuring to take us for our guns and whatever money we might have on us," Fraser

45

suggested. "There's enough of 'em around here."

"Well, whoever it was, he got away clean, and I don't aim to lose any sleep worrying about him," Longarm said. "If he sees me again, he'll try again, and next time it might be a different story."

"You take it real calm, getting shot at," Fraser observed. "Now, there's times when I'm out scouting for hostiles when I figure I'm going to get shot at, but at least I got an idea that there's somebody around who's after me. I ain't real sure I could learn to put up with it the way you do."

"A man can get used to it," Longarm said, knocking the ash off his cigar. "Now, it's getting late, Buck, and we better be hitting that trail we're on before it gets too dark to see. Come on. Let's head back for the horses and be moving."

Chapter 6

"I guess you've seen enough here to satisfy yourself?" Fraser asked after they'd returned to the wagon.

Longarm said thoughtfully, "Whoever that bushwhacker was, he didn't give me time to do much looking. I better nosey around a little bit before we go on to the reservation border."

"It's getting on for late, Longarm. I studied this place here for the best part of two hours yesterday, when I first come onto the wagon. If you're willing to take my word as good, I can likely tell you anything you'd want to know while we ride," Fraser suggested.

"Makes sense," Longarm agreed. "We'll mount up, and I'll listen while you do the talking."

"What you're looking for is five men and six horses," Fraser began after they'd started northeast again. "All the men are whites, no redskins or breeds or Mexicans. You'd already know that two of 'em have got on cavalry boots with big heels. The other three is wearing range boots, high heels."

"You figure the two that've got on regulation boots have served in the cavalry before?"

"Not likely. It don't take long for cavalrymen to start walking spraddle-legged, and these don't. Comes down to that, I'd be surprised if any of 'em ever done any kind of soldiering, because their paces all measure different. If they'd been in the infantry, theyd've got the habit of taking them regulation twenty-seven-inch steps. A course, they mighta been in the artillery, but my best guess is the whole bunch of 'em was ranch hands."

"Did you see enough boot prints to figure out how they'd move, or how they'd look?"

"Well, one of them's got on boots that's wore down on the left outside edge. I'd say he sorta lurches when he walks, maybe even got a limp. One of the fellows is a lot bigger than the other ones; he sinks into the ground more. He's a cigar smoker, the two-for-a-nickel kind. There's one I got tagged as a cowhand for sure; he toes in and walks on the outsides of his feet. I can't help you much about the others, except one's a tobacco chewer." When Longarm said nothing, the scout looked at him questioningly and asked, "You figure that'll give you enough to spot 'em?"

"It's a hell of a lot more'n the officers in charge of the depot could tell me, Buck."

Fraser went on, "Well, after I'd asked about a thousand questions from the soldier boys back there, I found out that the riding horses is two roans, two browns and a dapple. The wagon horse is a grey; it left some tail hairs in the shafts. A course, you can spot it by the calks on its shoes."

Longarm nodded. "Anything special about the shoes on the other ones?" he asked.

"Oh, sure. After you've followed the trail a little ways you won't have no trouble telling 'em apart. There's one that's carrying a heavier load than the others. I'd imagine the biggest man of the five is mounted on it, because it sure leaves a deeper mark than even the wagon horse does. Now, one of the other ones has got a loose nail sticking outa the shoe on its off hind hoof. There's another one with a chip gone in the shoe on its near front hoof. One of the nags limps a little bit, favors its near hind leg when the going's rough. The shoes on the other one is wore down so bad that the heel calks just barely makes a mark."

Longarm did not ask how the scout had arrived at his conclusions. He did not need to; he knew and used the same deductive processes himself.

If he'd taken the time to study the ground around the wagon, he would have found the same footprints, the same clues that basically came from studying the hoofprints of the horses and the boot prints of the escaping bandits. He could almost see the army scout discovering a cigar butt or two, a wad of spat-out chewing tobacco, and, from the position of the footprints, distinguishing the man who smoked from the one who chewed.

"You give me a lot of help, Buck," Longarm said. "I'd like nothing better'n to have you ride on with me till I catch up with them fellows, but you know why I can't."

"Sure. Orders is orders in your line, just like it is in mine. Except I cut mine pretty thin sometimes."

"Oh, so do I, but this is one time when I can't."

Except for an occasional word or two when Fraser pointed to a set of the tracks they were following, they rode on in silence as the sun dropped closer to the western mountains. After a bit more than an hour, Fraser pulled up his horse. Longarm stopped, too. The scout waved at the vast expanse of arid tan soil that stretched ahead of them and said, "Well, there it is. Everything in front of us to the east and north is Navajo Reservation land, so here's where I got to say goodbye."

Easing back in his saddle, Longarm surveyed the vista. The expanse of country in front of the two riders was relatively smooth, a uniform sand-hued tan broken only by an occasional dark rock outcrop. It seemed to roll in gigantic swells, like huge tidal bulges on the surface of an ocher-colored ocean, and stretched for what seemed to be an endless distance to the line of an infinitely far horizon.

In the west the sun had dropped close to the jagged peaks that rose beyond the humps of a stretch of foothills. The peaks, the more distant silhouettes of the rugged San Francisco Mountains, dominated the horizon until they merged with and became lost in the shadowed shoulders of the vast Coconino Plateau.

On the east, the rainbow hues of the Painted Desert were more intense in the slanting sunlight than they'd been in early afternoon. They glowed with an endless array of colors, surface blotches in streaks and stripes that rose from a generally level surface. Everywhere he looked there was color, not only across the flats, but in the places where buttes jutted and broken humps of rock formations rose and low cliffs no higher than a man's knees rippled across the rainbowed land. There was no pattern to the colors. They ran in all directions in strips and stripes and uneven blotches of yellow and orange, pink and rosy red, and pale lavender shading to deep purple.

"All I got to say is, I sure hope them fellows that robbed the depot payroll ain't smart enough to take off in that Painted Desert," Longarm observed. "A man couldn't see a damn elephant wandering around there, with all them colors to confuse him."

"You noticed the outlaws moved this far in a pretty straight line," Fraser said. "My hunch is they're making for the Little Colorado. That'd be about fifteen miles ahead."

"You've scouted along the river, I suppose?"

"Oh, sure, before the War Department begun keeping us off the Navajos' lands."

"Last night I looked at that ordnance map I carry in my saddlebags," Longarm went on. "But I didn't see any crossings marked close by here. Where's the best ones?"

"There ain't any best ones." Fraser smiled mirthlessly. "A man can get down the gorge to the river in two or three places between here and where the Little Colorado flows into the big one, but anyplace you cross, you're going to wish you'd picked out another one."

"It's that bad, is it?"

"Oh, I guess I pulled my bowstring back a mite far when I said that, Longarm. If you've travelled west of the Mississippi as much as me, and I reckon you have from what I've heard about you, the Little Colorado ain't going to bother you. Just take your time and let your nag pick his way, and don't try to ford the damn river anyplace where you can't see signs others has crossed there. You do that, you'll be all right."

"Thanks for the tip, Buck. I'll be riding on, then. See you if you're still here when I get back."

"Sure. But chances are I'll be sent back to Wingate by the time you show up here again. Good luck to you."

Longarm nodded, touched the brim of his tobacco-colored Stetson with a forefinger, and toed the gelding ahead. The chestnut set off at the deliberate walk a desert-wise animal learns to use on the trackless plains of the West. Fraser sat watching for a moment, then reined his own horse around and started back to the ordnance depot.

Longarm did not prod the chestnut gelding, but let it pick its own way and set its own pace. He divided his attention between the horizon and the ground in front of him. The horizon seemed the same distance ahead every time he looked, but his scanning of the ground was rewarded now and then by the sight of a shallow hoofprint in the hard-baked soil.

Usually the prints he spotted were more ghosts than anything else, shallow and almost invisible. Now and then, however, when he encountered an expanse of earth that was sandier than usual, or crossed one of the small depressions where water collected during a rare rainstorm had left a thin crust of mud, he could see sets of unusually distinct prints left by the hooves of the outlaws' horses.

After he'd seen them clearly once, he carried them in his

mind fully formed, and knew that whenever he saw them again he'd be sure to recognize them at once from his own memory rather than relying on Fraser's descriptions. As detailed as the scout's descriptions had been, Longarm preferred to trust the evidence of his own eyes.

By the time he'd followed the outlaws' track to the canyon of the Little Colorado River the sun had set, but on both sides of the yawning, ragged crevasse the plain was still bathed in the golden afterglow of the pre-dusk sky. Keeping a firm hand on the reins, Longarm nudged the horse to the edge of the river canyon. He looked down, and found that he was gazing into darkness. He could see the first ten or fifteen yards of the narrow, precipitous trail that zigzagged down the almost vertical wall, but only an occasional glint from the water's surface broke the gloom at the bottom.

Old son, he told himself, *that ain't no trail for a man who don't know it to take in the dark, especially when he's on a strange horse. The best thing you can do is camp up here on the rim and wait till it's full daylight before you try to get over to the other side of the river.*

In the final glow of the waning sunset, Longarm made camp a dozen yards away from the canyon's rim and a short distance off the trail. He tethered the horse to a sizeable boulder and put a scanty measure of oats in its nosebag. While the animal munched noisily, he spread his blanket roll, put his saddle at one end, and covered the saddle with his folded coat for a pillow. Sitting down with his legs folded Indian style, he ate a quick supper of jerky and parched corn.

By the time he'd finished eating, the light was completely gone, but his eyes had adjusted to the transition, and he moved swiftly to complete his preparations. Taking off his gunbelt, he slid the holstered Colt under the arch of the saddle, with the butt protruding where it would be ready to his hand. He laid his rifle at the edge of the blanket, the stock even with his chest. Before slipping out of his vest he lighted a final cigar and puffed it while he folded the vest, tucked it under the saddle, and laid his hat beside it.

Sliding between the folds of the blanket, fully dressed even to his boots, he lay staring through dissipating trails of cigar smoke at the stars that crowded the blue-black sky. In the stillness he could hear the faint murmur of the river a quarter of a mile below in the bottom of the canyon. Except for an occasional scraping of the horse's hooves, the low whisper of the river was the only sound that broke the quiet. Two minutes after he'd snuffed out the butt of his cigar on the ground beside his bed, Longarm was asleep.

Full daylight, the half-hour or so of translucent light that separates dawn from sunrise in the Western high country, found Longarm sitting the gelding at the canyon's edge, examining the area of soft soil around the spot where the trail started down the wall of the gorge. Here, where travellers usually stopped to give their mounts a brief rest before starting the trip to the floor of the gorge, the earth had been powdered and softened, the hard surface churned to fine sand.

Shod horses using the crossing were far outnumbered by the unshod ponies of the Navajos, and Longarm found the hoofprints he was looking for almost at once. Among the split-hoof prints of Navajo ponies, those of shod horses stood out in sharp relief. He quickly spotted the deep double-calked shoes of the wagon horse, the even deeper marks of the most heavily laden ridden pony, and the others with their identifying characteristics.

Manure piles were plentiful in the sanded area. Some of the droppings were obviously old, dessicated in the dry air and crumbling away to shreds. Others were fresher. Longarm prowled around the area of soft sand until he found a spot where the hoofprints of the wagon horse showed the animal had stood while voiding, and prodded the manure balls with his boot toe. The droppings were firmly crusted, but the crust was thin, the manure inside fresh and dark.

Them piles was dropped not more'n a day or two ago, old son, Longarm told himself. *That bunch of outlaws ain't moving fast as you can; they got too much of a load. If you get after 'em right away, chances are you can catch up to 'em about the middle of tomorrow morning.*

Swinging into the saddle, he nudged the cavalry mount ahead with his booted toe and started down the precipitous trail to the river.

Like a crumpled piece of ribbon that has been slashed at and wadded up before being hung on a nail to dangle by one end, the trail zigzagged down the almost vertical wall of the gorge. It was no path to be taken by the timid. The pathway worn on the face of the cliff passed through layers of earth and layers of stone, and both were treacherous under a horse's hooves.

Even metal horseshoes could not bite into the bared rock strata, and when rock gave way to dirt the soft, sandy soil was studded with rocks that ranged in size from those as big as a man's head to those as small as a clenched fist. The rocks shifted in the crumbly dirt, and caused the horse's hooves to slip even more dangerously than did the stretches of unyielding stone. In places the stone was a mere honeycomb, eroded by the currents when it had been exposed to the river's flow centuries earlier. The soft spots crumbled under the weight of horse and rider, throwing them off balance.

Longarm took his time in the lurching descent, keeping a firm hand on the reins, and when after almost an hour had passed the gelding finally stepped onto a wide stretch of moist sand at the bottom he was glad to rein in and dismount, leaving the horse to stand with its legs trembling and quaking.

That was sure some kinda trip, old son, he told himself, sliding a cheroot from his pocket and lighting it as he looked across the roiling surface of the Little Colorado at the steep cliff he would be faced with ascending to get out of the gorge. *Them outlaws must've had it worse, though, with all the money bags they was carrying. Wonder they ever made it at all.*

He did not have to search to find the tracks left by his quarry. They were impressed in the moist sand in front of him, among a maze of other prints made by unshod Navajo ponies. None of the hoofprints of the Indian horses overlaid those of the outlaws' mounts, and Longarm took this as evidence that he was the first to enter the gorge after they'd passed through. Leaving the gelding on the sandy strip to drink and rest, Longarm started along the bank on foot, following the trail left by the robbers.

Even though the soft sand that covered the ledge between the base of the cliff and the river soon gave way to a long stretch of stone, he had no trouble picking up their tracks beyond the rocky stretch, where he entered another strip of sandy bank. He'd covered fifty or sixty yards of the sandy section when he stopped and shook his head.

You're getting careless as a sleepy sheepdog, old son, his thoughts ran. *There's two sets of them fellows' tracks here. One set goes downriver, the other set shows they come back, too.*

Frowning, he kept moving downstream, curious to see why the outlaws had retraced their trail. He found the answer soon enough. The second section of sandy bank covered perhaps a quarter of a mile, then it gave way to a progressively narrowing ledge of rock, which ended in a fissure that ran up the sheer wall of the river's gorge.

Don't take much brains to see why they turned back, he thought as he turned and started retracing his steps. *There ain't no place to go but across the river.*

By this time the bottom of the gorge had grown much lighter as sunrise brightened the strip of sky visible above it. The river's surface, black and forbidding only a short time earlier, was now catching light and becoming transparent. As he walked along the bank, Longarm looked more closely at the stream and found that in shallow places he could see its bottom.

There were few shallow spots, he noted. Most of the stream flowed deep and fast through its narrow bed, and where he could see the bottom it was covered with loose stones on which the hooves of a horse would slip easily. A frown grew on his face as Longarm trudged back along the bank, but it vanished when he reached the first strip of sandy bank he'd traversed.

Here the sandbank shelved out into the river, and he saw what he'd been too engrossed in his exploration of the ledge to notice when he'd moved across it on his walk downstream. The prints of the outlaw's horses were plain, leading from the ledge into the river. By bending and squinting and changing the angle at which he looked, Longarm saw that the sandy shelf extended all the way across the stream to the opposite bank.

You got the answer now, old son, he told himself as he straightened up and lighted a cigar. *This is one of them fords that Buck Fraser told you to find. Looks like them fellows you're after found it, too, or knew about it already.*

Longarm moved swiftly now. He went on upstream to where the gelding was still standing and swung into the saddle. Toeing the animal ahead, he walked it to the sandspit and started crossing the river. The sandy strip under the cavalry horse's hooves was smooth, and the light had improved now to the point where he could see rounded dents on the bottom.

Though the scouring action of the current had washed away details, the dents were what remained of the hoofprints of horses that had used the ford in the past few days. Given a week, the current would have washed the bottom smooth again.

Longarm did not try to suppress the smile that came to his lips. He'd cut down very sharply the lead the outlaws had enjoyed. He settled back and began studying the east wall of the gorge, looking for the trail that led upward, as the gelding splashed through the shallow water to the river's east bank.

Ingrained habit born of many manhunts and chases led Longarm to look closely at the riverbank where the horse emerged from the water. The smile that had wreathed his sun-bronzed face turned into a thoughtful frown. There were no footprints of shod horses in the sand of the riverbank. All that dotted the surface were the split-hoof imprints of Navajo ponies.

Hold on here, old son, Longarm frowned, reining in at the water's edge. *Them damn horses went in on the other side, and there ain't no way they could've just dropped outa sight in the middle of the river. Question is, where'd they come out?*

Still frowning, he wheeled the gelding around and started retracing his path along the sandbar. The water was slightly roiled by his recent passage, but clear enough for him to see the prints made by the gelding's hooves as it crossed from the west to the east bank. The outlines of his horse's hooves were clear-cut and sharp, not yet eroded by the current as were the rounded dents made by the horses that had crossed earlier.

That just ain't possible, Longarm mused as he sat staring at the riverbed. *But the way I read them tracks, them outlaws and their horses just up and disappeared someplace in the middle of this damned river!*

Chapter 7

Reining up in midstream, Longarm studied the sandy bottom. He'd stopped where the water was shallowest, the highest point of the sandbank, and from the vantage point his saddle gave him he could see the underwater sandspit in its entirety, from the east bank to the west. The only hoofprints visible in the smooth sand through the glass-clear water were the partly washed-out ones he'd noted earlier and those made by his own mount. No prints led upstream or down; all had been made by horses crossing the Little Colorado.

Now, there's got to be an answer to this one, old son, he mused. Six horses don't just drop outa sight in a river where the bottom's like it is here. If it wasn't for the loads them animals was carrying, them outlaws might've swum the nags across, but they sure couldn't swim a horse that was toting a load of cartwheels or double eagles. No, swimming's out. Them bastards pulled some sorta trick, and unless you ain't as smart as they are, you oughta be able to figure out what it was.

For several minutes, Longarm sat silently in midstream, examining the prints. Then his face furrowed into a thoughtful frown and he walked the horse slowly to the west bank. Reining in, he looked closely again at the prints on the sand-covered ledge above the stream. There were plenty of them to study on the bank: his own, those of the outlaw gang's horses going downstream and returning, as well as others made when they'd milled around on shore before entering the water. There were also scores of older hoofprints made by unshod Navajo ponies.

Still frowning, Longarm recrossed to the east bank and took another close look at the prints his gelding had made when it left the stream. Then he studied once again the overlapping maze of hoofprints on the sandy ledge. When the answer he'd been seeking did come, it arrived in a sudden flash.

You was just about to be took in by the oldest trick in the world, old son, he told himself with a long sigh of relief. *There ain't but one way to account for them hoofprints changing in the middle of that river. Them outlaw sons of bitches took the shoes off their horses before they waded 'em across.*

Once he'd seen the answer, confirming its correctness was a simple matter. He crossed back over to the west bank and spent several minutes in an almost inch-by-inch examination of the sandy surface of the ledge. Knowing what he was looking for made it easy to confirm his deduction. The hoofprints and the prints of the outlaws' boots that before had been lost in the maze of overlapping impressions in the moist sand told their own story, and now he could read it in the yielding earth.

It took Longarm only a short time to find a spot where the mixture of hoofprints and boot prints indicated that the horse with the heaviest load had stood while its shoes were being pried off. Judging from the size and depth of the bootmarks, it was the big outlaw who'd handled the job. Longarm even found a spot where the outlaw had laid aside or dropped the horseshoeing hammer he was using; the soft sand held a clear impression of the hammer's stubby handle and extra-wide claws.

Though he was sure he'd find similar impressions elsewhere, Longarm wasted no time in looking for them. Now that the riddle which had puzzled him so greatly had been solved and confirmed once, no further evidence was needed.

At least one of them jackaroos has got some sense, Longarm thought as the chestnut gelding picked its way daintily along the sandbar to the east bank once again. *I got to give him credit for that, even if he did give me a bad time there for a few minutes. Might be he's given me a worse time than I can handle, though. It ain't going to be no easy job picking out the prints of them outlaws' horses from here on out. With no horseshoes on, they're going to look just like the prints them Navajo ponies leave, and that's sure as hell going to make for hard tracking.*

After he'd mounted the steep, torturous path that led up the eastern wall of the gorge, finding it even more difficult than the trail on the opposite side, Longarm found that his prediction had been correct. On the sun-baked crust of the desert soil it was very hard indeed for him to judge the difference in the depth of the prints made by the outlaw gang's horses and those which had been ridden by the constantly moving Navajos.

After he'd ridden a few miles, stopping wherever a group

of hoofprints branched off the trail he was following, Longarm decided that he could not depend on his keen eyesight alone to distinguish the tracks of the outlaws' mounts. He began stopping wherever one of the horses had dropped a pile of dung, then dismounting and breaking the manure balls with his boot heel to determine its age.

This was a more certain way of keeping on the right trail than trying to judge the depth of the tracks, but it also took a great deal more time. Each set of tracks that led off the main trail had to be investigated. All those he checked proved false trails, but the danger of making a mistake was so great that he dared not disregard them. Each time he investigated a branching trail meant the loss of many valuable minutes, and he pictured the outlaws stretching their lead on him.

As the long afternoon dragged slowly on, Longarm became so tired of jumping off the horse and remounting it every few miles that at the first blush of sunset he was more than ready to stop for the night. When he'd attended to his routine before-bedtime chores, feeding the gelding, eating his own sparse supper, and spreading his bedroll with the usual precaution of placing his weapons within easy reach, he was too out of sorts to enjoy a final cigar.

He'd already slid one out of his vest pocket and was reaching for a match when he realized that he needed sleep more than he did a smoke. His feet were hot and aching after the dozens of times he'd dismounted and remounted during the day, and after replacing the cigar in his pocket and tucking his folded vest in its usual place he slipped the boots off. Bone-weary, he pulled up his blanket and before a dozen seconds had ticked off was sound asleep.

Even Longarm's muscular and resilient physique had been strained by the long and unusually active day he'd just put in. He slept soundly and did not wake until the first rays of the rising sun crept across the Painted Desert. Accustomed by long habit to waking at the first hint of dawn, Longarm sat up in his blankets and rubbed his eyes.

Automatically, he reached for his vest and took out the cheroot he hadn't lighted the night before. With the cigar held firmly between his big, strong teeth, he was reaching for a match when he suddenly realized there was something wrong. He blinked and looked around. The chestnut gelding was missing.

Instantly Longarm was fully awake and alert. He glanced around, swivelling his torso to cover the entire landscape, but there was no sign of the chestnut. Stopping only long enough to pull on his boots, the unlighted cigar still in his jaws, he got to his feet, but even with his eyes higher above ground level than when he'd been sitting down, he could see no sign of the missing horse.

Frowning thoughtfully, Longarm strapped on his pistol belt and started walking slowly in a wide circle around his campsite. The circuit took only a moment to complete, but his close scrutiny of the ground had satisfied him that no one had crept up during the hours of darkness and stolen the gelding. He stepped over to the spot where he'd left the chestnut, with a big rock rolled on top of its lead rope to anchor the tether in place, and examined the ground around the rock.

A freshly cut groove underneath the boulder told him what had happened. At some time during the night the gelding had snaked the lead rope from beneath the stone and wandered off. While he stood gazing at the groove that explained how the horse had freed itself, Longarm lighted the cheroot in his mouth. Through a coil of blue smoke he scolded himself in one of those silent conversations in which he habitually indulged when he was alone.

Old son, somebody oughta kick your tailbone so hard you could reach up and pick a star outa the sky.

Thinking of the sky reminded Longarm; he glanced at the sun, already losing its red sunrise hue as it hung low above the vivid colors of the Painted Desert. The day would be a hot one. He could tell that already, for the air was warming rapidly.

Sure you was tired last night, but that ain't no reason why you had to sleep as sound as a field hand who'd done a day's hard plowing.

With a reflective shudder, a picture flashed through Longarm's memory of how the sweat drained off his skinny young body when as a lad not yet in his teens he'd wrestled the handles of a plow trying to cut a straight furrow through the stony hillside fields of a hardscrabble West Virginia farm.

Now you let them outlaws get a better start on you than they already had. If they're figuring on scattering, like gangs do after they pull off a job, you might not ever catch all of 'em.

His lips tightening, Longarm could almost see the gang's

members sitting around a campfire before splitting up, while they divided the money it was his job to recover.

And just suppose somebody'd snuck up on you while you was sawing wood. They could've had their gun on you before you knew there was anybody within ten miles.

He shook his head soberly. It had been a long time since he'd dropped his guard so badly while on a case. There'd been very few times when anybody could have surprised him, whether he was awake or asleep. In Longarm's book, however, past successes were no excuse for present failure.

But getting mad at yourself ain't going to help none, old son. It ain't going to be such a much of a trick to trail that chestnut gelding. It's got shoes on its hooves, and all the other horses that's passed over that trail's been unshod.

Even that small sop to ultimate success cheered him measurably. *You better hurry up and put some grub down your gullet, old son, and get ready to limber up a little bit, because you got a long ways to go and shank's mare's the only way to make it.*

Relieved to be going into action instead of thinking about his mistakes, Longarm discarded the thoughts that bothered him. He dug the ordnance map out of his saddlebags and unfolded it. The map was old, of pre-War vintage, but it showed the main features of the area. As closely as he could, Longarm located his present position on the map and then looked from it in all directions to find his options.

Except for the Navajo and Hopi settlements a good distance to the east, the nearest towns shown on the map were one named Tuba City, which lay almost due north about forty miles away, and Lee's Ferry, another fifty miles farther and to the northwest.

Now, that Tuba City place might be where them outlaws is heading for. Longarm mused thoughtfully. *It'd be natural for 'em to make for the only place where they could spend some of that money they stole. This trail don't seem to lead that way, but likely there'll be a branch off it someplace up ahead that'll take a man there. Which being the case, that's the best place you can aim for, old son.*

He folded his blankets into a long flat roll that would cushion his shoulders and, in spite of the heat that the day would bring later on, put on his coat. It was easier to wear the garment than to carry it, and its pockets were needed to hold his everyday

60

requirements. He lifted his saddle to one shoulder, hung his canteen on the opposite shoulder, and picked up his rifle as another counterbalance to the saddle's weight. Grim-faced, he started walking.

At first Longarm rather enjoyed the unfamiliar sensation of seeing the terrain around him at closer range and with more time to examine it than was possible on horseback. The morning was still cool; the sun had not yet heated the air and soil.

As he swung along at a steady, ground-eating pace, Longarm kept close watch on the tracks that marked his path. There were too many hoofprints of unshod horses for him to be certain he could pick out those made by the heavily loaded animals the outlaws were riding, but in two of the softer patches of ground he crossed he saw tracks made by the shod hooves of the strayed chestnut, which gave him more incentive to keep moving steadily.

More often than on the previous day, Longarm saw less heavily marked trails leading off the one which obviously was used the most. These branches, he decided, must lead to one or another of the Navajo settlements which lay east of the river, while the main trail led to the main Colorado River.

He checked each of the branches, however. Whenever he came to one he dropped his gear to the ground and, carrying only his rifle, followed the branch trail until he'd found and investigated enough manure balls to make sure that none of them was fresh. He was still far enough behind the outlaws to make this precaution necessary. The hot sunshine and extremely dry air of the high Moenkopi Plateau he was crossing caused fresh manure piles to begin fading within a few hours after a horse had dropped them, and within two or three days the interior of the balls had dried and faded as well.

Twice during the long morning he saw the hoofprints of the chestnut gelding crossing and re-crossing the trail, proof that the animal was still wandering somewhere ahead of him. When he stopped at noon, however, he had not gotten a glimpse of the strayed horse. Hunkering down beside the trail, Longarm ate a few bites of jerky, chewing it for a long time to get the saliva flowing in his mouth. Then, after taking a scant swallow of water and lighting the only cheroot he'd allowed himself since breakfast, he picked up his load and resumed walking.

* * *

Sunset was still an hour away, and the blazing orb was just beginning to take on an orange hue. To the east, its low-slanted rays added a new dimension to the Painted Desert by creating black patches of shadows where rock formations rose or where the ground was ridged or great boulders stood. Against the darkening blue of the eastern sky the multitude of colors seemed even more vivid than they had at high noon.

Longarm had no time to stop and admire the handiwork of nature which created the fantastic spectacle. The low-hanging sun was sending its rays under the broad brim of his hat, and even his deeply tanned skin was beginning to feel parched and drawn. Still he walked steadily ahead, watching the trail, until he saw the only shelter he'd noticed since setting out.

A short distance ahead and a few yards off the trail an isolated rock outcrop thrust up from the bare ground. A yard or so above its base a ledge extended like a narrow shelf, creating beneath it a slender line of shade. For a brief moment Longarm debated with himself. Daylight would hold for another hour, perhaps a bit more, and even at his progressively slower pace he could cover another mile or two before darkness forced him to stop. Another look at the shaded spot convinced him that the extra distance was less important than getting out of the sun and resting. He left the trail and headed for the rock formation.

Shade had never before been as welcome. After dropping his saddle and laying his rifle carefully beside it, Longarm hunkered down under the ledge. The shaded area was too shallow to allow him to shelter his entire body, and after the long day in the sun's blazing rays any heat at all was too much for comfort.

After a moment of experimenting, Longarm found that by stretching out along the base of the outcrop he could not only get completely into the strip of shade, but that when he pressed against the rock it transferred a welcome coolness to his body. After he'd lain quietly for a few moments, surrounded by the vast stillness of the barren desert, he fell asleep.

Darkness had fallen when he woke, vaguely aware that a noise of some sort had roused him. Fully alert from the time his eyes opened, Longarm lay motionless, listening. The desert night was still except for a distant whispering of the wind. A few thin clouds were scudding across the sky, veiling the moon from time to time, but in the intervals when the clouds passed by he could see almost as well as during daylight.

He heard the noise again, a horse whinnying, and when the sky cleared again he was looking in the direction from which the sound had come. He saw the chestnut gelding as the cloud veil left the moon. The horse was a quarter of a mile away, standing motionless, looking in his direction.

Longarm whistled, and even at that distance the moonlight was bright enough for him to see that the chestnut pricked up its ears. He whistled again and the horse took a tentative step toward him. Longarm rolled out of his shelter and stood up. The gelding started toward him, and Longarm took a few steps in the direction of the horse. The moment he moved, the animal turned and began retreating.

Longarm stopped and whistled once more. The horse turned to look, tossed its head, and, at Longarm's next whistle, stopped and stood as though waiting. Longarm began running toward the horse. The gelding swivelled in its tracks and started trotting away. Longarm ran faster, but the horse did not stop again. Knowing he could not match the beast's pace, Longarm halted once more. This time the gelding did not follow suit, but kept moving until it was lost in the darkness and the distance.

Realizing that anger was a futile waste of time and energy, Longarm held his temper in check. He stood where he'd stopped, and now and then whistled softly, coaxingly, but the gelding did not return. Frustrated, Longarm walked slowly back to the rock outcrop and hunkered down beside his gear. During his short walk he'd had time to think and to remember, and while he took out a cigar and lighted it, he held a silent, thoughtful conference with himself.

Old son, that damned hostler back at the ordnance depot played you for a fool. No wonder he give you such a fine, fancy horse! The damn critter's a runaway teaser!

Longarm had encountered such horses before, animals which through some quirk in their own brains, or because they'd been badly trained, became chronic runaways. Whether the habit was a throwback or one acquired as a colt, the runaways could not be trusted. Some of them even learned to trip the latches of a corral gate in order to make their escape.

Some trainers refused to try to break runaways of their bad habit, but ordered the animals destroyed. Those most familiar with horse traits claimed that no training routine, no amount of extra care, would ever cure a chronic runaway. A few patient trainers worked to cure the flaw in the runaways' makeup, but Longarm could not recall any who had succeeded.

Now that hostler knew damn well what kind of horse he was giving you, old son, Longarm's thoughts ran on. *What you got to figure out is why in hell he done it.*

For a moment, Longarm puffed his cheroot thoughtfully, trying to recall exactly what the hostler had said in response when he'd asked the man why the army was providing him with such an exceptionally fine horse.

He just as good as come out and said somebody told him to palm that runaway off on you, old son, Longarm frowned. *Said something about how he was supposed to make sure you got special attention.*

Longarm racked his brain trying to recall the hostler's exact words, but the incident hadn't seemed important at the time it occurred, and he had taken no special note of what the soldier at the stables had said.

Well, maybe it'll come back and maybe it won't, he told himself philosophically. *But if the hostler was told to give you that runaway nag, who in hell told him? He started to say something about the remount sergeant, but then he stopped right quick and never did go on.*

Again Longarm tried to recall the scene at the stables, but it had seemed so trivial and unimportant at the time, and he'd been so interested in the gelding, that he'd let it pass by.

Now, whoever it was set you up to get the gelding had to know where you was setting out to go and why. But that could be just about anybody on the damn post. There's one thing certain sure, old son. It wasn't no accident you got that runaway. Somebody back on that Army post wanted you to wind up just the way you are right now, high and dry in the middle of the desert. And when you get back to the depot after you catch up with them outlaws, you got to find out who's to blame, because whoever it was, the chances are the gang put 'em up to it!

Chapter 8

Chasing the chestnut gelding had taken up most of the morning, and Longarm ate a combined breakfast and lunch before starting again. His saddle and rifle seemed heavier today, and his pace a bit slower, but he did not think of abandoning his gear or changing the routine he'd established the day before. He continued to investigate each trail that branched off the main track, and though he'd covered only six or seven miles before dusk arrived and forced him to stop for the night, he was satisfied that the outlaws and their loot were still somewhere ahead of him. He did not even try to estimate how much of a lead they had by now.

Shortly after sunrise, Longarm was on the move again. He plodded doggedly along, his eyes fixed on the faint prints of unshod horse hooves that marked the trail. The going today was more difficult than it had been the day before, and his leg muscles ached with each step. Longarm kept his eyes fixed on the trail, for each time he raised his eyes to sweep the vast expanse of baked earth he was reminded of the many painful steps that still lay ahead.

His stomach was also reminding him that the few bites of jerky and parched corn he'd eaten before starting out were a poor substitute for a hot breakfast, and the fragrant smoke of the cheroot he was puffing rasped his dry throat. His saddle seemed to drag down his right shoulder in a way he hadn't noticed before, and the rifle he carried in his left hand to counterbalance the saddle's weight felt heavier than usual.

Setting his jaw a bit more firmly, Longarm continued his slow but steady progress. He felt a bit better near the end of the first two hours or so when he came across the tracks of the runaway chestnut gelding for the first time that day. The marks of the horse's shod hooves stood out clear and sharp against the blurred prints of the shoeless ponies that crisscrossed and overlapped on the main trail.

Letting his saddle slide to the ground, Longarm leaned his rifle across it and followed the hoofprints for a short distance on both sides of the trail. The chestnut's prints slanted across the unmarked desert soil in the same kind of pattern that had marked them from the beginning, a path of aimless wandering.

Reading the silent messages the prints conveyed to his experienced eyes, Longarm could see that the strayed gelding's gait was as steady as ever. Apparently the horse had not yet begun to suffer greatly from lack of feed and water, but Longarm knew that the time was near when the animal would begin to fade unless it had both.

And you ain't much better off than that damn runaway nag, old son, he reminded himself as he returned to his gear. *A man or animal in this kinda country's living on borrowed time unless he gets water and enough of the kinda grub he's got to have.*

Thinking of water, Longarm lifted his canteen. It was much lighter than it had been when he started from the Little Colorado and its felt cover was warm to his touch. He opened the canteen and took a small sip. The dehydrated tissues of his mouth absorbed the water like a blotter, and he swallowed nothing but empty air. He took another sip, and this time the water trickled down his throat. His parched feeling relieved, Longarm slung the canteen in place, picked up his load, and started walking again along what had thus far been a frustrating trail.

Shortly before noon a dry breeze began to stir the usually still air. Longarm had been plodding along slowly, his eyes fixed on the ground. He lifted them now and looked around. To the west, the Painted Desert glowed in its usual crazy-quilt patchwork of unlikely colors, but instead of a sharp horizon line wavering in the heat haze at the eastern rim, the air there was murky and obscured the sky halfway to the zenith where the sun hung. There was no change in its usual clear-cut white blaze, but east of it the sky was tinged with a light brownish stain.

Longarm had seen the West's high desert country in all its aspects, and recognized this one at once. A sandstorm was moving toward him, and moving fast. He watched the hazing sky to the east for a moment or two, gauging the movement of the blow. The sky was darkening rapidly, the haze on the horizon increasing in depth as the face of the storm front approached. He had perhaps a quarter of an hour before the first gusts would reach him.

Looking around for a place to shelter, Longarm saw nothing except barren ground. Under the entire broad bowl of the horizon there was not a rock outcrop, not a hillock, not a gully. In every direction the land stretched flat and featureless. There was no place visible that would provide a refuge.

Stepping a few paces off the trail, Longarm laid his gear on the ground and took out his pocketknife. Even its largest blade was small, but it was the best digging tool he had. With quick, sure strokes he slashed the outline of a rectangle on the hard soil. The lines enclosed an area roughly six feet by three feet. Stabbing and hacking at the baked earth, he deepened and widened the lines, scraping the loose dirt into a line parallel with the miniature trenches he'd dug.

Inside the rectangle he placed his saddlebags and saddle, his rifle and canteen. Unfolding his blanket, he fitted one edge into the trench and filled the trench with the loose dirt he'd scraped while digging. With his boot heels he tamped the soil as solidly as possible to anchor the blanket's edge. He pulled the blanket loosely over the rectangle and folded one end under, reaching beneath the blanket to shift his saddle until it lay on the section he'd folded under, weighting it down.

Folding the remaining long side of the blanket was harder, but he finally managed to get its full length tucked under and in place. He slid his rifle between the folds and maneuvered the gun until it rested in the shallow trench, then piled dirt on top of the blanket's fold that was now held in the trench by the weight of the Winchester. Then, with his boot heels, he tamped the loose soil as firmly as he could over the bulge made by the rifle and along the edge of the blanket, adding more dirt until it was level with the ground.

Now Longarm had a loose cocoon into which he wriggled with slow, careful moves. When he was finally stretched full-length on the blanket, he tucked the loose side sections under his body. His final move was to slide his hat down beside his feet and pull the last loose flap of the blanket over his head and tuck its ends under his broad shoulders. He maneuvered his canteen up over one shoulder and his saddlebags over the other to weight down the top fold. Then he stretched out and waited for the storm to reach him.

He did not have long to wait. Already dim, the interior of

his cocoon grew darker as the sandstorm came closer. Gusts of wind rippled the blanket, tugging at it. A low humming sound came through the thick sturdy fabric. The humming increased and grew higher in pitch until it became a shriek, then a wild howl.

Minute after minute the raging cry of the wind grew louder and its gusts grew stronger. The blanket billowed as the loose dirt in the outside trench where the rifle anchored the edge was picked up by the gusts. A thin stream of gritty dust found its way through a gap formed when the pulses of the gusting wind lifted the blanket's edge.

Longarm managed to get the toe of his boot on the loose edge in time to anchor it before his frail protective cover was ripped away. He'd seen men and animals caught in such storms before, men whom the abrasive grains of sand had left half blinded, their faces pitted and scoured raw, horses that had choked and died when their nostrils and mouths filled with sand. He'd seen guns that had been left out in these desert sand gales, the bluing scoured from their barrels to expose streaks of bright steel, the stocks stripped to the bare wood, the actions so jammed with microscopic grains of dust that the weapons were useless except as clubs.

He did not try to keep track of the length of time the storm raged above his precarious shelter. At its peak, fine streams of dust were forced through the thick, closely woven fabric, dust grains almost too small to see, but which coated his skin and clothing and filled his nostrils and mouth when he tried to breathe through the protective bandana he'd wrapped around the lower part of his face.

Whatever the duration of the storm, it lasted long enough so that he was exhausted from the tension of keeping his shelter intact while the blow peaked and waned. Longarm could not see the storm's passing, but he'd witnessed enough such blows to know what was taking place as the howling of the wild wind diminished slowly, almost imperceptibly, and finally died away. The sand no longer swept across the soil in an almost solid wall; the sky turned from black to brown to yellow and then became blue again.

As soon as the blanket no longer pulsed above him and tried to fly away in response to the wind's wild gusting, Longarm came out of his shelter. The terrain around him bore no signs of the storm except for a few small drifts of sand caught in the hoofprints of the trail. There were no boulders against which the sand could have drifted, no shrubs or trees to have been uprooted, no grass to be scoured away by the abrasive, wind-blown grains. Looking at his surroundings, Longarm would not have known a gale had passed over had he not been caught in it.

Neither the Painted Desert to the east nor the high bare tableland of the Moenkopi Plateau gave any evidence of the windstorm's sudden passage. Longarm wiped his face as clear as possible of the dust that clung to it, opened his canteen, and let two small sips of water trickle slowly down his throat. Then he lighted a cheroot to puff on while he reasssambled his gear. This was a simple job, requiring only a few minutes. Shouldering his saddle once more, Longarm started off at the same slow, steady pace that had brought him from the Little Colorado. He still followed the hoof-pocked trail that led north.

As he trudged steadily through the afternoon, Longarm made fewer stops than had been necessary earlier when he checked out the off-branching trails. The sun was dropping low when he saw what he took at first to be a large rock outcrop on the horizon. He paid scant attention to the vague shape until the distance lessened and he realized that its geometrically exact corners were foreign to nature and belonged to a man-made structure.

Gradually the formless hump took shape as he drew closer to it, and he suppressed a sigh of relief when he could tell at last that he was drawing close to the first sign of civilization he'd encountered since crossing the Little Colorado. Even at a distance he could recognize the structure as a traditional Navajo dwelling, a double hogan. The twin hogans, made of peeled logs laid to form eight-sided walls, were roofed with earth piled into the form of a low dome. The dwelling, actually two hogans that shared a common wall on one of their octagonal sides, were common in Navajo country. The hogan stood half a mile west of the trail and Longarm began angling toward it at once.

Approaching the hogan, he saw that behind it there was a small corral which had been hidden by the structure, and as he drew closer he could get an occasional glimpse of horses moving around in the pole enclosure. Seeing the horses raised Longarm's spirits at once. He walked faster, deciding as he approached that no matter whether he had to rent or buy a horse, or to get one by issuing an unauthorized government requisition, he was going to ride away from this place.

In spite of his weariness and the heavy load he carried, Longarm increased his pace. He looked in vain for some sign of life around the dwelling, but saw none. There was no smoke rising from the stovepipe chimney that protruded from one side of the hogan, and except for one small window with board shutters there was no opening on the sides of the structure that he could see. He pressed on, forcing his aching leg muscles to keep up the brisk pace he'd set.

Longarm was within a hundred yards of the hogans when the shutters opened a crack. The muzzle of a rifle was thrust through the slitted opening and the rifle barked. Its slug kicked up a puff of dust half a dozen paces to one side of Longarm's feet. Before he could drop his gear and get his Winchester into action the rifle spoke again and a second bullet plowed into the ground on his other side.

Even before the second shot sounded, Longarm had let his saddle and saddlebags slide to the ground. He did not waste time shouldering his Winchester, but fired from the hip. He heard his slug thunk into the board shutters of the window. Then a third shot rang out from the cabin and the bullet raised a puff of dust from the ground a couple of yards from his feet.

Longarm hit the dirt. He peered over his rifle sights for a target, but all that he could see was a six-inch-wide slit in the cabin's window shutters with the barrel of the rifle sticking out through the crack. He drew a bead on the black slit, but before triggering another shot the thought struck him that whoever was in the cabin had missed three easy shots.

That wasn't no accident, old son, he told himself. *Whoever that is inside ain't trying to hit you. They're just telling you to stop and palaver.*

He raised the rifle in one hand, its muzzle pointing to the sky, and shouted, "I ain't come looking for trouble! If you let me get up closer, I can prove that to you real quick."

Silence followed Longarm's shout. He lay motionless, his rifle still pointing straight up, and waited while the seconds ticked away. Then, to his complete surprise, a woman's voice replied.

"How're you going to prove what you said?"

Longarm's surprise delayed his answer for only a moment. "You'll see that when I show you my papers," he called. "But

I got to be close enough so you can read 'em."

Again there was a long silence from the hogan. At last the woman's voice was raised in reply. "All right. I'll look."

Longarm started to stand up, but dropped quickly and lay prone again when the rifle rang out. With the buzzing of an angry wasp a bullet buried itself in the earth directly in front of him and only half a dozen paces distant.

"I didn't say you could move, damn you!" the woman called angrily. "You lay right where you are!"

"How're you going to look at my papers if you won't let me bring 'em to you?" Longarm asked.

"You'll see, soon enough. First thing you've got to do is lay that rifle down on the ground and back away from it. Soon as you're out of reach of the gun, you can stand up."

Longarm hesitated only momentarily before obeying. When he'd crawfished backward away from the Winchester and gotten to his feet, the woman spoke again.

"Now get out whatever it is you want me to look at."

Wondering how the speaker was going to get his credentials, Longarm took out the leather wallet which held his federal marshal's badge and the travel vouchers he'd been given in Denver. He held the wallet high, where it would be easily seen.

"Here's what I want you to see," he called.

"All right. Just stay still and don't move."

Still wondering, Longarm obeyed. A few moments later a dog appeared around the corner of the hogan. The animal was of a breed Longarm did not recognize, some variant of the shepherds' dogs he'd seen in sheepherding country.

It was a big dog. As it started toward him, Longarm judged that it would stand mid-thigh to his long legs. The dog had a rough, straggly dark coat, a deep grey that was almost black, with fur a few shades lighter under its belly and on the back side of its long plumed tail. There was also a sprinkle of light fur on the animals' long, blunt muzzle.

Without hesitating, but with its head reared cautiously, the dog came toward Longarm. It stopped when it was a dozen feet away and stood looking at him for a moment, then whined.

"All right, Yatzee," the woman called. "Go on to the man." After a moment's silence she added, "He won't hurt you."

Longarm could not decide whether she was speaking to him or to the dog, but he did not move. Cautiously, its dark brown eyes fixed on Longarm, the dog advanced slowly. It did not

71

stop until it was an arm's length away from where Longarm waited.

"Move slow, now, mister," the woman commanded Longarm. "Hold out that wallet where Yatzee can take it in her mouth."

With slow deliberation, Longarm bent forward and extended the wallet. The dog did not move or shift its eyes from him.

"Take, Yatzee!" the woman commanded.

Still eyeing Longarm, the dog stretched out its head and took the wallet into its mouth.

"Good girl!" the woman called. "Now fetch, Yatzee!"

Obediently, the dog turned and trotted back to the hogan. It disappeared around the corner of the building. Longarm waited patiently. After a moment, the woman spoke again.

"Your name's Custis Long?" she called.

"That's right, ma'am," Longarm replied. "And if you'll look at them papers in the wallet you'll find my travel orders. And there's some federal vouchers in there, too, that I can cash for expense money. They're all signed by my chief in Denver."

"How do I know you're telling me the truth?" she asked. "For all I know, you could be another one of them damn outlaws that's trying to catch up with his friends. You could've killed the real Custis Long and taken the wallet off his body."

"Well, I got to allow that's what could've happened," Longarm agreed, "only it didn't."

"If you're a U. S. marshal, how come you've showed up here on foot, toting your saddle?"

"Because some fool hostler back at the Navajo Ordnance Depot in Flagstaff give me a horse that strays. The critter wandered off a couple of nights ago when I got careless and didn't tether it tight enough."

"What kind of horse was it?"

"Chestnut gelding, stood about fifteen hands at the withers. Had a U. S. Cavalry brand on the off side of its rump."

"What kind of tether was you using?"

"Hard-braided rope with a wove-in neck loop," Longarm replied with a frown, trying to figure out the purpose of the question.

Again there was a long silence from the cabin before the woman spoke once more. She said, "If you're a U. S. marshal, I guess you'd be carrying more than one gun. Have you got on a pistol belt under that coat?"

72

"Yes, ma'am. I have," Longarm answered.

"All right," she said at last. "Now you do exactly what I tell you to. You understand me, mister? Because if you don't, I'm not going to aim to miss the next time I pull the trigger."

"You tell me what you want me to do, and I'll guarantee to do it just like you say," Longarm assured her.

"First thing is, you get out your pistol and hold it where I can watch while you take the cartridges out of the cylinder. I'm going to be counting, and you take them out one at a time."

Without protesting, Longarm drew his Colt slowly and held the weapon up in front of him while he unloaded it. He held up the empty revolver.

"Fine. Now you can drop the cartridges in your pocket and put your gun back in the holster."

After he'd obeyed the woman's orders, Longarm held out his empty hands. "You can see I ain't afraid to do what you tell me to," he called. "Is it all right for me to come up to the house now, ma'am?"

"Come ahead. Leave your rifle where it's at, and walk slow. Me and Yatzee will be watching. You'll have to come around the west end of the hogan to get to the door. I'll open it for you, but when you walk through it I'll be standing there covering you with my rifle if you try to pull anything off."

Chapter 9

"You don't have to worry, ma'am," Longarm said. "I don't aim to try to pull no tricks on you."

"Come along, then," she replied. "If you're really who you say you are, we need to do some talking, you and me."

Moving slowly and deliberately, Longarm walked to the hogan and around its end, just as he'd been instructed to do. A door yawned open in the wall. He stepped inside. The interior was dim compared to the bright sunlight he'd just left and for a moment he stood just inside the door blinking, waiting for his eyes to adjust to the changed light.

As his vision cleared, he glanced quickly around the room, getting an impression of bareness, but his attention was concentrated on the woman he was seeing for the first time. She stood in the doorway that connected the two hogans, her rifle ready at her shoulder, a finger on the trigger. The dog stood beside her. She said nothing for a moment, but stood taking stock of Longarm, while at the same time he studied her.

He saw a woman no longer young, put poised in those middle years of maturity when she has accepted as normal a thickening waistline and a rounding layer of flesh on her face. There was no grey in her light brown hair. Her eyes were a startlingly bright blue above high cheekbones, but shadowed now with dark circles underneath them. Her nose was small and not quite short enough or flared enough at the nostrils to be called a pug. Her lips were a trifle too full, and had deep lines running from their corners to her nostrils, giving the impression that her cheeks were apple-rounded. Her hairline was high, and defined her brow almost as a semicircle.

Belatedly, Longarm became aware of the impression she was getting of him. He was suddenly conscious that he hadn't been able to shave for several days, that lack of water had allowed several layers of desert dust to accumulate on his face, and that instead of holding its usual impeccably curved lines like the horns of a Longhorn steer, his moustache drooped at the ends and was ragged in the middle. His clothes were dusty and wrinkled, his boots scarred and unpolished.

He said, "I don't look like such a much, I guess, but I been afoot on that desert out there ever since my horse strayed away from camp three nights ago."

She nodded. "Well, I've seen men come off the desert too many times to be fooled by the way they look. I'm ready to accept your word—and your badge, Marshal Long."

"That eases my mind, but I'd feel a little bit better if you'd let down the muzzle of that rifle, ma'am."

"Of course. I'm sorry." She smiled, lowering the gun. "I'm Leota Toh, Marshal. Welcome to my house. There's a pot of hot coffee on the stove, if you'd like a cup."

"Now, that's something I'd really relish, if it won't put you to no trouble."

"Coffee's my one indulgence, Marshal Long. It's dreadfully expensive and I make the long trip to the trading post more often than I ought to, just to be sure of having it fresh ground, but I'd be lost without it. Come on in the other room."

Longarm followed her into the second hogan. It was the same size as the other. The walls of the hogan were formed of clay-chinked logs, notched to interlock at each end, and were barely higher than Longarm's broad shoulders, but the ceiling rose steeply above them and gave enough headroom even for a man as tall as he was. The ceiling was a study in carefully planned primitive building. It was made of smaller logs laid in an intricate crisscross pattern that formed an arch which was self-supporting except for a center pole.

On the supporting pole a few articles of clothing hung. The room was sparsely furnished. A big double bed stood along one of the walls, a small square table and two plain wooden chairs were in the center. Across the octagonal room from the bed was an open-faced cabinet made from unpainted boards. It held a few airtights and boxes and small bags. Next to it stood a cast-iron kitchen range; a coffeepot was on one burner, a heavy skillet turned upside down lay along one edge. The stovepipe rose and passed through the roof. Yatzee went to the stove and stretched out on the floor behind it.

Leota Toh motioned to one of the chairs. "Sit down while

I get some cups, Marshal. Your wallet with your badge is there on the table. I've seen all I need to convince me."

"You're a mighty cautious lady, Mrs. Toh. That's a good way to be, though, while your husband's gone. I take it he ain't around, or it'd've been him carrying that rifle instead of you."

"My husband's dead, Marshal. I live here alone." Without pausing, just as though she was continuing the statement about her late husband, she went on, "I hope you don't take your coffee with sugar, because I haven't any."

Longarm decided that since Mrs. Toh had informed him of her husband's death in such a casual manner, any comment he might make would be out of place. He said, "Just plain black's the way I like it, ma'am. But if it's all the same to you, instead of setting down right now, I'd better go out and pick up my rifle. Not that there's much chance of anybody passing by here and picking it up, but—"

She interrupted. "Do go after your gun, Marshal Long. There might be more chance than you think of somebody lurking around here. Two nights ago, I had to run off a bunch of horse thieves who broke into my corral."

Longarm had already turned to start for the door, but he swivelled at once to face her as he asked, "How many of them were there? Or did you get time to count?"

"I'm sure there were five. I didn't get an accurate count, because I was too busy fighting them off, but I know I counted five sets of muzzle flashes while we were swapping shots, and if any of the men outside had changed positions, I'd've seen them."

Longarm gaped. "You fought off five men all by yourself, ma'am?" he asked.

"Of course," she said coolly. "It wasn't all that much of a fight, though. They'd already gotten what they came for before I had sense enough to realize that Yatzee was growling at men instead of a skunk or some kind of animal outside. Not that they weren't skunks!"

"Did you get a close look at any of 'em?"

"No. The moonlight wasn't all that bright. But you go on and pick up your rifle and the rest of your gear. We can talk about those men later on."

Longarm nodded and went on out to perform his errand. When he got back inside the hogan Leota Toh had filled two

76

cups with coffee and placed them on the table, together with a thin round crusty loaf of Navajo bread and a dish of some kind of jelly.

"Unless you're carrying a lot of food in your saddlebags, I don't imagine you've been eating too well. This is prickly pear jelly," she said. "I always have a bite about this time of day and eat supper late, after dark. When I eat later, it seems like the evenings don't drag out so long. Now go ahead and help yourself. Just tear off a piece of bread and start in. We'll talk while we're eating."

Longarm pulled a piece of bread off the loaf and put a dab of jelly on it. While he was eating it, Mrs. Toh took a piece for herself. Longarm found both the bread and the jelly so tasty that he helped himself to a second piece. Before popping it into his mouth, he asked a question to satisfy the curiosity that had been nagging at him.

"You been—" he said, then stopped short and started again. "That's mighty fine bread you make, Mrs. Toh. Good jelly, too."

"Thank you. Help yourself to more whenever you feel like it. I'm just glad to have somebody to sit down and eat with. It gets pretty lonely out here all by myself."

Now Longarm asked the question he'd started to ask a moment earlier. "You been living here by yourself a long time?"

"Long enough. It's been four years since Todisini—that was my husband's name—since he died. He and our little son were killed when they got caught in a rock slide while they were herding sheep."

"I'm sorry."

"Yes. So am I." She shook her head, an almost imperceptible move, then went on, "But things like that happen."

Longarm changed the subject quickly. "You was going to tell me about the shooting match you had with them fellows you called horse thieves. I'm real interested. The gang I'm after has got five men in it, and they'd just about have got here a couple of nights back. I figure they're running three or four days ahead of me, and they were heading in this direction. Chances are it was them that stole your stock."

Leota Toh frowned thoughtfully. "I suppose it could have been. What kind of crime are they wanted for?"

"Stealing an Army payroll from the ordnance depot down at Flagstaff."

"That'd be the Navajo depot? The one south of town?"

"Far as I know, it's the only one around."

"Of course it is, now. There used to be one right in the middle of Flagstaff, but I guess you wouldn't know about it. I'm sorry I interrupted you, Marshal. Go ahead and tell me about the robbery. The men that pulled it didn't kill anybody, did they?"

"No. There wasn't a shot fired. They just flummoxed the soldiers good and got away scot-free. I got on their trail two or three days after they'd pulled off the job, and I been after 'em ever since, until my horse got away the other night."

"You said that the runaway horse is a chestnut gelding about fifteen hands high, as I recall," Mrs. Toh said.

"That's right. Got an Army brand on it. Far as I know, it's still got its halter on, too."

"You don't look like the kind of man who'd be careless about tethering a horse, Marshal." Mrs. Toh smiled.

"Oh, it was my own fault for not staking the critter out better. But the thing is, I got that horse figured for one of them runaway teasers. I guess you know the kind I mean?"

"I've never run into one, but I've heard about them. Once in a while the Navajos get an animal that runs away all the time, but after it's done that two or three times, they just shoot it when they catch it."

"I'd be tempted to shoot this one if I ever catch up with it," Longarm said ruefully.

"Don't say anything you'll regret, Marshal, because if you'll look in my corral, I think you'll find your runaway gelding there."

Longarm's jaw dropped. "How in—how in tunket did it get there?"

"That's something of a long story. Here, let me fill your cup again, and I'll tell you how it came about."

"I don't guess you'd mind if I light up a cigar to smoke while you're telling me?"

"Of course not. Go right ahead." Leota Toh waited until Longarm had taken out a stogie and touched a match to it, then began, "I've already told you that when those horse thieves raided my corral the other night, I didn't wake up right away."

"Yes. I recall you saying that."

"Well, they must have been there for a long time before I realized it, because when I got outside they'd already switched saddles on four of their horses to my animals. Soon as I started shooting they scattered. Oh, they let off a few shots at me, but by the time they got their guns working, I'd ducked back inside the house, here. Then I was shooting from a window, and when they realized I was in better shape to hurt them than they were to get at me, they took off."

"You didn't hit any of 'em, I guess?"

"If I did, I don't know about it. There was only a quarter moon, so the light wasn't very good. If they'd waited another half hour or so it'd have been daylight. Or even if there'd been a full moon, I'd have wiped them out. I don't know whether or not you believe a woman can handle a gun, Marshal, but I'm a pretty good shot."

"Oh, I seen some women that can hit a fly at twenty paces. I don't sell you ladies short, Mrs. Toh. Go on."

"Let me ask you a favor first, Marshal."

"Sure. Go right ahead."

"Please call me Leota. I don't enjoy being called by my husband's name now that I'm a widow."

"If you'd like me to, why, sure." Longarm hesitated, then went on. "If we ain't going to be formal, I got a sorta nickname my friends call me. I answer to it better'n I do anything else."

"What is it?"

"Longarm."

"Marshal Custis Long, long arm of the law!" she exclaimed, smiling. "Of course. Longarm."

"Now that we got that settled, go on and finish telling me what happened," Longarm invited.

"Well, nothing else happened that night when my horses were stolen. The thieves got away before it was daylight, and I didn't have anybody to look after my place, so I didn't follow them and try to get my horses back."

"You mean you'd've done that?"

"I certainly would! And I'll bet I'd've gotten them, too."

"You know, I sorta think you might've," Longarm agreed.

"Oh, I was mad enough to chase them, even if they did leave the horses they'd been riding."

"You mean they put their nags in your corral?"

"Oh, no. They left them roaming around outside on the desert. I saw them at daylight and went out and herded them into the corral."

"You got all five of 'em?"

79

"No. There were only four strays. But, you see, I only had four horses, so they had to keep one of theirs."

"I don't reckon you followed their tracks?"

"I tracked them about half a mile, just far enough to be sure they'd left. That was at daylight, after I'd corraled the horses they'd left behind."

"I still don't see how that stray chestnut figures in this, Leota. You ain't said a word about it yet."

"I haven't gotten to that part. By the time I'd caught one of the strays to ride and hazed the others into the corral, the morning was pretty well along. I knew I didn't have a chance to catch up with the horse thieves, so I just followed their trail a little way before I turned around and came home. When I got here, the chestnut gelding was standing in front of the corral, just like he was waiting to be let inside it."

"So you let it in?"

"Of course I did! I opened the corral gate and it walked right in and made itself at home, just like it belonged here."

Longarm shook his head. "After the trouble that chestnut give me on the trail, I just don't see how you could've corraled him so easy."

"Well, I did," Leota assured him. "Step over to the window there and open the shutters if you want to see for yourself that it's your horse."

"Oh, I'm sure it is, but I guess I will look." Longarm went to the window Leota had indicated and opened the wooden shutters. The chestnut stood in the corral, still trailing its halter, seemingly none the worse for its solo wandering. "Yep," he said as he closed the shutter and came back to the table. "That's it, all right."

"It's a beautiful animal, Longarm."

"Oh, I'll give you that. A real nice piece of horseflesh, except for that one bad habit it's got."

"I don't suppose there's any way to break it of straying, is there?"

"None that I know about. A horse that does that can be trained to do most anything else except to stop wandering away."

"That's too bad."

An idea had been forming in Longarm's mind. He said, "You like the gelding pretty good, the way you talk about it."

"Yes, I do. You'd understand why if you'd seen the horses

80

those robbers took. They're Navajo ponies, shaggy and still about half wild."

"How'd you feel about us making a trade?"

"I thought the chestnut belongs to the Army."

"It does."

"Then how can you trade it?"

"Why, there'd be a lot of paperwork to do, but I can take care of that, provided you're agreeable to trading."

"You haven't looked at those horses the robbers left, but I have. I'll be honest about it, Longarm. There's not one of them as good as that chestnut. You'd be giving me the best of the swap, if we were to trade."

"Maybe so, but I'd be getting a horse I can depend on. In my line of work that means a lot."

"And you wouldn't get into any trouble for disposing of Army property without permission?"

"Look at it this way, Leota. If I was to get in a gunfight with them outlaws and my horse got killed, all I'd have to do would be to fill in a report telling what had happened."

"Suppose somebody found out the chestnut gelding didn't get killed, though?" she frowned. "Then you'd be in a lot of trouble."

"Why, I wouldn't lie about it," Longarm told her. "That ain't my way of doing things."

"You don't strike me as being a liar, Longarm." Leota nodded. "What would you do, if you traded with me?"

"I'd put it this way," Longarm said thoughtfully. "I'd put in a report that the hostler at the ordnance depot give me a horse that slowed down when I was trailing the robbers because it strayed. Then I'd come right out flat and say I traded with you to get a horse I could use in the kind of job I had to do."

"And you're sure trading wouldn't get you in trouble?"

"Certain sure," he assured her. "By the time the pen-pushers get hold of my report, it'll be too late for 'em to do anything. There'll never be a word said."

"Well, if you're sure you won't get into trouble, I'll keep the chestnut and you can have your pick of the four horses the robbers left," she said.

"That's fair enough. I'll go out and look 'em over, and soon as I pick one out, I'll be moving on."

"This evening?" Leota frowned. "As late as it is now, you wouldn't make much more than three or four miles before it'll be too dark for you to see the tracks the robbers left."

"It ain't all that late." Longarm went to the window and looked out at the sun, low on the horizon. "I guess it's later than I figured, at that," he said.

Leota said quickly, "I thought you'd like to take a good hot bath and have supper with me and stay the night."

Longarm rubbed the stubble on his chin. He asked, "If I was to take a bath and a shave, it wouldn't run you short of water, would it?"

"Of course not. We built the hogan here because there's a good spring. Even in the middle of summer it doesn't dry up."

"Well, then, I'll just take you up on that kind offer, Leota. I'll admit that after weathering that sandstorm I'm carrying a load of grit I'd be thankful to get rid of."

"Good," she said. "Now, from the way you move and look, you've had a few rough days. Why don't you just let everything go tonight except your bath and shave? There'll be plenty of time in the morning for you to pick out a horse. Tired as I imagine you are, you might make a mistake, and you wouldn't want to do that, would you?"

"I guess that's the best advice I've had in a long time." Longarm smiled. "Seems to me I'd be a fool not to take it. All right, Leota. I'll do just what you say."

Chapter 10

Longarm bathed quickly in a wooden tub that Leota had put in the room adjoining the kitchen half of the hogan, and followed the bath with a quick shave. He returned to the kitchen section to find Leota changing the sheets on the bed that stood along the wall across from the stove. From the uncared-for aspect of the room in which he'd bathed, he'd already deduced that she used the kitchen half as her living quarters.

"Now, hold on!" he said. "I didn't aim to walk in here off the desert and take your bed away from you, Leota!"

"Don't worry about me, Longarm. I'll fix myself a place to sleep in the other room."

"Unless you want me to saddle up and ride outa here right now, I'm going to be the one that uses whatever kind of shakedown you fix in the other room, and you're going to sleep in your own bed," Longarm said firmly.

Leota looked questioningly at him, saw that he was serious and shrugged. "Well, I can't force you," she said. "If that's what you want, that's what you'll get."

She went into the other half of the hogan, Longarm following her. A pile of perhaps two dozen thick, closely woven Navajo blankets was piled against one of the walls. She pulled a half dozen or so of the colorful blankets to the floor, knelt beside them, and began folding them down their long dimension and arranging them in a neat stack.

"You're a very stubborn man, Longarm," she said as she worked. "Do you always get your way about everything?"

"Not all the time. If I had my way, I'd've caught up with that gang of outlaws by now, they'd be in jail, and I'd be on my way back to Denver."

"You don't like the desert?" she asked, smoothing out his bedroll on top of the blankets. "I love it, myself."

. It's home to you."

". . . home, you know," she told him, hunk-
. . . . heels to inspect the finished pallet. "I'm only
. . . . . he rest of me is Cherokee. I grew up in the
. . . . . . ation, where my mother moved after my father
. . . . . ent to the Baptist Mission School, and was just getting
rea. . . to start teaching when I got married."

"Then, how'd you happen to come here?"

"It's a long story, and I'm not going to bore you with it."
Leota stood up, brushing a strand of her hair away from her
oval face, flushed now with the exertion of bed-making. She
went on, "I'll tell you the main part. I met my husband, Todisini, when his family brought him to the Nation to visit
relatives. We didn't really have much in common, and I still
don't understand how it happened that we fell in love. Our
parents didn't want to see another mixed Cherokee–Navajo
marriage, but both of us knew what we wanted, so we had our
way after all the arguing was finished."

"I guess you're lucky. A lot of folks don't always get what
they want," Longarm said. "It looks like you did, though."

"Yes, I did. I didn't know what the desert was like until
after I married Todisini and we came here. But I loved the
bare, harsh country from the first minute I saw it, and—and
I still love it, even knowing how cruel it can be now and then."

"Oh, it's right pretty sometimes, especially that part you
call the Painted Desert. I guess I'm just sorta tired after that
sandstorm and having my horse stray and all the rest of it."

"Well, I'm sure you'll be a lot more comfortable in here
than you would be out on the desert," she said. "But I still
wish you'd sleep in the bed in the other room and let me take
this pallet."

"Now, I ain't the kind of man who just walks in here and
takes your bed away from you, Leota," Longarm said. "Them
blankets will sure be a whole lot softer than the ground, but
you didn't have to go to all this trouble. I was just aiming to
spread my bedroll on the floor and turn in."

"It wasn't any trouble at all, and nobody's going to sleep
on the floor in my hogan as long as I have all these spare
blankets," she said firmly. "Since Todisini died, I've been
swapping the sheep herd a few at a time for the blankets the
women on the reservation weave."

"You don't like sheepherding, then?"

"Not especially. I didn't mind it, except that I couldn't take care of the size herd we had. But I've been too busy lately to take the blankets to the trading post to sell."

"Well, they'll make the first soft bed I've had for the last few days." Longarm took out a cheroot and fumbled in his vest pocket for a match.

"Save your cigar for after supper, Longarm," Leota said. "It's all ready, so let's go in and eat."

Their supper was simple, a stew of varicolored kernels of dried desert corn, potatoes and squash and slivers of venison jerky simmered with tomatoes from one of the air-tights Longarm had seen on the shelf near the stove. A thin round loaf of crusty Navajo bread went with the stew, and after he'd eaten two helpings, Longarm pushed his plate back and lighted the cigar he'd postponed smoking earlier.

"That was a real tasty meal," he told Leota. "And I'm so full now that soon as I finish this cigar and drink my coffee, I'm aiming to go to bed. I ain't much of a one for going to bed early, and I know it ain't polite, but now I've slowed down all I can think about is stretching out and closing my eyes."

Leota stood up and began clearing the table. "Go on to bed whenever you feel like it, Longarm," she said. "I'm sure that after all the walking you've been doing, you need to rest."

She took a coal-oil lamp from the shelf beside the stock and put it on the table and was reaching for the lantern that hung on the center post.

"Now, don't bother with that," Longarm protested. "I don't need no light to find that bed you fixed me." He stood up. "I guess I better find it pretty quick, because if I don't, I'm going to go to sleep sitting down."

"Good night, then, Longarm," she said. "I get up at first daylight, so I'll have breakfast cooked any time you're ready to start out."

Longarm wasted little time preparing for the night. He laid his holstered Colt on the floor beside the pallet where it would be convenient to his hand and put his vest on the opposite side to have his derringer and cigars within easy reach. Slipping out of his clothes and longjohns, he stretched out on the improvised bed. The cushion of springy wool blankets under him felt better than any mattress he'd ever slept on.

A rectangle of lamplight outlined the door that connected the two hogans, and through the planks he could hear an occasional small noise made by Leota as she got ready to retire.

She's a nice lady, old son, he mused. *Cherokee and Navajo, that's a funny mixture. I guess that accounts for her pale skin and light hair. And you was real lucky she took a fancy to that chestnut. Now you'll be riding a horse that ain't going to wander away any time it takes a notion to, and leave you afoot again.*

Reaching to the floor, Longarm groped for the pocket of his vest to take out a cigar. Before his fingers found the pocket, the relaxation of the tension that had been his constant companion since taking up the trail of the outlaw gang finished its work on him. His arm still extended, he fell asleep.

A tentative fingertip, soft as the wings of a butterfly, ran across Longarm's cheek. Even that light touch aroused him. Before he was fully awake, his right hand dropped by instinct to the holstered Colt on the floor beside him. He had it drawn and was bringing it up when a hand grasped his wrist.

"You don't need the pistol, Longarm," Leota whispered. "If you don't want me to visit you, I'll go back to my own bed."

"Leota?" he asked. "What's wrong?"

"Nothing's wrong, unless it's me."

"I don't rightly follow you."

"I couldn't go to sleep. I lay in the other room awake, thinking what a waste the night would be if both of us slept through it in separate beds." When Longarm released her wrist, but did not speak at once, she went on, "If you've got a woman you're being true to—"

"I ain't. It'd be hard for me to ask a woman to wait for me and worry about me, the kinda job I got."

Leota went on as though he hadn't spoken. "If you don't want me to join you, I'll go on back to my own bed."

"Now, wait a minute. I didn't say that."

"You haven't said much of anything, so far."

"That's because you took me by surprise."

"It shouldn't surprise you that I'm here. I'm a lonesome woman, Longarm. I've been sleeping by myself for four long years, but I still can't get used to it. I was hoping you'd come to my bed, but since you didn't . . ."

"I went to sleep before I could think much about anything."

"Then you don't mind?" she asked.

"You're welcome as the flowers in May, Leota." Longarm threw off the blanket that covered him. "I'd be proud to have you lie down here with me."

Leota did not lie down beside Longarm at once. Still on her knees on the floor, she bent over him and her mouth found his lips. Longarm took her in his arms as their kiss began, and was surprised to find that she was naked. He rubbed his callused hands down her sides to the swell of her hips, her skin smooth and yielding to his firm caress. Her tongue sought his and he slipped his hands up to her breasts.

They were surprisingly small and firm for a mature woman, and he rubbed his thumbs over her rosettes, feeling them grow pebbled as he caressed them. Then her nipples began to thrust out firm and hard under his touch. Her hand rippled over Longarm's chest and his flat muscle-corded belly to his groin. He felt himself begin to swell and become erect as she fondled him with her warm palms and busy fingertips.

Longarm grasped Leota's waist in his big hands to lift her on to the pallet, but she twisted away from him. "Not yet, Longarm. Let me be on top for now," she whispered.

"Sure, if that's what you enjoy," he replied.

Throwing a leg across his thighs, she kneeled above him and reached down to guide his erection while she lowered herself, sinking down slowly, moaning softly in her throat, until the full weight of her body rested on his hips.

"Oh, you're filling me like I haven't been filled for a long time," she said softly. "Don't move for a while yet, Longarm. I just want to feel you inside me."

"I won't do a thing until you say the word, Leota," he told her. "Go on and take your pleasure."

After a few moments, Leota began rocking her body back and forth, her hands resting on Longarm's broad chest. True to his promise, Longarm did not move. He lay quietly while Leota swayed above him, her sighs of pleasure filling the darkness. After a few minutes her movements grew erratic, then frantic. She leaned forward, her mouth seeking his, and their tongues entwined as her hips rose and fell, impaling her on his rigid shaft with a rhythm that grew faster and faster as the moments passed until she was gyrating frantically.

Leota lifted her torso, breaking their kiss, holding herself erect now, her cries of pleasure rising and falling until they became a shrill ululation of pleasure that rose to a climactic shriek. For a moment she held her position above him, trembling and shaking. Then, as her cries faded to soft moans, she fell forward, limp and quivering.

"I'm sorry, Longarm," she sighed after she'd lain quietly for several minutes. "I didn't wait for you. I couldn't."

"Don't bother about me," he told her. "I ain't in a bit of a hurry."

"You're still hard," she said. "If you feel like keeping on, so do I."

Longarm sat up on the pallet, then lifted Leota bodily without breaking the bond of rigid flesh that connected them. He held her in a firm embrace while he reversed their positions on the springy blankets. Then he started driving, slow, steady strokes that soon brought a response from Leota. She wriggled beneath his thrusts, her hips rising and falling, as again the soft sighs of pleasure bubbled from her full lips.

Longarm did not hurry. He stopped thrusting when Leota's sighs became small shrieks, and held himself motionless still buried deep within her moistly clinging warmth, until her cries faded and she no longer tried to match the tempo of his stroking. Then he began thrusting again in slow, measured movements, until once again she began to squirm and cry out. When he stopped for the second time, Leota grabbed his biceps and shook him.

"No, no, Longarm! Don't stop now!" she urged. "Can't you feel that I'm more than ready?"

"You don't need to worry," he assured her. "Let go again, if you want to. I'm still good for a little while yet."

"No. I'll wait with you," she said. "You're so big and you drive so hard that I don't think I could stand letting go again until you're ready to stop."

After a few moments, Longarm began lunging again, slowly at first, letting himself build this time. He paced himself by Leota's response, and as she mounted to her peak and started to shriek and cry out in the growing throes of ecstasy he released his restraint and pounded with deep hard thrusts. He drove hard, his own urge for satisfaction mounting, while Leota's cries rose in the darkness until she loosed a final throbbing scream. Then he released himself and jetted and drained and lurched forward on her full, generous body to rest at last.

• • •

"You pick out the one you want, Longarm," Leota said. "I don't care which you choose, as long as you're leaving me the chestnut."

They were standing inside the corral in the first hush of dawn. Longarm's saddle gear lay at one side, and the horses were lined up at the feed trough munching the hay she'd tossed in for them. In the east the soft grey dawnlight was slowly turning to pink as the time for sunrise approached.

"I got a notion to take that little filly," Longarm said thoughtfully. "She ain't as big as the others, but she oughta be faster, and I ain't packing much gear with me."

"She's well muscled for her size," Leota said. "If that's your choice, go ahead and saddle up, and I'll go back inside and finish fixing breakfast."

By the time Longarm had the mare saddled and ready to go and went back into the hogan, a stack of hotcakes was smoking on a platter on the table and the fragrant aroma of freshly brewed coffee filled the air.

"You've been busy," Leota said, looking up from the stove.

Though she'd spoken in a noncommittal tone, Longarm was quick to recognize the symptoms she was displaying. He'd coped with them before.

"Now, listen to me, Leota," he said gently. "I know you get lonesome here, and I guess you feel put out that I can't stay with you for a while. But don't fret because I got to move along. Sorta send me on my way with a smile, will you? You're too pretty a woman for me to remember frowning and mad."

Leota's reply was oblique. "You know, Longarm, I'm not quite sure whether I'm glad or sorry that you stopped here."

"You was happy enough last night. There ain't a thing changed that I can see."

"Except that you're going on to chase those robbers today. And after last night, I want you to stay."

"I still got my job to do, Leota. You wouldn't want me to let them rascals get away, after they stole your horses and all."

"If you'd just stay here with me, I wouldn't care what happened to them," Leota sighed. Then she smiled and added, "But I know you can't. You're not the kind of man to bury yourself on a sheep ranch in the desert when you've got the kind of job you have."

"Well, I got to admit I like my work," Longarm told her. "There's times, like when I got here yesterday, that I'm pretty

89

wore down, but things always look better the next day."

"I don't suppose you've got any plan? I mean, will you be coming back this way?"

"Leota, I ain't got a plan in the world except to catch up with them outlaws and get back the money they stole. It might take me just a few days, or it might take me a month."

"Well, you'll go off with a good breakfast under your belt," she said, forcing a smile. "Sit down and eat, now."

After he'd taken the first edge off his hunger, Longarm said, "You know, it might help me finish my job quicker if you'd tell me a little bit about the country hereabouts. Where would a bunch of outlaws be heading for to hide out? A canyon, maybe, or a town?"

"There are plenty of canyons around here where outlaws do hide," Leota replied. "Or did, before the Navajo Police got busy."

"I know a little bit about them Navajo Police," Longarm nodded. "There was one of 'em named Toshi Nez that give me a hand on a case I had over east on the reservation a while back."

"I know him," Leota said. "He's very good. You should have him helping you now."

"There wasn't time," Longarm replied. "Anyhow, this case don't have a thing to do with the Navajos. It's Army business—and mine, now."

"In country like this there are plenty of places where a bunch of outlaws can hide," Leota said, frowning thoughtfully. "But my guess is that they'd head for Tuba City to stock up on food and whatever else they need before they hole up."

"What sorta place is this Tuba City?"

"Oh, just a little crossroads, even if the roads that meet there are more like trails."

"The trails go anyplace in particular?"

"One goes north to Lee's Ferry, where there's a bridge over the Colorado River gorge. Another one goes south to Cameron, that's almost due east of here. And there's a road that dips down to the Little Colorado where there's a ford. It's a real road; the stagecoaches use it regularly."

"Stagecoaches? Where do they run between?"

"They don't run between anyplace. They just go to the Grand Canyon and take a trail along the rim, then go back to Tuba City."

"Eastern dudes?" Longarm asked.

"You guessed it. There's almost always three or four coaches full. They come from the D&RG railhead at Grand Junction and take the dudes back after they've looked at the canyon."

"And there ain't no places—no towns, that is—outside of Tuba City and Cameron?"

"A few little trading posts. But they're not the kind of place a bunch of outlaws would stop at. None of them sell liquor, and about all they have is trade goods for the Navajos."

"How far are they, Leota?"

"Cameron's only a long day's ride. Tuba City's a day and a half, without pushing too hard."

"Well, if I can't pick up the trail that bunch left, or if I lose it, I'll look for 'em in Cameron or Tuba City. You been a big help, Leota." Longarm stood up and glanced out the window. The sky was blue now instead of grey, and the sunrise light was washing out its color in the east. He went on, "There's light enough now to see the tracks them fellows left, so I guess it's time for me to be riding."

Leota came and stood beside him. "Kiss me goodbye now," she said. "I won't come out and wave goodbye, if you don't mind. And don't look back, or you might find me following you."

Longarm kissed her, and in spite of her clinging to him, gently pulled away and went outside. He'd led the filly outside the corral after saddling up, and as he took up the trail of the outlaws he glanced back only once. Leota's face was framed in the window. He quickly turned his head forward and rode on.

Chapter 11

Riding slowly north along the trail after he'd left the hogan, Longarm examined with more than usual care the hoofprints that marked its surface. Most of the Navajo settlements now lay behind him, and there were fewer prints on the trail. Without the maze of overlapping impressions to confuse things now, and since he'd spent some time in Leota's corral, studying the marks made by the hooves of the horses taken by the outlaws, he had little trouble in picking out the prints he must follow.

Although all the prints including those of the animals taken from Leota's corral had been made by unshod Navajo ponies, one of the animals now ridden by the fugitives had a split front hoof and another had a swollen frog which caused it to favor its near foreleg when going up a slope. Longarm looked for these distinctive hoofprints first, and with such readily noticed characteristics he lost little time in finding them.

He made good progress, and when he came to the point where the trail forked, the west fork leading to the little settlement of Cameron, he had only to glance at the ground to learn that the outlaw gang was continuing north to Tuba City.

Longarm had followed the northwest trail only a few hundred yards when he noticed two sets of new prints. These were made by shod horses, and had not appeared below the fork; obviously they were made by horses coming from Cameron. Reining in, he swung out of his saddle and bent down to study the new prints more closely. A quick look was all that was necessary to tell him that they were very fresh indeed.

Looks like you might run into company up the way, old son, he told himself as he mounted again and toed the filly into motion. *Fresh as them prints are, the fellows that made 'em ain't very far ahead*.

He made good time as he rode on. The cool flow of the

morning air began to become warmed as the sunlight increased from a gentle morning glow to a blinding glare. But he did not see the new riders on the trail ahead. Longarm was not too surprised by this. The country had grown progressively rockier and rougher as he moved north. By noon the Painted Desert had dwindled in the increasing distance to a narrow strip of color that occasionally shrank thread-thin, only to widen again and spread in a maze of blues and reds, purples and yellows, past the point where he could see.

Ahead, the generally level terrain to which he'd become accustomed was giving way to a land of rock outcrops and boulders that ranged from the size of a man's head to those bigger than a house. A short distance in front of him and off the trail, Longarm saw a formation that had an overhanging ledge which offered shade from the sun's hot glare. He reined the mare off the trail and pulled up in front of the towering mass of porous volcanic rock. Dismounting, he took his bag of trail rations out of his saddlebag, lifted his canteen from the saddlehorn, and sought the shade cast by the high ledge.

There was no breeze now. The cool breath that had wafted over the land at sunrise had died away, and the air was hot even in the shade. Longarm settled down in the sun-free strip below the ledge and leaned back against the rough rock wall. He was not really hungry—the generous breakfast he'd eaten before leaving Leota's hogan would have carried him for another hour or so—but the filly needed to rest, and time lost in resting might as well be spent eating to avoid a second stop later.

While he idly scanned the deserted landscape through eyes slitted against the sun's bright glare, Longarm chewed at a strip of jerky, chomped on a few grains of corn, and tucked the remainder of the food back in its sack. After swallowing a mouthful of water, he capped the canteen and put it aside. He fished a cigar out of his pocket and rasped his horn-hard thumbnail over the head. When the match burst into flame, Longarm cupped it in his hands and leaned forward to light the cigar.

With the high-pitched buzz of an angry hornet a rifle slug whizzed past his ear, passing through the air where his head had been a split second before. The grinding spat of the bullet burying itself in the soft, porous rock behind him sounded at almost the same instant that the sharp bark of the rifle broke the desert stillness.

Longarm's reflexes took over. Before the quick echoes of the shot had died away he fell forward and began belly-crawling across the two or three yards of space that separated him from his horse. The filly had flinched at the sound of the shot, but had not bolted. Longarm picked up the trailing reins and, still edging along flat on his belly, led the horse around the outcrop.

A second bullet kicked up a spurt of sand before he got the horse safely behind the shelter of the tall rock. Springing to his feet, Longarm whipped his rifle out of its saddle scabbard and with two long strides reached the far side of the outcrop. As he moved he levered a shell into the Winchester's chamber.

Crouched on one knee behind the outcrop, Longarm waited for several moments, counting on the curiosity of the invisible sniper to make the man show himself. When he decided enough time had passed, he peered cautiously around the edge of the high pinnacle. There was no sign of movement visible anywhere within his field of vision.

Longarm was not surprised. The broken country he'd been travelling through for the past few hours offered scores of huge boulders and rock outcrops behind which a sniper could hide after letting off a fast shot or two at his target.

Old son, he told himself, *looks like you're up against a cagey customer out there. Whoever it was let off them shots, he's got brains enough to stay still so if he missed he won't get spotted so easy.*

Lighting the cheroot which had saved him from the first surprise shot, Longarm leaned against the rough hot surface of the outcrop and waited.

Question is, his thoughts ran, *who in hell is doing that shooting? It ain't likely to be them outlaws. They got a full day's lead; they oughta be twelve, fifteen miles ahead, about halfway to Tuba City, and that's about the likeliest place for them to be heading. Now, that don't leave nobody you know about but them two riders that turned onto the trail where it branched off towards Cameron.*

Deciding he'd get no answers to the questions that were puzzling him unless he took some action to force the sniper to show himself, Longarm stretched out on the ground. Taking off his hat, he poised the broad-brimmed felt on the muzzle of his rifle and inched up to the edge of the outcrop, holding the rifle slanted behind the high formation to keep the hat from being seen until he was in place and ready.

When his head was beyond the edge of the outcrop, Longarm tensed himself to be ready to leap up quickly and then slowly brought his rifle erect until the edge of his hatbrim protruded beyond the rock. He held the gun steady for a moment, then exposed a bit of the crown.

A few seconds ticked off. Longarm held the hat motionless for those instants and was just about to give up his ruse as being a bad idea when the hidden sniper took the bait.

A shot broke the noon stillness. Longarm was on his knees an instant after the sniper's slug sang off the edge of the rock, while the sound of the shot was still echoing in his ears. He brought the muzzle of his rifle down, his eyes flicking over the broken terrain, seeking the sniper's hiding place.

He caught a flicker of movement, a flash of some bright color, red or purple, disappearing behind a huge boulder that stood off the trail fifty or sixty yards ahead. Aiming by instinct, Longarm fired. He saw his slug kick up dust from the rising ground a few feet behind the boulder, but no sign of movement anywhere in the field of his vision.

Then, from one side, another rifle barked, but Longarm did not hear the angry hissing of the bullet, nor did he see where the shot landed. He was too busy levering another shell into his Winchester while throwing himself backward into the shelter of the rock outcrop.

There's two of 'em out there, old son, he thought. *But they ain't got you in a crossfire—at least not yet. And if you got the brains God give a constipated jackass, you ain't going to let 'em whipsaw you, either.*

Darting back around the rock formation, he risked making a target of himself by leaning out and letting off a random shot. He had no point at which to aim, just a general impression of the area from which the second rifleman had fired. As soon as he'd squeezed off the round, he ran back to the other side of the outcrop and peered cautiously around its edge.

He saw a man's back disappearing behind a distant boulder. The fleeing sniper was moving fast, and Longarm had no time to aim before the man had reached cover. Longarm drew a bead on the boulder and waited. The sound of stones disturbed by running feet reached his ears from a spot at right angles to the rock behind which the man he'd seen was sheltered. The new sound drew his attention and he leaned forward to try to locate it.

His effort to spot the source of the noise failed. There were too many rock outcrops in the direction from which it had come. By the time he looked back toward the spot where the first runner had sheltered, that target was on the move again, and once again frustrated Longarm's attempt to bring him down by diving behind another boulder before Longarm could swing his rifle around.

They whipsawed you, old son, Longarm told himself angrily as he waited vainly for one or the other of the running men to show himself again. *You might as well stop wasting shells, because they're far enough away now so's to be plumb outa range. They suckered you, but there wasn't no help for it; you couldn't see all the openings they was able to spot. By now they're cutting a shuck so fast you ain't likely to spot either one of 'em.*

No man to accept frustration, Longarm swung into the saddle and started after the fugitives. He had no guide except the general direction in which he'd seen one of the mysterious attackers disappear. After much searching he managed to pick up the hoofprints of the man's horse in spite of the hard-baked nature of the soil with its frequent rock outcrops, but following it proved to be another matter.

Like other sections of the Moenkopi Plateau, the area he was crossing was cut by frequent washes. Mapmakers had adopted the name given by early explorers to a geographical peculiarity of the Western desert country to describe the beds of old rivers that had dried up perhaps centuries ago, but which still existed as broad, shallow gullies whose bottoms consisted of a thick layer of loose, shifting stones.

A rider willing to risk his neck and the legs of his horse to hide his tracks could use the washes as a road in spite of the shifting, uncertain, and dangerous footing they provided. On the unstable bed of loose stones, ranging from thumb-sized pebbles to big boulders the size of a man's head, not even the big pads of an elephant would have left recognizable prints.

As soon as he realized that the man he was after had made his getaway by riding down the center of the first wash he came to, Longarm reluctantly gave up. Once in the past, when he'd been on the Navajo Reservation investigating a case, he'd had experience trying to track lawbreakers who'd ridden down washes to avoid leaving a trail.

Whoever them men was, they sure didn't want to let you

catch up to 'em, old son, he mused as he studied the hoofprints at the point where they entered the wash. *They wasn't as set on killing you as they was on getting clear without giving you a good look at 'em, and that's a funny thing in itself.*

Lighting a cheroot, Longarm rode very slowly beside the wash for perhaps a mile. Both banks were sandy and dry and fairly steep. It would have been as impossible to miss the hoofprints of a horse leaving the wash as it was to overlook the point at which it had entered.

Now, a man that'll take a dry wash to keep from leaving a trail knows he's likely to lose a horse and maybe get himself killed riding down it, Longarm considered. That's a lot of chance to take just to keep from being seen up close, and nobody'd do it without good reason.

Returning to the point where the hoofprints had gone into the wash, Longarm dismounted and studied them. The horse making the prints had been freshly shod. The shoes had clean-cut edges and the nail groove was also very clearly marked. In places even the heads of the nails had left their dents in the track.

Them tracks would sure be easy to follow, Longarm told himself as he examined the hoofprints. *And from what you seen since you been on this trail, old son, there ain't all that many riders taking it. You're running behind that outfit toting the Army loot, but there ain't much place up ahead except Tuba City where they can stop to buy the grub they'll be needing by now, so you won't be apt to lose their trail. It'd likely be time well spent if you backtracked to that little town on the branch trail they come through and see what you can find out about the two that made this set of tracks.*

Backtracking the hoofprints on the trail to Cameron proved to be an easy job. Aside from the few occasional marks left by unshod Navajo ponies, the tracks in which Longarm was interested were the only fresh prints on the dry, dusty, seldom-travelled path. An occasional glance at the trail was all Longarm needed to assure himself that the trail he was following had been taken earlier by the two riders who'd attacked him.

Cameron was a tiny town, essentially a trading post with a dozen or so houses, a general store, and a saloon added to it. As was his habit, Longarm headed for the clearing house of local news and gossip, the saloon. There was no Maryland rye—no rye at all—in its limited stock, and he carried on his seemingly casual conversation with the barkeep between sips of bourbon which to his taste was cloyingly sweet.

"That trail coming down here from Tuba City's about the lonesomest stretch of road I ever seen," he said, pocketing his change from the twenty-five-cent piece he'd laid on the bar. "I only run into two fellows on it the whole way, and they went right on past me without even stopping to pass the time of day."

"They must've been the two that stayed at Miz Lewis's house last night," the barkeep frowned. "Maybe they didn't want to stop and visit because the old fellow was feeling sick again. He complained his chest was hurting when him and the fellow with him come in for a drink, so I sent 'em over to see her."

"I figured they must've stopped here last night. I couldn't tell about one of 'em being sick, of course."

"Oh, it's bound to be the same ones. They're the only white men been through here for a week."

"This lady, Miz Lewis—I take it she's a sorta doctor?" Longarm asked.

"She's the closest thing we got to one. She done a lot of midwifing back in Illinois, where she come from."

"You know, maybe I oughta go talk to her myself. You think she could give a man something for a riled-up belly?"

"Sure. She keeps all sorts of yarbs and concoctions. Her folks back East sends her plants and things that don't grow here," the barkeep replied. "She's right pricey, charges you two bits for a dose of whatever she figures out ails you, but I guess it's worth the price if you got some kind of bad misery."

"I better go see her, then." Longarm stood up and rubbed his stomach. Quite truthfully, he added, "Not finding fault with your liquor, but that drink I had ain't setting too well, and a man sure don't want to get sick when he's by himself on a lonesome trail like these you got around here."

"Her house is the next to last one on the trail out south," the barkeep volunteered. "Tell her I sent you to see her. She'll come up with some kinda dose that'll fix you up so you can keep on travelling."

Mrs. Lewis was a tall, stringy woman with sparse white hair that she gathered into a tiny knob at the nape of her neck. She led Longarm into her kitchen, where shelves laden with crocks and bottles of various liquids lined the walls and bundles

98

of roots and leaves and plant stems dangled from the rafters. After she'd listened to his somewhat sketchy explanation of his totally imaginary symptoms, she nodded wisely.

"You likely just got all bound up, travelling the way you been doing," she told him. "You don't have to tell me what you men eat on the trail when there ain't a woman along to look after you."

"Well, now, I don't feel all that bad, but when the barkeep told me you fixed up a fellow yesterday who was having stomach miseries, I figured I might as well stop and see if you could give me whatever it was that fixed him up."

"It wasn't a stomach misery bothering that poor man," she said. "He was having trouble catching his breath, and ever' once in a while he'd get a terrible pain that'd just double him over."

"But you give him something that eased him, did you?"

"Why, sure. I fixed him some hyssop and burdock and kohosh root brew. That's a prime cure for what was bothering him. Him and his friend slept in my barn loft last night, and they must've left real early, because they was gone when I got up at daybreak. But he taken his medicine with him, so he'll be all right."

"I'm pretty sure it was him and the fellow with him I met on the way down here. He didn't tell you his name, did he?"

Mrs. Lewis frowned. "Now, that's funny, Mr. Long. Most folks I tend, that's the first thing they tell me, but him and the other man didn't and, now I recall, they never called each other by name."

"If they was headed for Tuba City, they'd be the ones I met, all right."

"Oh, you couldn't mistake them. The one who was sick was pretty well along in years—looked a little puny, which is what a body'd expect. The other man was big, real big, and kind of rough-looking. What I recall about him best was that he had a real bright-colored bandana around his throat."

"That's them," Longarm nodded. "So I guess whatever you fixed for him done him some good. Now, if you'll just fix me a bottle of the same—"

"No, sir!" she interrupted. "That man had a bad misery in his chest. Yours is in your belly, so I'll mix you up some stomach tea. That's made out of steepings off of sumac and blackberry leaves, and some scraped smartweed root, and it's got a little bit of chokecherry juice in it."

Mrs. Lewis stepped over to the wall and began walking along the shelves, selecting a bottle here and a crock there. She put her burden on the table. Longarm watched her for a moment as she measured liquids from the various containers in a bottle. Then he walked over to the window and looked out. The sun was dropping low and the Painted Desert's riotous colors were blending into a mellowness that somehow merged them into harmony. He thought of the oncoming night and turned back to Mrs. Lewis, who was shaking the bottle to blend the mixture she'd concocted.

He said, "You mentioned that them men that was here yesterday bedded down in your barn last night. You think I can sleep there tonight? It's pretty late for me to start out again."

"Why, sure." She handed him the bottle. "Now, that'll be a quarter, Mr. Long. I get a quarter for supper, and a dime for sleeping in the barn, but that takes in the hay your horse eats. I'll tell you what. I'll only charge you fifty cents for all of it. Does that sound fair?"

"It sure does, Mrs. Lewis." Longarm fished a half-dollar out of his pocket. "And, considering all you've done for me, I got an idea I'm really getting my money's worth."

Chapter 12

Knowing he'd dropped another full day behind the gang escaping with the gold and that he was also a day behind the pair of bushwhackers spurred Longarm to step up his pace when he started out from Cameron the next morning. Both he and the filly had benefited from the extra rest and the change from trail rations, and he felt safe in setting a faster pace.

When he reached the main trail to Tuba City, and the tracks of the bushwhackers overlaid those of the outlaws, Longarm nodded to himself with the satisfaction of having been correct: both were obviously heading for the same place. Tuba City was the gateway to the arid, almost impassable Utah desert that had for many years been the safest haven for wanted men.

You ain't on a cold trail now, old son, he cautioned himself. *Just because them fellows that tried to dry-gulch you is in front of you now, that don't mean they might not still be laying for you up ahead. You been a mite careless up till now, and you can't afford to run on a slack rope no longer.*

For the balance of the day he stayed with the beaten trail, and just before sunset found a stopping place that appealed to him. A little distance to one side of the trail an extensive outcrop of porous lava rock rose in a maze of humps and jagged clusters and low pinnacles. There were enough odd shapes in the half-mile square the outcrop covered to camouflage the silhouettes of both Longarm and the horse.

He fed the filly and after giving her a measure of water in her nosebag led the horse to a cluster of low, pyramid-like formations that offered the best cover available. Tethering the filly a few yards from the center of the cluster, Longarm found a rising stone close to the edge that felt comfortable to his back. Settling himself against it, his rifle across his knees, he lighted a cheroot. He kept watch until the light was gone, then slept sitting up for the rest of the night.

There were no alarms during the night. Longarm's sleep was interrupted two or three times by the small desert deer wandering close by over the hard ground in the darkness, and once by the filly's nervous movements when the animal stamped several times in quick succession on the hard-baked ground. Longarm stood up and walked around the formation, but he neither saw nor heard anything in the darkness.

At daybreak Longarm fed and watered the filly again while he chewed more jerky and parched corn, then set out again, still following the tracks of the unshod horses ridden by the outlaws. Although he scanned both sides of the trail carefully, he saw no sign of the two mysterious riders who had attacked him the day before. Except for a few stops at the top of steep inclines to rest the filly, he made steady progress under the blazing sun.

Since midday the trail north had grown wider and more firmly packed as the hoofprints of riders, singly and in groups, converged on the beaten path and joined it. The tracks of the two identifiable horses ridden by the outlaws and the clean-cut prints of those ridden by the mysterious bushwhackers had become more and more difficult to follow, but he could still pick out the swollen frog and the edge-chipped hoof and occasionally the trail bore a full, clear print or two of the freshly shod animals ridden by the pair who'd attacked him.

Near mid-afternoon, Longarm saw buildings in the distance. Allowing for the illusion of nearness created by the clear desert air, he judged them to be three or four miles away. Assuming that he was closer to Tuba City than he'd thought, he turned the filly toward them and kept his eyes on the cluster of houses instead of on the trail.

He was still a mile from the structures when he glanced down at the ground and realized with a start that except for the now-familiar tracks left by the outlaws' animals, he was following an old, dim trail on which no other fresh tracks appeared. He reined in and gazed thoughtfully at the clump of adobes ahead.

He could see now that what he'd taken for a town was a desert illusion created by haze and distance. There was no town ahead, only one large adobe and three small hogans. All the structures showed signs of long disuse. There were cracks in the walls of the big adobe, and all the glass panes were gone from the weather-worn frames in its windows. The doors of all the hogans as well as those of the adobe sagged in their casings and the paint was peeling off the wood. The logs of the hogans were cracked and split and the roof of one was collapsing.

You played the fool, old son, Longarm told himself disgustedly. *Them fellows just turned off the trail to shelter in that old deserted 'dobe for the night. No use you going on. You can save a mile or more and cut your losses just by riding straight ahead and picking up the place where they slanted on back to the main trail.*

Toeing the filly ahead, Longarm rode slowly forward, sure that by doing so he'd pick up the tracks of the outlaws once again. His hunch had been right. When he'd ridden a quarter of a mile past the ruins of the trading post, he found what he'd expected: fresh prints of the pony with the cracked hoof and of the one with a swollen frog appeared superimposed on the old trace left from the time when the trading post had been used.

He'd ridden a hundred yards or so following the outlaws' tracks back to the Tuba City trail when he turned in his saddle for a final glance at the ruins. A flutter of white between two of the hogans caught his eye. He reined in for a longer look and this time saw something that had been invisible from the angle at which he'd approached the old structures. A streamer of white cloth fluttered against one of the walls, although there was no breeze, and strange grey lumps lay scattered over the ground between the adobe and the hogans.

"Now that just plain ain't possible," he muttered under his breath. "Rags don't blow unless there's a breeze to stir 'em, and damned if them grey things don't look like dead sheep. Old son, you better not be in too big a hurry to ride on. As long as you're so close, it might be a good idea to go take a closer look at them buildings."

As the filly drew closer to the dilapidated structures, Longarm could see that the grey lumps were indeed dead sheep. The animals were scattered willy-nilly on the ground, and he counted eleven before he could make out the source of the strange fluttering white cloth. A man was propped against the wall of one of the hogans, and now and then he raised his arm for a moment and waved it feebly. Longarm dug his boot toe into the filly's flank and in a few moments he was swinging out of his saddle and bending over the man who lay propped against the wall.

At first glance, Longarm could not determine his age. The man's face was a pulpy mass streaked with thick swaths of dried blood. Out of the crushed, ruined face one dark eye peered through lids so crusted with dried blood that he could barely hold them open. His lips were grotesquely swollen, and when he opened his mouth Longarm could see bloody gaps between the stubs of broken teeth.

One of his arms lay twisted and limp across his thighs. The other arm was raised against the wall of the building, the hand dangling useless, bent against his forearm. The remains of a shirtsleeve covered the upraised arm. It was the fluttering of the sleeve's fabric that had drawn Longarm's attention.

"Oo-ah," the man groaned. "Oo-ah."

Only after he'd stepped to the filly and taken his canteen from the saddlehorn did it occur to Longarm that the man had been trying to say *"agua,"* the Spanish for "water." By that time he was starting back to the wall, his every movement followed by the wounded man's single eye.

Taking out his bandana, Longarm soaked it in water and very carefully squeezed a few drops into the man's gaping lips. He waited and followed it with a bit more. The injured man gulped and his eye wavered as he tried to use it to signal some kind of message. Longarm knew that getting water into the man's system was the first thing to be done. He ignored the eye and continued to squeeze small trickles of water between the man's pulped lips.

When he'd given the injured man all the liquid he judged safe, Longarm wet the bandana again and began trying to mop the dried blood away from his face. The man shook his head feebly and his upraised arm flopped in what would normally have been urgent gestures. Longarm frowned, trying to understand the signals the man was obviously trying to send him.

"Is there somebody else around here in the same shape you are?" he asked at last. A gabble of unintelligible stammers came from the man's lips. "Inside, maybe?" Longarm asked.

When the man managed a nod, Longarm told him, "I'll go

take a look. I'll be right back."

Longarm went around two sides of the octagonal hogan before he found the east side with its entrance door. The door hung by its bottom hinge; the top had been torn away. Longarm dragged it open and looked inside. His gorge rose and he stood staring in disbelief for a moment before forcing himself to enter.

Broken pieces of wood and tatters of torn cloth strewed the earthen floor. The only furniture in the room was a stove that stood against one wall and a square table. It soot in the center of the octagonal enclosure. A woman's naked body lay on the table. Her face was so battered that it was impossible to judge what she had looked life in life or to guess her age.

Her body spoke of youth in spite of the abuse it had suffered. Her back was arched as though she had been frozen in a moment of either ecstasy or agony, but Longarm had no doubt what she had been feeling in the moments before her death, for the evidence of how she had died was appallingly apparent.

Her arms were outstretched and bound with thongs to the table legs. Her chin pointed to the ceiling, her mouth was open, her bruised lips swollen and twisted. Ropes had been tied to her ankles and thrown over the angled roof supports that stretched halfway across the room from the big center post. The ropes had been drawn at an angle that pulled her legs apart, spreading her thighs wide. Her sparse pubic brush was stiff with matted blood and her abdomen and flattened breasts streaked with red. A stream of blood had run down the table legs to form a congealing puddle on the floor.

Longarm had seen violent death in most of its ugly forms, but this sight brought a twist of nausea to his stomach and he swallowed hard to force the rising bile from gushing up his throat. He touched the woman's shoulder with the back of his hand and found it cold. Then he left the hogan quickly.

Although the man had not moved, he could work his lips now, and when he saw Longarm he asked in a thick-voiced whisper, "Ro-la?"

Longarm frowned, worked the garbled word through his mind and asked, "Rosalie?"

"Ro-LA," the man repeated.

"Rosalia?" Longarm guessed.

"Thee. E-po-tha."

"Esposa? Your wife? The lady in—in the house?"

"Thee."

Longarm shook his head. "She's dead. You must've knowed."

After a moment, the man managed a feeble nod. Longarm went on, "Now, don't try to talk to me, just nod or—well, I'll know if you're trying to tell me yes or no." When the man inclined his head again, Longarm asked, "Was it five men done this to you and your wife?" The man made minimal inclination of his head. "Three nights ago?" Again the tiny movement. "They moved off to the north?" Longarm asked.

This time there was no answering motion. Longarm hunkered down and pressed a finger to the man's throat. There was no pulse. For a moment, Longarm held his position, then he stood up. "Poor son of a bitch," he muttered. "He kept himself alive just long enough so's he could tell somebody who done this. And I had to be the one he told."

For several minutes Longarm studied the corpse and the hogan. Then he carried the man's body inside and laid it on the table beside the woman. An axe leaned against the wall behind the stove. Longarm gashed the log walls with the axe, tearing out huge splinters. He scraped up the pieces of wood on the floor and split some of them for kindling. He arranged the kindling around the center post, where the flames would lick along the ceiling braces and from them to the walls. Then he touched a match to the kindling and left the hogan quickly.

Perhaps an hour of daylight remained when Longarm sighted Tuba City, and as he watched the details of the town slowly become visible as he drew closer he knew that this time he had not made a mistake. He could see at a glance that the town was small and very new.

Only three or four of its two dozen buildings and houses had been painted, and the lumber used in those which were still untouched by a paintbrush had not yet been darkened by the scorching sunshine, but still glowed with the bright shade of new wood. He checked the trail for the hoofprints he was looking for as he continued toward the town, and spotted both the chipped hoof and the swollen frog prints within the next few yards.

Now, certain of the identity of the town lying just ahead, sure that the outlaw gang had gone there, and with the sun dropping closer to the sheer towering face of the Kaibab Plateau fifty miles away, Longarm reined in and lighted a cigar while he took stock of his situation.

Them outlaws was damn fools to head from that trading post right into Tuba City and not even try to hide their tracks. Even if they pushed on, they'll be easy to follow.

Except them two bushwhackers didn't belong to that gang; not the way them prints read. What it looks like, old son, is that you got two different bunches on your hands.

Seeing the problem helped, but seeing a solution would have helped even more, Longarm thought sourly as he tossed away the butt of his smoked-down cigar and rode on into Tuba City.

Because the supper hour was at hand, Longarm was prepared to find the town deserted. He'd seen Tuba City's equivalent in many places to which his cases had taken him before. It was a one-street town, with most of the buildings strung out in a long line along one side, their faces to the south, their backs to the direction from which the thin cold wind would blow in winter.

Perhaps forty or fifty houses made up the town. About half of them stretched along the street beyond the ten or fifteen commercial buildings. The other houses were scattered out across the high mesa. The street was unpaved, but Longarm did not waste time looking for hoofprints on the churned dust of its surface. He rode along the street looking for a hotel or rooming house.

He walked the filly slowly, noting the street's features. There were very few. First there was the livery stable, on the edge of town, as usual. A short distance further, a down-at-the-heels structure of unpainted boards bore a sign DELUXE SALOON, and still further along a much larger building was labelled simply GENERAL STORE. A bit beyond it a tiny frame structure that could have contained only a single room had POST OFFICE on the false front that rose above its narrow tin awning.

Looking ahead, Longarm saw the red-and-white-striped pole of a barbershop, and beyond that a two-story building that was the town's most imposing structure. As he drew closer he saw that the big building bore the legend RITZ SALOON and, in smaller letters just past it at the edge of the facade, RITZ ROOMS. Beyond the big building, a sign on a smaller announced the place to be a CAFÉ.

107

There were a few other business buildings farther down the street, but he could not make out the signs that identified them. In front of the big building with the twin "Ritz" signs, Longarm pulled up, swung out of his saddle, and looped the filly's reins around the hitch rail. He looked along the building's front, but saw no entrance except the swinging doors leading to the saloon. After a final glance both ways along the deserted street, he pushed through the batwings.

Like the street, the saloon was deserted. Not even a barkeep was visible. Looking around, Longarm saw the place was smaller than he'd expected it to be, given the size of the building it occupied. At the back, a stairway led to a balcony off which half a dozen doors opened. The front edge of the balcony dropped in a straight line to the floor, forming a wall broken by the stairs leading to the balcony and by two doors, both of which were closed.

There were four small round tables along the wall on one side and the bar occupied the opposite wall. The bar was short. It could accommodate perhaps a dozen men if they crowded shoulder to shoulder. The array of bottles on the shelves flanking a small mirror was not encouraging. Longarm studied them while he waited; more than half the bottles bore no labels at all, and most of the labels on those identified were strange to him.

Tired of waiting, Longarm tossed a cartwheel on the bar. Almost before the coin's mellow ringing died away a man came through a door at the rear of the saloon. He wore the white apron, ribboned shirtsleeve holders, and curled waxed moustache that had been adopted as their unofficial uniform by bartenders.

"I hope you ain't been waiting long, friend," he said apologetically. "We don't get many customers this time of day. Most of the men in Tuba City stops by for a drink before they go home to supper, so I have a bite myself while trade's slack."

"No harm done," Longarm said. He picked up the cartwheel and went on, "I'll have a drink later on. What I really come in here for was to see about renting a room. You got a sign out in front, but I didn't see no door to go through except your batwings."

"Oh, the main door to the rooming house is around the side of the building," the barkeep explained. "You don't have to go outside again, though. You can go up the stairs back there and down on the other side, but since there's nobody around, use that door on the right under the balcony, the one I came in by. Knock on the door at the end of the passage. That's the office. Mrs. O'Reilley's there, and she'll fix you up with a room."

Mrs. O'Reilley was a buxom woman with full, pink cheeks and a firm jutting chin. Strands of grey were beginning to show in her coal-black hair. She eyed Longarm narrowly and said, "You're sure you just want a room, mister? Because I run a decent place here—no flip-skirt floozies or fancy women."

"A room's all I'm looking for, ma'am," Longarm replied.

"It'll be two dollars for tonight and tomorrow night," she said. "If you stay past then, it goes up to five dollars a day."

"That sounds sorta steep to me," Longarm frowned. "You mind telling me why?"

"Day after tomorrow the rubbernecks come in on the stage from the railroad," Mrs. O'Reilley replied. "Prices always go up in Tuba City when they're in town."

"I guess I don't follow you, ma'am," Longarm said.

"Sightseers from the East. A stage brings them here from the railroad and then to the Grand Canyon for two or three days. All them Eastern folks is used to paying big prices back where they come from, so we just charge them what they expect when they come to Tuba City."

"But I didn't come rubbernecking," Longarm pointed out.

His remark brought a puzzled frown to the landlady's face. After a moment she said, "Well, I guess that's right. I'll tell you, Mr.—"

"My name's Long, ma'am. Custis Long. I'm here on business, not to sightsee."

"You let me think on it, Mr. Long," Mrs. O'Reilley said. "I guess we can work something out. Now, you can go up to your room, number five, at the top of the stairs. You can go in and out through the saloon, or you can take the stairs that lead down to the hall and use the side door. We had to put that in because some of the ladies with the rubbernecks didn't want to go in and out through the saloon."

"That'll be just fine," Longarm said. "I'll get my gear off my horse and move right in, if there's no objection."

"Do what you please, Mr. Long," Mrs. O'Reilley said. "But

I'll take the first two nights' rent now, if you don't mind."

Longarm found the room neat but bare—a bed, a dresser with a washbowl on it, and a single straight chair. He looked around it and shook his head.

Well, you got here, old son, he told himself. *Now all you got to do is find the men you're after. Because if I was them and was looking for a place to hide out where nobody'd think of looking for me, there wouldn't be a better place anywhere than Tuba City.*

Chapter 13

After carrying his rifle and saddlebags up to the bare little room, Longarm rode down Tuba City's main street to the livery stable and left the filly there to be cared for. The attendant spoke more Spanish and Navajo than he did English, and Longarm wasn't sure that his instructions to shoe the animal had been understood. By the time he'd finished trying to get his wishes across, dusk had crept up over the town.

Lights were showing in the stores when Longarm left the livery stable, but Tuba City's single street was still deserted. Walking back toward his lodgings, he glanced into the scruffy-looking Deluxe Saloon. It was as empty as the more imposing one where he'd rented the room had been at the time he'd left. He passed the place by. Looking in the general store, he saw more clerks than customers, and he did not stop there, either.

Reaching the Ritz, he recalled the barkeep's remark about the supper hour, and went on past it into the café. Tuba City was evidently a town where the residents ate at home, for the café was as bare of customers as the saloons and the store had been.

Longarm sat at the counter, ate a thin, overdone steak and a few slices of the fried potatoes that came with his order, and drank a cup of coffee. Though the meal had filled his stomach, it had not fully satisfied him. When he'd drained his coffee cup, he returned to the saloon.

The barkeep was on duty but the place was still bare of other customers. With a welcoming smile, the man started down the bar, wiping his hands on his white apron. Longarm looked at the bottles displayed on the backbar and flicked a finger at them.

"I hope you got a bottle of good Maryland rye up there," he told the waiting barkeep.

"You won't see none on show, but I got a bottle I keep under the bar," the man said, reaching. He brought out an almost full quart of Tom Moore and set it in front of Longarm. "How does this suit you?"

"Right down to a tee," Longarm told him. A sliver of memory began prodding his mind. He caught and retained it, and while the barkeep poured, went on, "Not that it's any of my business, but how come you keep your rye put away like you do?"

"Oh, we don't have much call for it. Fact is, I just keep it on hand for a regular customer." The barkeep picked up the dollar Longarm had tossed on the bar and put a fifty-cent piece in its place. "It ain't his personal bottle, though. He pays for it a drink at a time, just like you or anybody else."

Looking at his change, Longarm said mildly, "This rye's mighty expensive whiskey. Not complaining, you understand, just remarking."

"Special order liquor usually is. If a man's got a taste for a good whiskey, he ought not mind paying the price."

Longarm did not believe in coincidence. He recalled the similar answer he'd gotten when asking about Tom Moore rye at a saloon in Flagstaff, but deferred questioning the barkeep about the bottle until later. Picking up the glass, he swallowed half the whiskey and put the glass back on the bar while he lighted a cigar.

"That special customer of yours knows good rye whiskey," he told the barkeep. "You figure he'll be in later? Seeing as how he's the reason I'm getting a sip of good rye, I figure I owe him a drink."

"It ain't likely he'll show up, friend. He don't live here in Tuba City, but he comes up from Flagstaff pretty regular."

"Well, I'm going to be around a few days. Maybe he'll show up before I leave."

"You'd be in town on business, I guess?" the barkeep asked, his voice carefully casual. "Mrs. O'Reilley mentioned you was planning to stay a while."

Longarm matched the man's seeming lack of interest. "I got a few little things I need to tend to up this way. It might take me a few days to get 'em all wound up."

"Well, if there's anything you'd like to know, I guess I'm acquainted with just about everybody that lives within a hundred miles of here," the man offered. "My name's Al Scanlon, by the way."

"Mine's Long," Longarm replied. "And I'll keep you in mind if I need to ask some questions." He drained the glass and put it on the bar. "Now, I've rode a long ways, and that bed in my room upstairs looked mighty good to me."

"You better enjoy sleeping while you can," Scanlon told him. "There's a new bunch of rubbernecks due in here the day after tomorrow, and they sorta lift the lid while they're around."

"Mrs. O'Reilley was saying something about the sightseers. Whereabouts do they come from?"

"Why, they're mostly from the East. They ride out to the end of rail on the Denver & Rio Grande—it runs on past Grand Junction now, you know. Then they take special stagecoaches the rest of the way. Going and coming, the stages stop here for a night to let the rubbernecks rest."

"I guess Tuba City really does some business when the stages are here."

"I tell you, Long, it's been a lifesaver for this little old town. There wouldn't be much business without it, now the Navajo trading's so slack. But more rubbernecks come every year. That canyon's getting quite a name as a place folks oughta see. If you ain't seen it, you might like to go on one of the stages and take a look."

"I been there, thanks. And I got to admit it's a real sight to behold. Once you've seen it, though, there ain't much point in going back for a second look."

"That's about the way I feel," Scanlon agreed.

"I don't guess you get many new people in here besides them sightseers, do you?" Longarm asked.

"Well, you've seen the town. There ain't a hell of a lot of reason for anybody except a wool buyer or a Navajo trader to want to move here or even come here for a visit, is there?"

"I couldn't say about that. But judging from the way the trail up from the south looks, you get a lot passing through."

"Oh, sure. But most of them passes through in a real big hurry, when you come down to that."

"I had a hunch that might be the case. Men on the dodge?"

"Yep. We're right on one of the old outlaw trails. It's not used so much now, but there's still owlhoots moving over it." The barkeep frowned. "I don't mean to pry, Long, but is that

113

why you're here? You wouldn't by any chance be a bounty hunter, would you?"

Longarm grasped at the chance to give himself a believable reason for asking questions without revealing his real identity. He said, "You wouldn't expect me to go around bragging about it if I was, now would you?"

"Well, no, I guess not."

Dropping his voice and leaning across the bar, Longarm went on, "If you was to know about a bunch of men that come this way yesterday or the day before, I might be interested, though."

"A bunch of 'em?" Scanlon asked, lowering his voice to match Longarm's confidential tone.

"That's right. They'd be moving north or east, and their horses would be real heavy loaded, if it's the bunch I got in mind. I've got a pretty good idea they'd have to stop here and stock up on grub, things like that."

Before Scanlon could answer, two men pushed through the batwings. The barkeep called a greeting to the newcomers, but before going to serve them he refilled Longarm's glass and said, "On the house this time." Then, dropping his voice to a half-whisper, he added, "We better have a little talk later on, Long. Might be I could help you, if there's enough in it for me."

"Whenever you're ready," Longarm replied. "And better sooner than later."

Finishing his drink, Longarm left with a wave to Scanlon, who was talking to the two new arrivals. Outside, he looked up and down the street. There were two or three men standing in front of the general store, and he turned in that direction, hoping the livery stable proprietor might be back on the job by now and in a mood to answer a few questions about travellers who had stopped there recently.

He detoured around the group standing in front of the store and glanced into the Deluxe Saloon as he passed, but all he could see below the batwings were the legs of men lined up along the bar. He looked at the horses tethered to the hitch rail, but none of them appeared familiar. Deciding he'd stop and take a look at the faces of the men inside after he'd finished his business at the livery stable, Longarm moved on without stopping.

At the livery stable, the proprietor had returned from supper.

Longarm said, "My name's Long. You own this place?"

"I sure do. Name's Sam Church, like it reads on the sign."

"Well, I brought a horse in a little while ago, need to board it here for a few days."

"I know your horse, Long," Church nodded. "A nice little filly. Something wrong with her? She need to be doctored?"

"Not that I know of, but she needs to be shod," Longarm said. "I wasn't sure that fellow you had working here when I brought her in could understand me too good, so I decided I'd wait until you got back to talk about shoeing her."

"Oh, old Belai doesn't talk much English, but he understands it all right," Church replied. "I'll get your filly shod, but it'll be a day or two before I can get around to it."

Longarm frowned. "That's a long time to wait. Can't you get the job done tomorrow? Suppose I need her, sudden-like?"

"Ride her and bring her back, unless she's got sore feet. If she has, I'll lend you a mount," the liveryman said. "I can't do the job sooner. There's a man bringing four animals in sometime tomorrow, and the rubberneck stages'll be here next day. There's always something their teams needs."

Church's mention of four horses struck a chord in Longarm's mind at once; the four horses stolen from Leota Toh's corral were unshod, and this was the first place the outlaws had reached where the job could be done. He said to the liveryman, "I guess the fellow with the four horses wanted you to do the job right away?"

"You guessed right, Long. He started out wanting six horses shod, then said he'd settle for having shoes put on four. He didn't like it a bit when I told him it didn't matter whether he had four or six or ten—I couldn't do the job any sooner."

"I'm in a little bit of a hurry myself," Longarm said. He was sure after Church's remark about six horses that he'd now caught up with the outlaw gang, and that they weren't going to be moving on for at least a day or two. He asked Church, "If I was to go ask that fellow to wait until you get shoes on my filly, you reckon he'd be of a mind to?"

Church shook his head. "Not likely. He started giving me the rough edge of his tongue, till I told him if he didn't feel like waiting he could take his animals someplace else."

"You got any idea where I could find him if I wanted to give it a try?"

"Nope," Church replied. "All I know is that him and his

115

outfit's camped around here somewhere."

"How'd I know him if I run onto him?" Longarm asked.

"Oh, he's a big man. Maybe not as tall as you, but a lot wider, running to fat. Had a week's beard when I talked to him, but I'd imagine he's found the barbershop now and got shaved."

"I'll keep my eyes out, then. If he's still hanging around town, maybe I'll run into him."

"You do that. And if I can see a way to do it, I'll get your filly shod sooner than I figured. That's not a promise, but if you get in a bind and need a horse, I'll be glad to oblige you with one."

"Thanks, Mr. Church. That's real helpful, and I appreciate the offer."

Leaving the livery stable, Longarm started back toward town. He'd covered almost half the distance to the Ritz Saloon when he saw a man approaching him on the dark street. Wishing that Tuba City offered such refinements as street lights, Longarm stopped until he could see the oncoming walker more clearly. As the man drew closer, Longarm stepped out of the street into the shadows of the nearest building.

Hoping the gloom was deep enough to hide him, he watched and waited. He got his first clear glimpse when the approaching man passed through the rectangle of light that poured through the open door of the general store. Though the moment when the man was brightly lighted was very brief, shorter than it had been on their first encounter, Longarm instinctively moved to draw his Colt.

Even without the clear recollection of the approaching man's distinctive build, Longarm knew he'd never forget the off-color purple-pink of the bandana around his throat. Added to the memory of the bandana around his throat. Added to the memory of the bandana was the line-by-line recollection of the set of his shoulders, the angle at which he carried his head, and the swing of his arms as he walked. The sum of these provided all the identification needed.

There was no room for doubt in Longarm's mind. The man who was approaching was the one who, with a hidden companion providing crossfire, had tried to murder him on the trip north from Flagstaff.

For a stretched-out moment, Longarm's hand tightened on the butt of his Colt. Then common sense regained control over anger, and he let his hand fall away. Somehow, Longarm resolved, he'd find a way to track the would-be assassin to wherever he was staying in Tuba City. The job that was more important at the moment was to find the gang of five members. Not only was it his job to recover the loot from the ordnance depot robbery, but Longarm had a personal grudge to settle with them. The memory of the hogan at the deserted trading post still rankled in his memory. After the five outlaws had been brought in, he'd have plenty of time to pick up the trail of the bushwhackers.

Taking half a step forward, Longarm started toward the Deluxe Saloon to carry out his plan to watch for the big outlaw who'd been his original quarry. Before he could leave the gloom that concealed him, he settled back into the shadows again as he saw someone else approaching the pool of light from the store door.

This time the man who was briefly visible as he passed through the lighted area was big and wide and fitted Sam Church's description of the outlaw Longarm was seeking. He was as tall as Longarm and quite a bit bulkier, and, as the liveryman had noted, beginning to run to fat.

Once again Longarm's hand sought the butt of his Colt in its cross-draw holster. He waited while the big man strode toward him unhurriedly. Before he was close enough to catch sight of Longarm in the darkness, the man turned when he reached the broken panel of light spilling from the Deluxe and pushed through the batwings.

That's likely the fellow you're after, old son, Longarm told himself as he stood in the darkness. *He's big enough to weight a horse down real good, all right, especially if he was carrying a few bags of silver dollars. Now, all you got to do is settle down here and wait till he starts back to wherever the rest of the gang's holed up, and that's where you'll find them five murdering bastards and the money they stole. After that, you can hunt down the sons of bitches that tried to bushwhack you.*

Even as the thought passed through his mind, Longarm became aware that he'd almost overlooked an important fact.

Old son, you just missed coming down with a bad case of the stupids, he scolded himself. *It ain't no accident them two men both headed for that saloon. They had it all set up beforehand. They was going in there to meet each other!*

Suddenly the attempt made by the bushwhackers to kill him

117

on the trail fell into the pattern. It formed the section that had been missing in the theft of the Army payroll. Longarm slid a cigar from his pocket; with both men in the saloon, he did not need to worry about hiding any longer. Lighting the cheroot, he hunkered down again and began thinking.

You was only chasing part of that gang of outlaws on the way up here from Flagstaff, his thoughts ran. *The rest of the gang was covering the back of the bunch carrying the loot, which means they was chasing you. Now the chips is all finally in the pot and it's time to lay the cards face up on the table. But you got the wild card in your hand, old son, because they don't know yet that you've put their scheme all together.*

For several moments Longarm did not move. Then he stood up and started for the Deluxe Saloon. There were four horses at the hitch rail now, but he remembered the two that had stood there earlier. A quick look revealed that one was unshod. Bending down, he examined the hooves of the unshod horse.

He could see no chip missing from its hoof, and the prints it had made in the dusty street showed no sign of a swollen frog. Longarm reminded himself that two of the four stolen horses had left no distinctive tracks. Though he had no way of proving his suspicions, he would have bet a sizeable sum that the horse was one of those stolen from Leota's corral. Moving to one side of the panels of light streaming above and below the swinging doors of the Deluxe, Longarm took off his hat and peered inside.

He blinked to adjust his vision to the lighted interior and flicked his eyes over the small room. There were several men standing in a group along the bar close to the door. At the far end, their heads close together, the big outlaw and the bushwhacker with the bright purple-pink neckerchief stood talking.

Longarm looked at them for a moment. Then he quietly backed off the narrow porch and retraced his steps to the livery stable.

Chapter 14

Sam Church did not seem at all surprised when Longarm came back so soon after he'd left and asked that the filly be saddled. The liveryman led the horse out of its stall, took Longarm's McClellan saddle off the partition wall where it rested, and proceeded silently with the job of securing it on the filly's back.

While the liveryman was securing the cinch straps, Longarm said, "I might not be back till pretty late. I guess you'll have a night man on, though?"

"Even if this ain't a big city, Long, I run a good stable here," Church replied tartly. "After I go home, old Belai will be sleeping in the hayloft. You might have to yell for him a few times, but he'll wake up and take care of you."

Leading the filly, Longarm started back toward the Deluxe. He stopped in the shadows fifty yards from the saloon's door. Peering through the darkness, he saw that there were still four horses at the hitch rail. He settled down to wait.

Minutes ticked away. A man came out of the saloon and made his way unsteadily toward town, and after another long period of inactivity another pushed through the batwings, mounted one of the horses, and rode off. Longarm began to wonder if the men in whom he was interested had left while he'd been at the livery stable.

Both of them emerged. There was no mistaking their identity. Even though he could only see their silhouettes against the light from the swinging door, Longarm relaxed. They stood on the narrow porch for a few moments, then the fat outlaw went to the hitch rail and swung into the saddle while the second man started walking toward the center of town.

Longarm mounted and waited. The outlaw on horseback passed the second man with a wave, but Longarm still made

119

no move to follow him. He knew from long experience that trailing a man on horseback in the darkness was a tricky job at best. Eyes were of little use. If he got near enough to the outlaw to keep him in sight, it would be equally easy for the outlaw to see him. Even trailing by the sound of hoofbeats ahead meant the follower's hoofbeats could be heard by the quarry.

Counting on the drinks the fat outlaw must have put away to dull the man's sense of caution, Longarm waited until he saw the man pass through the lighted area created in the street by the glow coming from the batwings of the Ritz Saloon. Then he toed his horse into the street and followed.

As he came near the fat man's companion, he slumped forward in the saddle, his hatbrim almost touching the saddle-horn as he swayed from side to side in what he hoped was a convincing imitation of a drunken rider. Longarm's sham must have been more than adequate, for the man wearing the fancy neck scarf merely glanced up as the filly passed.

As he came abreast of the Ritz, Longarm risked a quick glance back. The bushwhacker was still making his way along the street with slow deliberation, neither hurrying nor lolly-gagging. For a moment Longarm debated reining in and going up to his room to pick up his rifle, but he discarded the idea after another quick backward glance. By the time he'd reached his room and picked up the gun, the bushwhacker would be passing in front of the place. He let the filly keep moving and within a few moments had passed through the lighted area and was in darkness again.

There were very few lights spilling into the street ahead after he'd left the Ritz and its neighboring café behind. Here and there a chink in a shuttered window sent a thin spear of light into the street, but for the most part the windows merely marked the location of a house and helped Longarm keep track of the outlaw's progress by watching him block out the window lights as he passed each one in turn. Then the street and the town ended. The street became a trail again, and there were no more lights from houses ahead.

As they entered the open country beyond the town, Longarm changed his tracking tactics. Cautiously, signalling the filly to move a bit faster by nudging her gently with his heels, he closed the gap between himself and the fat outlaw. By bending forward in the saddle every few minutes and squinting ahead at a slight upward angle, he kept track of his quarry's progress by locating the dark blob of the outlaw's body where it blocked out the stars. When he saw the distant glow of a fire against the night sky, Longarm relaxed and reined in. The fat man had led him to the spot where the outlaws were camped.

As anxious as he was to get to the gang's camp, Longarm waited. He dismounted and led his mount forward, moving only a few yards at a time, stopping to listen while he tried to pierce the blackness with his eyes. When the glow of the campfire was cut to a sharp edge by the rim of the canyon in which the outlaws had made their camp, Longarm tethered the filly and went on with slow, careful steps.

In the silent darkness that surrounded him, Longarm moved stealthily forward until he could hear the muted voices from the canyon. Now the night became his friend. He moved faster and with less caution, for he knew the men's voices would drown any faint sounds he might make, and with their eyes contracted by the fire they could not see him in the gloom. Just the same, he slid his Colt out of its cross-draw holster as he drew closer to the voices. He could not disregard the possibility that the outlaws had posted a sentry between the canyon and the trail.

Despite his confidence, Longarm took no chances. Before he reached the rim of the little canyon he dropped to his hands and knees and made the last ten yards of his approach by crawling. He could both see and hear plainly now. The outlaws were sitting around a small campfire, a bottle on the ground beside each man. Longarm counted them quickly. All five were present.

Longarm studied the canyon below him. It was the kind of small canyon common to that part of the country, barren of brush and trees, with only an occasional tuft of short weedy grass showing on the ocher-colored soil. The horses were secured to a picket line at one side, where a spring ran a few yards to form a small pool. A tarpaulin had been staked to create a spot of shade, but it was like a tent without sides and would provide no cover for a man trying to approach unseen.

With a sigh, he put his Colt back in its holster. Now he regretted his failure to stop at his room and pick up his Winchester. Expert marksman that he was, he'd realized instantly that the men around the fire were out of certain range for his revolver. With five of them armed with rifles firing at his muzzle flashes, he'd stand no chance of coming out alive if he started a gunfight. Settling down, he shrugged off his frustration and gave his full attention to what the fat outlaw was saying.

"So we oughta get the money split up in the next three or four days and be on our way," the fat man said. "The boss don't want to make no kinda move till he can get rid of that damn Longarm, though."

"How's he aiming to do that, Joe?" one of the men asked.

"He was supposed to gun Longarm down someplace along the way up here from Flagstaff, but now you say the bastard's still poking around."

"Yeah," another chimed in. "Simms is right. I say we take our shares and get out. I'm aiming to head for the Hole in the Wall up by Goblin Valley and lay low a while. It ain't but a two or three day ride from here."

Longarm smiled in the darkness. He was intimately acquainted with three of the several hideouts known on the outlaw trail as "Hole in the Wall." He also had identities now for two of the five men around the campfire; he knew the fat man's name was Joe, and he recognized Simms's name as being one of the two deserters who'd assisted in the robbery at the ordnance depot.

"If the boss couldn't get rid of Longarm on the way up here, I don't see as he'll do any better now," a third man objected.

"Now, hold on, Karp," Joe said quickly. "Tuba City ain't like Flagstaff. It'll be easier to get at Longarm up here."

"I don't see how he figures that," Simms said. "Longarm got here two days after we pulled in. That's gotta mean he come damn close to us on the trail."

Longarm now knew the identity of the second deserter, Karp. Only the other two now needed names, and he was sure these would be forthcoming before very long. He was not disappointed, for one of the two he'd not yet identified was the next to object.

"You reckon he seen that mess we left at the old trading post?" one of the unidentified outlaws asked.

"Now, shut up, Slocum!" Joe snapped. "You know all of us agreed we wasn't gonna talk about that."

"Damn it, that wouldn't've happened if we could've gone someplace where we could spend some of that money we got in them bags!" Slocum said. "We been hauling it all over the country long enough! Joe, why don't you shell out a few dollars apiece so we can go to town like you do?"

"Because we all agreed to go about this job the way the head man had it planned," Joe replied. "And I'll tell you this right now, Slocum: it don't do a man much good to go into a little town like Tuba City when he knows there's a smart son of a bitch of a U. S. marshal on the lookout for him!"

"Sounds to me like you'd turn and run if you was to meet Longarm," the man sitting next to Joe commented.

"Not by a damn sight!" Joe retorted. "But I'm smart enough to be careful and follow orders. That's why the boss put me in charge till he can take over."

"I never did see you go looking for a face-down, McGee," Slocum said. "Whether it was with that tinhorn gambler that backed you down in Gallup, or with somebody who's got the kind of name Longarm has."

"It wouldn't spook me one damn bit!" the man called McGee announced boastfully. "Longarm puts on his pants one leg at a time, just like anybody else. It sure as hell wouldn't scare me to face him down."

"Listen to big-mouth Bob!" Karp jeered. "They don't call you that for nothing, McGee! Any time you face down Longarm, I wanta be there to see it!"

"Just keep your eyes peeled, then!" McGee retorted. "Maybe you'll be surprised!"

"All right, damn it!" Joe broke in, his voice loud and angry. "All of you shut up! You're yelling before you're hurt!"

Longarm took advantage of the silence that followed the fat man's command to glance quickly at each of the men sitting around the fire and associate names with faces. He was sure he'd be able to spot each of them, and put the right name on the right man, the next time he saw them.

Joe broke the silence by saying, "Now here's what's gonna happen. Tomorrow a couple of you men has got to take them Navajo ponies to the livery stable and get 'em shod. We want 'em to be in good shape when we split up."

"Who's going to do that?" Simms asked.

"Whoever I tell to," Joe retorted. "I'll make up my mind tonight or early tomorrow. Then I'm going back late tomorrow and have a talk with the head man."

"Take the damn nags in yourself, then," McGee suggested.

Joe shook his head. "Not likely. They got to go in early tomorrow morning, and I already been in town once. Big as I am, folks sorta remember seeing me. The boss says it's too risky for me to go in twice on the same day."

"Hold on, Joe!" Slocum objected. "Never mind about people remembering you. There's likely to be wanted posters out on the rest of us by now."

"There's not," Joe assured him. "There'd have been one at the livery stable and likely the saloon, too. I'd've seen 'em if there'd been any."

"Hell, it's too far from Flagstaff for any flyers to be up here yet," McGee put in. "The Army won't do any better with a job like that than they do with anything else."

"Well, there's not any," Joe repeated. "So whoever goes in with the horses won't have to worry."

"What about Longarm?" Simms asked. "He knows who he's looking for by now, I bet."

"How in hell could he?" Joe asked. "He ain't seen us yet."

On the canyon rim, Longarm smiled thinly and wished again that he'd taken the risk involved in getting his Winchester.

"That don't mean he ain't looking for us," Karp pointed out. "Now that he's nosing around here, I wanta get my ass just as far away as I can as fast as I can travel!"

"You ain't the only one that feels that way, Karp," Slocum seconded. "I'm ready to move, too."

"Me, too," McGee said, "but I'll be damned if I move an inch until I get my share of that money we lugged all the way up here from Flagstaff. We stole it fair and square, and I want what's coming to me!"

"All right!" Joe snapped. "Shut up and let me finish. Then you can talk the rest of the night, for all I give a damn!" He looked angrily from one to the other of the gang. When he was sure they were ready to listen, he went on, "It's going to take that livery stable most of the day tomorrow to shoe all them horses. I don't want whoever takes 'em in to wait. I'll get the nags and bring 'em back myself after I get through."

"I thought you said it was too risky for you to go back to town tomorrow." McGee frowned.

"Sure it's a risk, but the boss figures I got to. After him and me get done talking, I'll come back out here and we'll divide up the money. Then I'll tell you men which way he wants you to go when we split up, and that'll be the end of it."

"Now, that ain't part of the deal!" Slocum objected.

"It sure as hell ain't!" McGee agreed. "When we planned this out, there wasn't a thing said about us having to take orders from anybody after we get our share of the money."

"Well, I'm telling you now!" Joe snapped. "And if you'll listen to me a minute, you'll see why it's got to be done the way the boss says."

"I'm ready to listen," Simms said. "But it better sound damn good before I go along with it."

"You'll see, all right," Joe promised. He paused for a moment, then went on. "Now, the Army's got records of everything there is to know about the four of you—"

"How about you, Joe?" Karp broke in. "You been telling us all about the hitch you put in in the Army. They'll have as much about you as they will about us."

"Sure. But it's been ten years since I got my discharge. That was up in Montana, and it was an honorable, so it ain't likely they'll even think about me. Now, McGee and Slocum got busted out right here in Arizona with dishonorable discharges not more'n a year ago. And you and Simms, you're down in the books now as deserters. They'll be after you worse than the rest of us on account of that."

"Damned if you don't make it sound like me and Karp ain't got much of a chance, Joe," Simms said.

"Oh, you got a chance," the fat man replied. "But if you don't do what the boss says for you to after we split up, chances are you'll get caught instead of getting way."

"When you put it that way it starts to make sense," Karp said thoughtfully.

"Damn right it makes sense!" Joe told him. "Now, I might not like to do what the boss says any better than you men do, but I got enough brains to know he understands how things work on the other side of the law a lot better than I do. So I listen to him when he says something, and you better do the same."

"You been talking about the boss ever since we begun to work on this scheme," McGee said. "Except none of us has ever seen him. Hell, we don't even know who he is. Maybe we'd listen better if you told us."

125

"That's the way he wants it," Joe answered. "If and when he wants you to know something, he tells me, and I tell you. And you got to admit, it's worked real good so far."

"Did he tell you we was going to have Longarm on our tails?" Simms asked.

"No, I got to admit he didn't," Joe said. "But as soon as he found it out, he come up with a way to give him the slip, didn't he? We're here, and he still ain't found us."

"All right, Joe," McGee said sullenly. "We've gone along this far, and you're right, everything's worked out. I'll go the rest of the way if you guarantee to wind things up tomorrow."

"That's fair enough," Joe agreed. "How about the rest of you men? You feel like McGee does?"

"It's all right with me," Simms said.

"Sure. I'll stick it out until tomorrow," Karp said.

"Well, if the rest of you are going along, it looks like I've got to, whether I like it or not," Slocum said grudgingly.

"That settles it, then," Joe said, trying without success to keep his voice from reflecting his relief. "Now let's have a drink or two and turn in. We got a lot to do tomorrow, and if it all works out, we'll all be on our way this time tomorrow night."

Longarm had no doubt that there'd be more said, but he was equally sure that he'd heard everything that was important. He gave the outlaws time to feel the effects of the liquor and then backed away from the edge of the cliff. Walking slowly and silently back to where he'd tethered his horse, he started back toward Tuba City. As soon as he'd settled into the rhythm of the filly's easy gait, he took out a cigar and lighted it.

What you just heard sure answers a lot of questions you been asking yourself, old son, he thought as he let the horse set her own pace through the dark night. *There ain't one of them men, except maybe the fat one, that'd have sense enough to pour sand out of a boot if there wasn't somebody around to tell 'em it had to be turned bottom up. That's why this case ain't made much sense from the start. You been chasing the men that stole that Army money chest when you oughta been thinking about the one that planned how they was to do it. And there ain't a lot of question who that was, and there ain't a lot of question why he done it. But what you got to do now is see that the case is closed up the right way. And that's going*

126

to call for a lot of real hard scheming.

He reached the outskirts of Tuba City. All the windows he'd seen lighted earlier now were dark. The lights of the two saloons were all that he could see along the street. He rode on past them and reached the livery stable. It was dark, but he followed Church's instructions and knocked at the barn door. He had to knock twice before the old attendant responded. Leaving the horse with the man, Longarm started walking slowly back toward the town.

He stopped at the Deluxe long enough to look inside. There were no horses at the hitch rail and only a pair of grizzle-faced desert rats inside, leaning against the bar. After a quick glance, Longarm moved on to the Ritz. He pushed through the swinging doors into the saloon section. There were three men at the bar and two at one of the tables along the wall. Al Scanlon came up to where Longarm had stopped and without a word placed a glass in front of him and reached under the bar and produced the bottle of Tom Moore.

"I didn't think I needed to ask you," he smiled.

"No need to at all." Longarm lighted a cigar and puffed it into an even glow before lifting the glass to his lips.

"Not meaning to be forward, Long," Scanlon said, dropping his voice to a confidential whisper, "but that talk we started earlier about that bunch of outlaws. You feel like going on with it now?"

"It's as good a time as any, I guess."

"We'd better do it now," Scanlon said. "If they're running on schedule, the rubberneck stages will be pulling in about noon tomorrow, and I'll be so busy pouring drinks there won't be any time for me to talk."

"Go on," Longarm invited. "I'm listening."

"I don't guess you've been around town much since we had our little conversation, but I found that Dirk Colby got back last night."

"Who's Colby?"

"Why, the town marshal. Haven't you heard about him?"

"Can't say I have. Last time I heard, the only law up in these parts was the Navajo Police and a deputy U.S. marshal down in Flagstaff."

"Well, Dirk's only been marshal a few months. Anyhow, he had to take a trip down to Flagstaff, and about noon today

127

he came in and got a bottle of this," Scanlon said, indicating the bottle of Maryland rye. "Now, that special customer I told you about, he's—"

Longarm broke in to say levelly, "His name's Paul Ferguson, and he's the deputy U.S. marshal at Flagstaff." When Scanlon's jaw dropped and he stared across the bar in amazement, Longarm went on, "You better pour a drink for yourself, Scanlon. You and me got a little bit of talking to do. There's some things happening that you ain't heard about yet."

Chapter 15

For a moment Scanlon was unable to speak. Then he asked, "How in hell did you come up with that? I know I didn't mention Ferguson's name."

"That's right, you didn't. You didn't need to, because you said exactly what a barkeep down in Flagstaff told me just before I left to come up here. Seems like he's got a regular customer who don't drink nothing but top-grade Maryland rye."

"You're saying his customer was Marshal Ferguson, too?"

"Now, he didn't call no names, but you didn't either."

"Then what made you think of Ferguson?"

"I just got reminded of a few things I oughta thought about before," Longarm replied.

"Maybe you'd better explain," Scanlon frowned.

"You said your town marshal picked up a bottle of Tom Moore for that special customer of yours the minute he got back from Flagstaff. Now, I don't figure there's likely to be more'n one man in Arizona Territory who's got taste like that. It popped into my mind that man's name is Paul Ferguson."

His voice taut, Scanlon said, "I'm not sure what you are or who you are, Long, but there's nothing wrong with the way your mind works. You make me feel like a fool."

"Which you ain't, Scanlon. And I ain't told you no lies. I just didn't correct you when you made some wrong guesses."

"Who the hell are you, anyhow? You're sure not any bounty hunter. What's your real name and what're you here for?"

"My name's Long, all right. And if you'll recall, I never claimed to be a bounty hunter. That was your idea."

"I guess it was, at that." The barkeep grinned ruefully. "You just let me go on and talk myself into a corner."

"There ain't no harm done. The fact is, I'm a deputy U. S. marshal myself, outa the Denver office." Taking out his wallet,

Longarm flipped it open to show Scanlon his badge. He said. "Just so you'll be sure I ain't fooling you again, you might as well have a look at this."

"Wait a minute!" Scanlon broke in. "I've heard about you before, when I was one of the barkeeps at the Cheyenne Club. You're the one they call Longarm."

"Some of my friends call me that, sorta like a nickname."

"Any time I make a damn fool of myself, it calls for a drink on me!" Scanlon refilled Longarm's glass, then said, "Even if you do seem to know more about what's going on than I do, did you really mean it when you said there's something you want to talk to me about?"

"There's a few things you can help me out with, if you've got a mind to."

"Whatever I can do. Go ahead."

"First thing I'm curious about is why Ferguson ain't staying here at the Ritz, if he's in town."

"That's easy. Right after we hired Dirk Colby, Ferguson came up to Tuba City on some kind of case. He just happened to get here right after the rubberneck stages had pulled in from the railhead. The dudes were knee-deep, like they are every time those stages are in town. There wasn't a room vacant here at the Ritz for Ferguson, so he slept at the jail in Colby's room."

"Now, that's a funny thing," Longarm said when Scanlon paused. "Being in the line of work I am, I generally notice where the jail is when I come into a strange town, but I don't recall seeing one here."

"It's not likely you'd notice it," Scanlon said with a smile. "Nobody in town wanted to have it next door to them, so we wound up putting it out behind the livery stable. You've got to look twice to see it behind Sam Church's big barn, but if you want to find Ferguson, I imagine you'll find him there."

"Ferguson gets up here pretty often, then?"

"Oh, four or five times a year. There's always cases that the Navajo Police can't handle, and Tuba City didn't have any kind of police or marshal until we hired Dirk Colby."

"How come you didn't mention this Colby before now?"

"Why, he wasn't in town when you got here, Long; he'd had to go to Flagstaff. And I guess I'm not used to having any kind of regular lawman here yet. I just didn't think about him when we were talking before."

"Of course, I wouldn't've known him, unless I'd seen him on the street with his uniform and badge on."

"He didn't want to wear a uniform, and I can't say I blame him. And he hasn't got a badge yet, either. We ordered one for him from Denver, but it hasn't been delivered."

"What's he look like?" Longarm was sure he already knew the answer, but he wanted Scanlon's confirmation of his suspicions.

"He's a big man." Scanlon measured Longarm with his eyes. "Not quite as big as you, but almost. You'd notice one thing about him right away. He's almost always got a red or purple bandana around his neck."

Longarm nodded. He could see no reason for taking Scanlon into his confidence at this point. He said, "I'll recognize him when I see him." He was silent while he lighted a cheroot, then asked, "You mind telling me who pays Colby's wages?"

"Well, Tuba City hasn't got any laws about collecting taxes to pay town officers or selectmen or a marshal," Scanlon replied. "So all the businesses along the street here got together and pitched in enough money to build a jail, with a room for Colby to sleep in, and we chip in to make up his salary every month."

"Who does he report to?"

Scanlon stared at Longarm, his face wrinkled into a bewildered frown. "What d'you mean, report to?"

"Well, Denver is my headquarters, and I report to the chief marshal in the office there. In Arizona Territory, there's a chief marshal in Prescott, and Ferguson reports to him. In a town where there's a real police force, the policemen all report to a sergeant or a captain or a chief. Who does Colby report to here?"

"Why, nobody in particular. If he needs something, he'll come to one of us and we'll talk it over and see if we feel like he needs it."

"Then he really hasn't got any boss, has he?" Longarm continued.

"When you put it that way, I'd have to say no. But he's a good man on the job. Keeps the drunks and Indians in line."

"How'd you happen to pick him out?"

"Why, your friend Ferguson recommended him for the job. We went to Flagstaff looking for a man to hire, and Ferguson said Colby was the best one he could think of."

"And that was just a little while back?"

"Not quite six months." Scanlon frowned. "What's all this leading up to, Long?"

"Maybe more'n I like to think about. Tell me something, Scanlon. When you took me for a bounty hunter, you'd seen somebody that looked like they was running, hadn't you?"

Scanlon did not reply for a moment. Then he nodded. "I saw five men riding through town the day before. If they weren't on the owlhoot trail, I'll cash my chips and stay out of the pot."

"Was one of 'em a fat man, broad as he is high?"

"Yes. I guess you know who they are?"

"I got a real good idea. You'd know that fat fellow if you was to see him again, I guess?"

"Sure. He's one nobody could mistake."

"He's likely to come in here and meet somebody tomorrow."

"You don't know who?"

"Not for sure." Longarm hesitated, reluctant to involve the barkeep in what he'd prefer to keep private. Seeing no way to avoid laying at least a few of his cards on the table, he went on, "I got an idea the fat one's going to meet either Ferguson or Colby."

"Ferguson? Colby?" Scanlon said, shaking his head. "But they're lawmen, like you! Surely you don't suspect them—"

"Scanlon," Longarm said quietly, "lawmen go wrong sometimes. Now, I got good reason for what I'm doing. Just do me a favor and go along on this without asking questions."

"But it doesn't make good sense! An outlaw and a lawman getting their heads together in a place like this, where anybody might walk in and see them?"

"You generally have a lot of customers here in the early part of the afternoon, Scanlon?"

"Well, no, not usually. Saturdays, maybe, or when the rubberneck stages are here, but most afternoons this place is as empty as a graveyard."

"There you are, then. If they sit down and talk in a place like this, nobody's going to think they got anything to hide."

After he'd thought about it for a moment, the barkeep nodded slowly. "Yes, I guess you're right. If they were to sneak off where they'd be by themselves and somebody saw them, it'd look suspicious to anybody who happened to see them."

"That's what I'm getting at."

132

"I suppose you know what they'll be talking about?"

"That's what I've got to make sure about. And I'm going to need some help to carry out a scheme I got."

Scanlon's mouth worked, but he could not speak for several seconds. Then he asked, "Where do I come in?"

"I need to hear what they talk about."

"You want me to listen to them and tell you what they said?"

"No. I want to hear what they say myself."

"I don't see how you can do that unless you hide under the bar. I guess I can clear a place that'd be big enough, but—"

"No," Longarm broke in. "There's a better way. You pile the bar up with glasses and bottles, like you're having a real housecleaning. Stack chairs on top of three of them tables and put the other one by the door back there. I'll be on the other side of the door, listening."

Scanlon studied the area by the door leading to the rooms. He nodded and said, "I guess that'd work. When do you look for them to get together?"

"Some time after noon tomorrow. I don't aim to show my face around town after daylight. You won't see me back of that door, but I'll be there, all right."

"I'm still not quite sure what I'm letting myself in for," Scanlon said slowly. "But I figure I owe you one, so you can count on me doing just exactly what you've told me to."

"Thanks. You ain't going to regret it, and I sure won't forget it," Longarm said. "Now, if you'll dig me out a bottle of that Tom Moore you got hid away someplace, I'll take it up to my room with me so I can have an eye-opener in the morning. But right now, I'm going to roll in and get some shuteye. It's been a real busy day."

Longarm woke fully alert at his usual hour, at daybreak, when his stomach began reminding him that it'd been a long time since supper the previous evening. Dressing hurriedly, he walked the few steps to the café down the street from the Ritz. The steak he ate was no better and no worse than the one he'd had the evening before, though the yolks of the two fried eggs helped cut the grease.

After a second cup of coffee, he went back to his room, took off his coat and vest, and laid his guns across the bed. Then he began stripping and cleaning the weapons, working deliberately and methodically. Unless he was wrong, he'd be

133

needing them before the day ended.

Though he worked as slowly as possible, the Winchester, Colt, and derringer were ready for action long before noon. Laying them aside, Longarm scoured the oil from his hands in the washbasin and lighted a cigar. He pulled the room's lone chair up to the bed and put the bottle of Tom Moore on its seat. Stretching out on the thin mattress, he sipped and smoked until his watch told him the time had come to get in position to listen to the conversation he was sure would take place between Joe and either Ferguson or Colby.

Going downstairs, Longarm moved silently into the passage between the saloon and the rooms. He cracked the door open until a hairline of light showed between door and jamb. Hearing no voices, Longarm risked opening the door wide enough to peer into the saloon.

A table had been placed where he'd asked Scanlon to put it, and by twisting his neck Longarm could see the barkeep busy behind the bar, which was piled high with glasses and bottles. Longarm resisted the temptation to open the door and tell the barkeep he was in place, and was glad that he had, for just then he heard the soft sound of the swinging doors followed by the thunk of boot heels on the wooden floor.

A trifle louder than was necessary, Scanlon said, "Well, Colby. I heard you got back to town, but I guess you been too busy catching up to stop in."

"Yeah, sure," Colby's grating voice replied. "You know how it is when you leave for a few days."

"Sorry I can't serve you here at the bar," Scanlon went on. "The rubberneck stages are due in tomorrow, and I needed to clean up before they get here. Have a seat over at the table, there. I guess you want your usual?"

"No hurry, Scanlon. Whenever you get around to it. I'm looking for a fellow to meet me here. I don't guess there's been anybody come asking for me, has there?"

"Not a soul. You're the first customer that's walked in since noon."

Longarm heard the scraping of a chair as Colby sat down, and almost at once the batwings flapped again and the town marshal said, "Over here, Joe. Scanlon, bring two glasses along with that bottle, will you?"

His face pressed to the doorjamb, Longarm translated the noises and scrapings that followed into Joe's progress to the table, Scanlon bringing the whiskey and glasses, and the small clinks and gurgles made as drinks were poured for the two men. Then there was a long silence.

Joe's voice broke the stillness. "Where are we going to go so we can talk?"

"We'll sit right here. Keep our voices low, nobody can hear us. The barkeep's busy. He's not paying us any mind."

"I don't like it, but I guess it's the best we can do."

"It's all right," Colby said. "As long as we just sit here and talk, nobody's going to look at us twice."

There was a long silence, and Longarm wondered what was delaying the start of the discussion. He understood the reason when he heard the thunk of glasses being put back on the table.

Colby said, "Pour another one if you want, Joe."

"I'll settle for what I've had. The time to drink's after we get away from this damn place."

"I guess you're about ready to move along?"

"Soon as we get our share of the money," Joe rasped.

"That'll be just after sundown."

"Sundown? I told the boys you or the boss would be coming back with me."

"Well, don't blame me, Joe," Colby said. "The boss decided to change the time. I didn't."

"Why'd he do a thing like that? We had it all set up."

"Him and me can't tote all them bags of money on our horses, the way you fellows did. We'll have to bring a wagon."

"What if you do? That don't mean you've got to wait so late," Joe protested.

"That's just what it does mean. The boss wants to wait till suppertime, when everybody in Tuba City's inside. That way it won't draw so much notice."

"I don't like it, Colby. The boys won't like it, either."

"Hell, that little bit of waiting won't make no difference."

"That reason you give me is mighty thin. Why're you putting it off, Colby?"

"I'm not. The boss put it off. He don't want everybody noticing what he's doing, and besides, he don't feel so good, Joe. Matter of fact, he's about half sick."

"Why can't you handle it, then? Me and the boys wanta get moving before dark."

"Because I got other things to do, and the boss wants to do the counting hisself," Colby said shortly.

"You keep putting us off, we won't get away before that damn Longarm gets here," Joe said, anger edging his voice.

"Pour yourself another drink and stop worrying about Longarm. Even if he was to pull in this minute, it'd take him a while to track you men down."

"Maybe. We're all of us a little bit edgy, just the same."

"Get over it, then. Now, here's what the boss has decided. The money's going to be split three ways."

"Three ways?" Joe's voice rose above the whisper in which he and Colby had been talking.

"Quit yelling, damn it!" Colby snapped. "You trying to tell the whole town what's going on?"

"You said we'd split fifty-fifty when we set this job up." Now the fat outlaw's tone told Longarm that he was hissing through tightened lips. "How'd you come up with three ways?"

"Half to the ones that set the job up. A fourth to the boss and me, and the other fourth to your bunch."

"Wait a minute, Colby! We was promised an even split! Where do you and the boss get off, changing things without even talking to us about it? Damn it, *we* done the dirty work!"

"Listen, there'll be more money in your share than any of you men has ever seen at one time!"

"Never mind that! We'll get what's coming to us, or all hell's going to bust loose!"

There was silence on the other side of the door for a minute. Then Longarm heard a chair scrape on the floor.

"Wait a minute, Joe!" Colby said. "Where do you think you're going?"

"I'm gonna find the boss! We don't aim to be cut short of our fair share!"

"Keep your prick in your pants, damn it!" Colby snapped. "Sit down and let's talk a minute more before you kite off!"

"Talking's not going to change a thing," Joe retorted hotly. "Look here, Colby, how'd you like it if me and the boys was to write a few letters that told how this job got set up?"

"You start writing letters, you'll open up a trail they can follow till they run your men down!" Colby blustered.

"Maybe so. But me and the boys ain't got as much to lose as you and the boss and his friends."

"Now, hold on, Joe!" Colby's voice was suddenly placating. "There's no reason for you and me to try to argue this out. You know the boss has got the last word."

"Let's go see him, then!"

"I told you, he's about half sick."

"He won't be too sick to talk."

"He's been taking some kind of medicine that makes him awful sleepy, Joe. It won't wear off for a long time. That's one reason he set the split-up time so late."

"You're lying, Colby!"

"I swear I'm not! Now, listen, you go on back out to the canyon and tell the boys we'll be out there right after sundown. After the boss talks to you, I'll bet he'll fix up a different split that'll give you what you want. Now, you know that's something I can't do."

"Suppose we just take all the money and go?" Joe asked.

"How far do you think you'd get?"

Again there was such a long silence that Longarm grew restive. Then the two resumed their talk.

"All right," Joe said reluctantly. "You and the boss come on out when you said you would. But you and him better be ready to give us our fair share, or I promise you that all hell's going to break loose!"

Chapter 16

Longarm waited until he could no longer hear the boot heels of the departing men thumping across the floor, then stepped into the saloon. Scanlon looked at him questioningly.

"How much could you hear of what they said?" Longarm asked.

"Not a lot, just a word here and there. But I heard enough to know we made a damn poor choice when we picked Colby to be our town marshal. Why, the son of a bitch is a crook!"

"He ain't the only crooked lawman around," Longarm said. "I guess you figured out who's bossing Colby."

"Well . . ." Scanlon hesitated. "I got an idea, but . . ."

"I'll say it for you. Ferguson. Just because you might say we belong to the same outfit don't mean I keep my eyes shut."

"It makes me feel a lot better to know that, Long, but how I feel is neither here nor there. Did you hear enough to put Colby and Ferguson behind bars?"

"Just about." Longarm spoke around the cheroot he'd just clamped between his teeth. He lighted the slim cigar and with a long exhalation of satisfaction puffed out a cloud of fragrant smoke. He went on, "I could nail Colby with what I got on him now, but there'd be a chance Ferguson could weasel out because he wasn't here."

"I kept waiting for you to push that door open and arrest them," Scanlon said. "It surprised me when you let them walk out without you nabbing them."

"All I had after listening to their talk was my word against theirs, Scanlon. I need to catch 'em with evidence that'll make an air-tight case."

"Is what you heard going to make it possible for you to get that kind of evidence?"

"Just as sure as God made little green apples it is! Now that

I know the moves they're going to make, I'll have what I need before daybreak, if everything works out."

"Are you going to need some help arresting them? I can get up a posse, if you feel like swearing one in," Scanlon said.

"Thanks for the offer," Longarm replied. He had no intention of revealing to Scanlon or anyone else his personal reason for wanting to have a lone hand—which meant a free hand—in handling the outlaw gang. He went on, "You see, I don't cotton much to posses. You put five or six men in a posse, and there's going to be somebody that'll shoot at the wrong time or shoot at the wrong man."

"There's a lot of good men in Tuba City, Long. Veterans, good shots, not afraid of anything. Counting Ferguson and Colby, you're going up against a gang that outnumbers you seven to one."

Longarm shook his head. "I don't mind bucking odds, but even if I did, I got a scheme to make things a little bit more equal. Without meaning to offend you none, a lone hand's what I play best, so I'll just go ahead and handle things without help."

"I won't ask any more questions, then. But remember, if you get into a tight spot and need somebody to back up your play, all you've got to do is say the word."

"Thanks again, Scanlon. Not just for the offer, but for what you already done. Now, I'm going to go next door and get me a bite to eat. It's been a long time since breakfast, and my belly thinks my throat's been cut."

Outside, during his short walk from the Ritz to the restaurant, Longarm glanced at the sun. It was well past the mid-point between noon and sunset, and he judged that he had almost three hours before Colby and Ferguson were due to meet with the outlaws in their canyon hideout.

He took his time eating, got his rifle from his room, and walked unhurriedly to the livery stable. Mounted, Longarm rode away from Tuba City in the same direction from which he'd entered the little town. Even though the most direct route to the outlaw hideout was in the opposite direction, riding down the town's main street would have called attention to his departure.

He was in no hurry, and let the filly set its own easy pace. He kept the sun at his back until well out of sight of the livery stable, then turned northwest and started across the broken country in a wide half-circle that would take him to the outlaw hideout in the canyon.

By the time Longarm's unerring sense of direction told him that he was close to his destination and he began scanning the western sky for the final sign he needed to guide him to the valley where the outlaws were waiting, the sun's bottom rim was almost touching the horizon. A wisp of smoke, barely visible against the reddening western sky, gave him the direction that he was looking for. Holding the filly to a slow, deliberate walk, Longarm headed for the faint shimmer that he was certain marked the outlaw band's supper fire.

He rode in a zigzag course that avoided the ridges and took him across the low ground. He was not sure whether the gang had posted lookouts on both sides of the canyon. It was a precaution any experienced group would have taken, but Longarm gambled that the greenhorns enlisted by Ferguson and Colby would not think of covering both approaches. While the going was rougher and his progress slower in the boulder-strewn washes and valleys, by taking the low ground he kept his silhouette from being outlined against the deepening blue of the pre-sunset sky.

When he judged he'd gotten to within a quarter of a mile of the canyon, Longarm reined in and dismounted. Tethering the filly, he slid his Winchester out of its saddle scabbard and started ahead on foot. Picking his way around the high rock outcrops and skirting wide areas of loose, shifting gravel, he made fast progress. Within a few minutes he could see the ragged line of the box canyon's rim.

Before reaching it, Longarm stopped and hunkered down. He touched a match to a cheroot and puffed it while he studied the lay of the land, imprinting its details in his memory. The sun was balanced on the horizon's rim by now, and Longarm had no intention of floundering across unfamiliar terrain in darkness when the time came for him to leave. When he was sure that he'd be able to find the spot easily, even in the dark and in a hurry, he tethered the filly and took a final puff from the cheroot before stubbing it out and resuming his careful advance.

Though he was sure that he'd have been challenged by a lookout if the gang had stationed one on the high ground, Longarm did not relax his vigilance. Nearing the canyon's rim,

140

where he could see the winding road from Tuba City and the short rough track leading off the road into the canyon, he dropped to the ground and crawled carefully forward on hands and knees until he could look down into the small oval depression.

Longarm's roundabout approach had eaten up twice as much time as a more straightforward one would have taken. The afternoon was merging into evening by now, and the canyon floor was already shadowed. Beyond the western wall where he was located the canyon was becoming obscured by a creeping veil of deepening darkness. The line of shadow had not yet reached the firepit, and he could see the outlaws in clear detail. They were gathered around the waning fire, not lounging comfortably now, but poised in tense impatience.

At one side of the fire their horses waited, saddled and ready. The tarpaulin shelter had been taken down, and where it had stood Longarm saw that the tarp had sheltered more than the outlaws. Now that it had been removed he could see the loot from the ordnance depot robbery, an untidy heap of white canvas sacks.

Joe, the fat outlaw, was sitting on the sacks. He held his rifle poised with the butt on his thigh, its muzzle pointing skyward.

"They're taking their time about getting here," McGee was saying sourly as Longarm came within earshot.

"Too damn much time," Slocum agreed. "Unless we get moving pretty soon, it'll be too dark to travel."

"You figure they're running late on purpose?" Simms asked. "I don't trust that Colby an inch further than I can see him."

"Hell, Ferguson's as bad as Colby, or worse," Karp said. "Hiding his crookedness behind his badge, telling us to be sure we didn't call his name, and all the time up to his belly button in figuring out how to pull off this job."

"Both of 'em are as tricky as they are crooked, too," McGee said. "I'm betting they got some kinda trick up their sleeve to keep from paying us off."

"What kind of scheme?" Karp asked.

"I'm betting they'll pull something, only I'm damned if I can figure how they'd work it, us being five to two against 'em," McGee answered. "But I sure don't intend to take my eyes off of them for a minute."

"One thing's for damn sure," Simms observed. "They've got to show up sooner or later, because we still got all the money."

"Don't start counting your share yet," Karp advised. "Wait'll we wind up figuring out how it's gonna be split up."

"Yeah," Slocum agreed. "But all we got to do is stick to what we decided after Joe got back."

"Don't worry about that," McGee said. "Even Joe over there got mad enough to spill their scheme and come in with us."

As though on signal, the four ex-soldiers turned to look at the fat man. "You think we can trust him?" Simms asked, making no effort to lower his voice.

"I don't think we got much choice," McGee said soberly.

Karp called to the fat man, "Hey, Joe, I thought you said Colby and the big boss was gonna be here before sundown. Where in hell are they?"

"You know as much as I do about that," Joe replied. "I told you what Colby said. It ain't my fault if they're late."

"How do we know you meant what you said when you told us you wasn't going to flunkey for them any more?" McGee asked. "You was on their side a lot longer'n you been on ours."

Joe stood up and started toward the fire. He said, "Don't worry about me. I got no use for them two any more. I told you I'd stand against 'em with you, and that's what I'll do."

As he listened to the outlaws, Longarm tried to think of a way to deepen the break between them and Ferguson and Colby. A dozen half-formed schemes tumbled through his mind, but as he considered the ideas carefully, each one showed flaws. He was still trying to work out an approach that might be successful when his time for planning ran out.

From his vantage point on the canyon rim, Longarm heard the creaking of the wagaon and saw its slow approach before the men in the canyon did. He was watching it crawl down the narrow trail into the canyon when the outlaws first became aware of its arrival and turned to look. The vehicle was drawn by two mules, and only one man occupied the seat. Even from across the canyon, Longarm recognized Ferguson.

"Hey, it looks like they finally got here!" Karp called to his fellows. "Maybe we'll get away while it's still light enough to travel, after all."

"That'll depend on how much arguing we got to do," McGee said. "But even if it takes time, we've got to stick together and not let 'em talk us into cutting down our split!"

"Don't worry," Simms said. "If anybody gives in, it'll be them, not us!"

"Remember, now," Karp cautioned. "We don't take a penny less than we was supposed to get when we agreed to this job."

"That's for damn sure," Slocum chimed in.

Longarm watched the approach of the wagon with almost as much interest as the outlaws did. Unlike them, he had more than one thing to watch. As the high-sided conveyance navigated the steep, winding trail off the road and into the canyon he divided his attention between the wagon and the Tuba City road, looking for Colby to be following on horseback. Then, as the wagon rolled out onto the flat valley floor and Colby still did not appear, he decided that he'd see an approaching rider readily enough, and concentrated his attention on Ferguson.

Ferguson reined the wagon around the dying campfire and pulled the team to a halt midway between the fire and the heap of money bags. Joe stood up and started toward it, and the outlaws left the fire and moved up to it as well.

Ferguson made no effort to get out of the wagon seat. From his high vantage point on the canyon wall, Longarm could see that except for a crumpled tarpaulin the wagon bed was bare. He wondered why the tarpaulin was there until it occurred to him that it had been brought to hide the money bags after they'd been loaded. He returned his attention to the outlaws. They had reached the wagon now and stood around it in a straggled group.

"Sorry I kept you men waiting such a long time," Ferguson said. "I guess Joe told you, I been a little bit under the weather, and it took me a while to get going."

"Where's Colby?" Joe asked. "He said he'd be here, too."

"Oh, he'll show up in a few minutes," Ferguson replied. "I decided we better come separate, so we'll have a horse to hand if it turns out we need one."

"We ain't in much of a mind to wait any longer," McGee told Ferguson. "We'd figured on being out of here and getting some miles put behind us by dark."

"You'll be able to ride out pretty quick, now," Ferguson said. "All we got to do is count out the shares. Then you can take yours and go on."

"We've got to do a lot more than that," Karp said, his voice edged with anger. "Joe told us what Colby said about you figuring on changing the way the money's going to be split."

"Well, now, it seems to me that's the fair way to handle it," Ferguson replied. "If you men will think about it a minute, you'll see that if it hadn't been for having somebody to plan the job, you wouldn't be getting a dime."

"Now, you think about the other side of the deal, Ferguson!" McGee snapped. "If we hadn't handled all the dirty work back at Flagstaff and hauled the payroll money up here for whatever damn reason that plan you gave us called for, you wouldn't be getting a dime, either!"

"Wait a minute, now!" Ferguson said placatingly. "I know you men are probably mad after Joe told you what Colby said when they met in town—"

Karp broke in, "We ain't going to stand for cutting our share, Ferguson. Don't try to fast-talk us, or there'll be some real trouble."

"All of us feel like McGee and Karp do," Simms said before Ferguson could reply to Karp. "We're standing together on this!"

Ferguson turned to Joe, who'd come up to stand at one side of the group, a little apart from both the wagon and the other members of the gang. "Joe, what in hell did you tell these men to get 'em so riled up?" he asked.

"I told 'em what Colby told me, Ferguson. And he said you and him had talked things over," Joe replied stolidly.

"You must not've understood right, then," Ferguson told the fat man.

"Ask Colby," Joe said curtly. "He'll tell you what I just said is right."

"Where is Colby, anyhow?" McGee asked. "You said he was following right behind the wagon."

"Well, he was," Ferguson replied. "He must've had some kind of trouble, or he'd be here by now."

"Maybe one of us better backtrack and see what's happened to him," Simms suggested.

"Oh, there's no reason to do that," Ferguson replied. "Colby can look after himself."

Longarm smelled trouble brewing. He could sense impatience growing in the outlaw gang, and Colby's continued absence was also beginning to start a nagging worry picking at his mind. He did not want to make a move until Colby arrived and he could capture the whole gang. He still had no fixed plan of action, but was certain that the tension growing in the canyon would give him the chance he was waiting for.

One explanation for Colby being missing struck him suddenly, and he took his eyes off the group on the canyon floor long enough to scan the perimeter of the rim on both sides of him. The light was better on the high ground, and he was sure that if Ferguson had sent Colby to hold the outlaws at gunpoint while he loaded the loot and drove off with it, he would see the renegade lawman. There was no cover on the rim where a man could hide. Satisfied, Longarm shifted his position on the hard ground and watched and listened patiently.

"Why in hell do we have to wait for Colby to get here, anyhow?" Karp asked. "Are you the boss, or is he?"

"Now, you know I am, Karp," Ferguson snapped. "Colby does what I tell him to—no more and no less."

"Then let's go on and make the split without waiting for him," Karp went on. "Anything between you and him you can get straightened out later."

"Well, if you put it that way, I don't see any reason why we have to wait," Ferguson replied. "All I'm interested in is making a split that'll be fair to everybody."

"We decided how the money was gonna be split up before we stole it," McGee said. "It wasn't our idea to change things."

"Yeah," Slocum seconded. "All we want is what you said we'd get when you propositioned us to do the job."

"None of us is gonna stand for being shortchanged," Simms warned. "Just hand over what we was promised at the start, and we'll be on our way."

"Fine, fine," Ferguson nodded. "That's exactly what we're going to do."

"I don't guess we've got anything to argue about, then," Slocum said. "Let's get started."

"I don't see why not," Ferguson agreed. "If you men will just bring those money bags and put 'em in the wagon bed, we'll get 'em opened up and start dividing the cash right away."

"What's wrong with dividing it right where they are?" Joe asked. "No use to handle 'em twice."

"Now, Joe, all those bags have got to be opened. Some of them have got silver in 'em, some are full of gold. We won't know how much is in each bag unless we count it."

"We don't have to move the bags to open 'em," Joe insisted.

"Open 'em where they're laying right now."

"No, that's not a good idea," Ferguson said. "Suppose we spill some money out on the ground? It'll fall down in the dirt and rocks and we might not be able to find it, the way it's getting dark. If we drop some in the wagon bed, it'll be easy to see and we can pick it up without any trouble."

"Well, I guess that makes sense," Joe agreed. "Come on, boys. If we're going to do it the way the boss says, we'd better get busy before it gets so dark we can't see what we're doing."

"Hell, there ain't all that many sacks to be moved," Slocum said. "Let's go, fellows. We wanta get away from here as soon as we can."

During their talk with Ferguson, the outlaws had left the fire and come up to the wagon, which now stood between them and the piled-up money bags. They started around the wagon toward the sacks. Joe was the only one carrying a rifle. He put the weapon down and moved to join the others.

From his vantage point on the edge of the valley rim, Longarm could see what was hidden from the outlaws. As they reached the stacked sacks, the tarpaulin in the wagon bed moved, then was thrown aside. Dirk Colby rose up with a sawed-off double-barrelled shotgun in his hands. For a moment Longarm did not see what the renegade lawman was holding. When he did, he brought his rifle up and started swinging it to cover Colby.

Getting to his knees, Colby brought the shotgun up and levelled it at the outlaws. They were in a tight group now, clustered around the sacks, bending to lift them. The shotgun roared once, spewing out its deadly buckshot pellets in a dense cloud of powder smoke. Through the haze of smoke Longarm saw at least two of the outlaws lurch forward and drop across the stack of canvas bags.

Even before the red flashing muzzle blast from the first shot faded the shotgun boomed again as Colby triggered its other barrel. The powder smoke thickened with the blast, but Longarm could hear the higher-pitched crack of revolver fire through the veil of smoke. Suddenly the shooting stopped. The ominous silence that follows sudden death settled over the valley.

Chapter 17

Longarm had Colby in the Winchester's sights within seconds after the deadly shotgun roared for the second time. He squeezed off his shot just as the renegade lawman opened the shotgun's breech to slide another pair of shells into the chambers. The slug tore into Colby's shoulder. The shotgun tumbled from his hands as the impact of the bullet knocked him sprawling on his face in the wagon bed.

In his concentration on Colby, Longarm had paid little attention to Ferguson. He'd seen Ferguson draw his revolver when Colby emerged from beneath the concealment of the tarpaulin, but Longarm knew that the handgun lacked the range to be effective against him. He heard the report of the shot Ferguson fired at him in the instant while he was drawing his bead on Colby, and when he saw Colby fall, turned his attention to the turncoat federal marshal. As Longarm swung his rifle to draw a bead on him, Ferguson rolled out of the wagon seat and crawfished beneath it before Longarm could trigger off a shot.

With both Ferguson and Colby out of the fight for the moment, Longarm shifted his attention to the outlaws. Three of the five had been mowed down by the shotgun slugs and he did not need a second glance to know they were dead. Too many times he'd seen men lying in the unnaturally twisted attitudes of the motionless forms on the ground around the heap of money bags. He took his eyes off the huddled figures, not sure whether he was glad or sorry Colby had robbed him of the personal vengeance he'd promised himself.

Lowering the Winchester, Longarm looked for the other two, and saw that they had rolled and belly-crawled up to the sacks, where they huddled behind the scanty protection provided by the bags of coins. They were stretched out prone,

147

revolvers ready in their hands, looking for targets. By now they could find none. Colby had not moved since he'd been knocked spread-eagled to the wagon bed by Longarm's bullet, and Ferguson remained hidden under the seat.

Although the heap of canvas bags provided a measure of protection from shots fired out of the wagon, the outlaws who'd sought cover behind them were totally exposed to shots fired from above them. Looking down from his vantage point on the rim of the valley wall, Longarm saw they were easy targets for his deadly Winchester in spite of the tricky shooting he'd have to do in the last traces of failing daylight.

He swung the rifle to get them in his sights, but as he drew a bead on the back of the nearest man his finger slackened on the trigger. During the years he'd been working on the side of the law, Longarm had killed men, but he'd never stooped to backshooting. They'd died with guns in their hands, facing him, with a chance that their skill might outmatch his. The idea of backshooting the outlaws, even though they'd shown themselves to be little more than animals, was too much like carrying out an execution. The idea made his gorge rise. He held his finger on the Winchester's trigger, but without pressure.

"All right, you men down there!" Longarm shouted. "All of you, whichever side you're on! Lay your guns down! My name's Long, I'm a deputy U. S. marshal, and I'm putting the whole bunch of you under arrest!" Then, to remove any impression the outlaws might have that he was going to give special treatment to Ferguson, he added, "Ferguson! I'm arresting you just like I am everybody else! And you know enough about me to know I mean every word I say!"

Longarm had not taken his eyes off the outlaws while he was talking. He got Ferguson's answer in the form of a rifle shot from beneath the wagon seat. The bullet was far wide. It thunked into the face of the valley wall ten feet to one side and a yard low, but Longarm realized at once that Paul Ferguson's wild, unaimed shot had given him the only answer he was likely to get to his demand for surrender.

He looked at the wagon, still covering the two outlaws. Colby was dragging himself behind the protection of the seat. Longarm knew that offering the two renegade lawmen another chance to surrender would be a waste of words. He shifted his aim from the outlaws. Sighting in on the wagon seat, he triggered off a round. The slug tore into the thick tough wood, sending splinters flying, but a second shot from beneath it told Longarm that his slug hadn't penetrated. Ferguson was still shooting blind, but Longarm knew that even an unaimed slug might find him by accident.

He shifted his position a few yards, rolling along the edge of the cliff, but when he stopped and squinted over his sights again he found that he had not improved his chances by moving. The unattended campfire was smouldering to extinction, smoking now as it burned itself out, and through the drifting wisps and the increasing darkness all that Longarm could see now was a vague outline of the wagon. Aiming from memory rather than vision, he tried another shot at the wagon before moving still further along the cliff rim.

In his new position, Longarm could see a tiny sliver of black between the front dash of the wagon and the bottom of the seat. He aimed for the black line and squeezed off his shot. He heard the metallic clank his slug made when it grazed the strap-steel binding around the top of the sideboard and saw another spray of splinters fly from the seat as the bullet ricocheted and flew harmlessly into the air. Deciding reluctantly that any further effort to reach the renegade lawmen in the wagon would be a waste of ammunition, Longarm held his fire. He was studying the wagon when the hail came from the canyon floor.

"Hey, Longarm!" one of the outlaws called.

Longarm was sure it was Karp who'd spoken, but from the distance it was impossible to tell. He replied, "Go on, I'm listening."

"It'll be too dark for you to shoot any more inside of the next few minutes. What's in it for us if we help you corral them bastards in the wagon?" the man asked.

Longarm had not expected the surviving outlaws to make an offer of that kind. He knew his position was not good. Darkness was closing down fast, the sudden ending of the day that marked the high desert country. He had little time now to get down to the canyon floor while there was still enough light to aim by. Within a very few minutes not only the surviving outlaws, but Ferguson and Colby as well, had a good chance to escape.

Accepting help from the outlaws rasped against his grain. Longarm told himself that even if he did, he'd make no promise that would keep him from arresting them for the murders they'd committed at the trading post. The thought that he could still make them pay for those crimes somehow seemed to offset his distaste for accepting their help in bringing Ferguson and Colby to justice. It was the only way he could see out of the dead end into which he'd been forced. While he was still debating how best to answer the outlaw, Ferguson raised his voice.

"You men better think again before you throw in with Long," he called. "I know what I'm talking about! My job's the same as his, and I can tell you that he can't make any kind of deal with you that a judge can't throw out when a case is being tried!"

Longarm decided instantly that truth was his best resource. He said, "He's right. The judge can wipe out a deal, but he damn sure can't bring a man back to life!"

"Then to hell with you both!" the outlaw shouted. "We've got along without help so far. We'll just go on and fight it out!"

Two booming gunshots in quick succession brought a cry of pain from one of the men barricaded behind the money bags. Longarm realized that he had not been watching the wagon as closely as he should. He dropped his cheek to the stock and raised the Winchester's muzzle. He'd waited too long. All he could see in his sights was a blur.

Longarm was sure he'd recognized Karp's voice a moment earlier. He called, "Karp, was that you taken a slug when Colby shot?"

"It was me, all right," Karp called back. "But don't count on it making me change my mind. I been hurt worse when I nicked my face shaving!"

A rifle cracked from the wagon and the wind from its slug cut the air above Longarm's head. He ducked instinctively, and snapshot blindly in the direction of the wagon. He knew the shot had come from either Ferguson or Colby, since neither of the outlaws had rifles. The crash of his bullet hitting the wagon's sideboard brought a taunting laugh from Colby.

"We got a Mexican standoff here, Long!" the renegade lawman called. "It ain't gonna last long, though! It's too dark to shoot now, and you can't get down here close enough to get us before we can hightail it!"

"That's what you think, Colby!" Karp called. "Longarm might be where he can't get to you, but me and Simms sure as hell can! And after that damn ambush you caught us in, we ain't going to let you stay alive to stand trial!"

"You men listen to me!" Ferguson said hoarsely. He kept his voice down, but in the evening quiet Longarm could still hear him plainly. The turncoat federal marshal went on, "There's a whole hell of a lot of money in them sacks. The way things have worked out, we don't need to split it but four ways. We can take our shares and be out of here free and clear before Long can make a move. In the dark, we can get away from him clean. Now, you think about that for a minute, and you'll see what's best for the two of you to do."

"You're wasting your breath, old man!" Simms replied. "We wouldn't trust you and Colby any more than we would a pair of rattlesnakes. Them three men you backshot might not've been much, but they were our friends."

Colby's harsh voice rose in reply. "Listen, you damned fools! Friendship don't mean shit when you're in the kind of tight spot we are right now. Don't you two see you're in the same boat with us? Do what Ferguson said. It's a lot better'n spending the rest of your life in a federal pen."

There was another long silence from the valley floor. Longarm could feel the small leverage given him by the two surviving outlaws was slipping away. Once gone, he could not be sure of making them pay for their murders at the trading post. Raising his voice, he called, "Karp! Simms! Listen to me a minute!"

After another silence, shorter this time, Karp called, "Go ahead, Longarm. Say what's on your mind."

"This deal ain't like it was at first," Longarm said. "It started out with me coming after you to arrest you and get back the money you stole from the Army. It's a lot more'n that now. You got two renegade lawmen down there with you, and I want them a lot worse than I do you others. If you keep Ferguson and Colby pinned down in that wagon till I get there, I'll see that you get off real light for stealing that Army money." To himself, he added, *But I'll see them swing for murder!*

This time Ferguson was quick to reply. He said, "You men tell Long you'll throw in with him, and Colby and me will cut you down before you finish talking."

As the silence following Ferguson's threat stretched into several minutes without the surviving outlaws replying to either him or Ferguson, Longarm realized that he was losing. He edged closer to the rim of the valley wall, peering down through the almost complete darkness for footholds that might enable him to descend. He could see a few projecting rocks and earthen ledges before the gloom obscured the lower section of the canyon wall, and had marked them in his mind when Karp spoke again.

"Ferguson! We want to make a deal with you!" he called.

"What kind of deal?" Ferguson asked.

"It's too dark for Longarm to shoot now, and Simms and me are ready to ride out by ourselves if you'll guarantee Colby won't cut us down with that shotgun."

There was a long silence. Then Ferguson called, "Go ahead, if that's what you want to do."

Longarm was busy using his bandana to tie his Winchester to his pistol belt when he heard the words that told him he'd lost. He had no illusions about Ferguson allowing Karp and Simms to escape. They were potential witnesses against him and Colby and the others who'd plotted the robbery. As little respect as he had for the two outlaws, he felt a duty to try to save them.

"Karp! Simms!" he shouted without stopping his work. "You men are fools if you think Ferguson and Colby are going to let you get away. You're the only witnesses left that can stand up in court and testify against them."

"Don't pay any mind to Long," Colby's harsh voice grated. "Remember, if you testify against us, you'll be testifying against yourselves, too. Go on, make your getaway while there's still time!"

Simms raised his voice now. "We're going to take one bag of money apiece, Ferguson. The rest is yours. Split it up any way you please. But we earned a share, so we aim to take it."

Again Ferguson waited a long while to answer. Then he said, "I guess you're entitled to it. It's worth that much to me and Colby to get you out of here. Go on, get as far away as you can, and don't show your faces in Arizona Territory again!"

Atop the valley wall, Longarm had stretched out on his belly and was lowering himself over the edge of the cliff when he heard the exchange between the outlaws and Ferguson that told him he'd lost. Setting his jaw, moving slowly and carefully, he began inching down its sheer face. As he began his precarious climb, clinging with little more than the tips of his fingers to stones that protruded from the almost vertical face, he listened to the final exchange of words between the men on the canyon floor.

Karp said, "All right, Ferguson! We're leaving now. And don't worry about us coming back here. As far as I'm concerned, if I never see this damn place or you and Colby again it'll suit me just fine."

"That goes for me, too!" Simms called.

Clinging precariously with one hand while he clawed for a place to lock his other hand or a toehold on which to rest his feet, Longarm shook his head sadly. A moment later he heard the roar of Colby's sawed-off shotgun, and saw the red of its muzzle blast light the face of the cliff for a fraction of a second.

At least the bastards didn't get away, old son, he told himself as he tried to hold himself closer to the almost vertical wall. *But don't waste time on what's past. If Ferguson and Colby got brains enough to light up a torch apiece while you're still stuck on this damn piece of up-and-down real estate, it might just be your turn next. Because if they was to spot you, it wouldn't be no trick at all for Colby to pick you off with that scattergun of his, even if there ain't much light.*

Clawing and scraping, Longarm continued his hazardous descent. Somehow he managed to find the handholds and toeholds he needed to work his way down another yard or two. Then the toehold he'd thought was safe crumbled away when he rested his full weight on it while feeling for another with one hand.

He felt his support going and scraped frantically at the cliff face, seeking another projection to grasp with his free hand, but there was no crevice, no protrusion. His foot slid free, throwing him out of balance. The slight lurch of his body tore his hand from the precarious grip he'd been maintaining on a knob of rock.

Arms and legs flailing, Longarm fell. He landed with a thud, and did not even feel the hard impact of his head on a boulder at the foot of the cliff. A blacker blackness than that of the night's darkness claimed his brain.

When he became aware of the world and the night again, Longarm did not remember at first where he was or how he'd gotten there, or why he should be lying on the hard ground. He tried to move. His Winchester was tangled in his legs. His back was sore and his head throbbed. Darkness and silence surrounded him, and for a few moments he lay motionless. Then from the blackness he heard the sounds of booted feet scraping on the baked earth and the mumbling of voices reached his ears.

Instinct told Longarm to lie still and make no noise. The voices came closer and he began to catch an occasional word. Then he recognized the voices and instantly he remembered everything.

Longarm still had no way of judging how long he'd lain unconscious. The voices were coming closer now, and hearing them spurred him into action. Moving silently, he disentangled his Winchester from his legs. He slid his hand around his chest and made sure that his Colt was secure in its cross-draw holster. Then he began working on the knots in the bandana that secured the rifle to his pistol belt.

With the rifle in his hands, Longarm rubbed his fingertips along the Winchester's breechplates. He could feel no cracks, and when he checked the hammer it felt straight. Running his hand down the stock, he encountered a few new rough places, but there were no breaks in the tough walnut. The footsteps came closer to him, then stopped. When a voice broke the silence, Longarm recognized it as Colby's.

"Damn this dark night! I'd swear Long hit the ground right around here someplace."

"Maybe he busted his neck," Ferguson said. "That cliff's a good sixty feet high."

"It'd be all right with me if he did," Colby rasped. "Save us having to hunt him down and finish him off."

Longarm judged the two men were standing fifty or sixty feet away. He tried to locate them in the darkness, but the faint starshine did not penetrate the pitch blackness that extended around the bottom of the canyon's walls. No matter how Longarm strained, he could not penetrate the all-embracing gloom.

"We'd've heard him stirring around for sure if he was up and moving," Ferguson said. "Maybe he got killed when he fell."

"Maybe. But we're damn fools if we don't make sure."

"I guess you're right," Ferguson agreed, his voice showing his reluctance.

"I know I'm right," Colby retorted. "Come on, let's move a little faster. This damn shoulder of mine's getting stiffer and

154

sorer by the minute. I need to get to a doctor soon as I can."

There was silence for a moment. Then Ferguson said thoughtfully, "You know, I keep thinking we'd better be loading that money on the wagon. If Long tries to jump us, the two of us ought to be able to handle him."

"Well, we ain't getting anyplace poking around in the dark this way," Colby said. "You might be right about loading them money bags. If we don't make any noise while we're doing it, we can hear Long if he's still alive and able to move."

"Come on, then," Ferguson said. "The moon will be up by the time we finish. We'll have another look for Long when we get through."

Longarm remained motionless while the footsteps of the two moved away. In the stillness of the night he could hear them even after they had reached the wagon and began carrying the bags of money to it and dropping them in its bed. Then he tried to stand up. The muscles in his bruised back protested, but he ignored them. Moving carefully, levering himself up with the aid of the rifle, he finally got to his feet and started toward the center of the canyon.

Once away from the deep darkness that shrouded the area at the base of the walls, he could see the objects vaguely, but only as darker blobs against the prevailing gloom. He placed his position by memory as he moved carefully forward. The horses belonging to the dead outlaws were still standing at one side of the dark oval made by the firepit. Ahead, he could make out the blocky shape of the wagon. He approached it cautiously, judging his distance by the noises Ferguson and Colby were making as they loaded the money bags into the wagon, and counting on the sounds they were making to cover his approach.

"This is the last one," he heard Ferguson say. "Now let's have another try at finding Long. I damn sure don't intend to leave this place until I know he's dead."

"He's either dead or stove up so bad he can't move," Colby said. "If he got killed when he pitched off of that cliff, so much the better. If he's still alive, we'll just put him outa his misery."

"Let's be at it, then," Ferguson said impatiently. "I want to be on my way to the D&RG railhead before daylight."

"Thought you had to go back to Flagstaff, to carry their split to—"

"Never mind what you thought," Ferguson broke in. "Just grab that scattergun and let's get moving."

Longarm had heard more than enough. By inching ahead while Ferguson and Colby talked, he'd gotten close enough now to make out the blurred shadows of their bodies as they stood beside the wagon. He raised his rifle and levelled it to shoot from the hip before he spoke.

"Don't either one of you move," Longarm commanded harshly. "I got you covered, and I can see you good enough to cut you both down before you can get your guns out."

Chapter 18

In their desperation neither Ferguson nor Colby obeyed Longarm's command. Their surprise did not inhibit their reactions. Longarm sensed rather than saw their movements as both men went for their pistols.

Longarm's finger closed on the Winchester's trigger, but the weapon did not fire. Dropping the rifle as he hit the dirt, he swept his Colt from its holster. It was in his hand before he landed full-length on the ground, but by then muzzle flashes from the guns drawn by Ferguson and Colby were cutting the darkness and their slugs were whistling around him.

Longarm rolled. He stopped after he'd covered a couple of yards and triggered two quick shots at the spots where he'd seen the muzzles of his enemies' weapons spurting red. He heard his bullets thunk into the side of the wagon and moved again, toward the wagon this time. He rolled under it and waited.

Ferguson and Colby had reacted in the manner of the expert gunfighters they were. When they fired again, one muzzle blast showed from Longarm's right side, the other far to his left.

Longarm had expected nothing less. He'd anticipated that the renegade lawmen would separate, presenting him with two widely spaced targets. He did not fire at either of them and by doing so give away his position. In his cover beneath the wagon he waited patiently for either Ferguson or Colby to reveal the new locations to which he was sure they'd moved.

His wait was not a long one. From his left side Ferguson called, "Colby! You got any idea where the son of a bitch is?"

Colby's reply came from Longarm's right. "No, damn it! If I did, I'd be doing something about it!"

Longarm decided to do something about it himself. Hearing Colby's voice at such close range was almost as good as being able to see him. Judging his enemy's position carefully, Longarm triggered his Colt, two fast shots, shifting his aim a few inches between them.

His second shot went home. He heard the deadly thunk of lead hitting soft flesh, then a gasping sigh, followed by the metallic thud of a revolver landing on the hard-baked soil and then the slow rustle of a body settling to the ground. Longarm let the sounds die away and the silence return before he crawled noiselessly from beneath the wagon and stood behind the protection of its bed.

From a different position from before, Ferguson's voice broke the stillness. "Colby!" he called anxiously. "Colby?"

There was no reply. Longarm let the silence drag on for several seconds, then said quietly, "He ain't going to answer you, Ferguson. You're by yourself now."

Ferguson's reply was a shot. The slug splintered the sideboard of the wagon, but this time Longarm neither moved nor replied to the shot with one of his own. He wanted Ferguson alive. He stood listening, following with his ears the scrabbling sounds that Ferguson's feet made, waiting for him to stop.

When the hushed grating of boot soles on the hard earth at last ended, Longarm called, "You might as well give up, Ferguson. I can last a hell of a lot longer'n you can, dodging around in the dark this way."

Longarm talked fast and ducked behind the wagon as soon as he'd finished speaking, in anticipation of a shot that was never fired. Instead, there was a creak of saddle leather and the night's silence was broken by the thudding of hoofbeats.

Dropping to one knee, Longarm watched the skyline. He saw the stars in the night sky blotted out by the silhouette of Ferguson, bending over the neck of the outlaw's horse he'd found and mounted.

Longarm took quick aim and fired. He knew the galloping rider offered a chancy target at best, and was not too surprised when he missed. Swearing silently at himself for having failed to take time to reload after each exchange of shots with the two renegades, he ejected the spent shells from his Colt and thumbed in fresh loads while the hoofbeats faded and died away in the darkness.

Holstering his Colt, Longarm whistled shrilly, the universal call of a rider to a horse. There was a whinnying in the darkness,

158

and two of the loose animals plodded up to where Longarm stood. He grasped the reins of the first one and led the horse while he zigzagged across the area where he'd fired last at Colby.

After a few minutes of searching he located the body and struck a match. While he gazed at the flickering flame reflected from Colby's sightless eyes, Longarm lighted a cheroot. Certain now that no one remained alive in the canyon besides himself, Longarm swung into the saddle and started toward Tuba City.

To his surprise, lights were still showing in many of the houses and most of the few business buildings along the street. Longarm fished for the chain that swung between the two bottom pockets of his vest and took out his watch. He glanced at it and saw that more than an hour remained before midnight. Returning the watch to his pocket, he rode on through Tuba City. He resisted the temptation to stop at the café, though seeing it made him suddenly aware that he was both hungry and thirsty, and rode on down the street until he reached the livery stable.

Turning the horse off the street, Longarm circled around the big livery barn. Behind it he saw the small building Scanlon had described, fifty or sixty feet away. A light gleamed from one of the little structure's high-set barred windows, and a saddled horse stood at the hitch rail at one side. Seeing the horse, Longarm pulled up at once. Swinging out of the saddle, he dropped his mount's reins over its head and started walking toward the building.

As he approached it, Longarm could see a door in the center of the wall nearest him, and on the other side of the door a second window, this one unlighted. He ignored the door and went directly to the lighted window. By standing on tiptoe and craning his neck, Longarm could peer over the bottom of the windowsill. The room into which he looked was a jail cell; the bars that enclosed it were visible as was the bunk that was fastened to a wall on one side. The cell was unoccupied, and beyond the bars the lamp burning in the corridor outside the cell was reflected off a blank wall.

A quick glance was all that Longarm got of the jail's interior. Before he'd finished his examination, a gun muzzle stabbed into his side and Ferguson's voice sounded in his ear. "I had a pretty good idea you'd be showing up here," the renegade marshal said. "It's where I'd have looked first, if I was in your boots."

"It seemed like a good idea to me," Longarm said.

Ferguson grunted. Then, in a hard-edged voice, he said, "I'd better warn you, Long. This Colt I've got in your ribs is full-cocked, and I filed the sear down myself till just breathing on it'll let the hammer drop."

"I got too much sense to put up a fight when I know a man's got me dead to rights," Longarm said.

"That's one of the first sensible things I've heard you say," Ferguson told him. "Now stand still while I get your sixgun out of your holster."

Longarm did not move while Ferguson grasped the butt of his Colt and snaked it out of his holster. He stuck the weapon in his belt and moved quickly away from Longarm.

Nodding toward the door that opened into the building, Ferguson said, "That door's not locked. Open it and walk inside. There's another door down the hall between the cells. It's not locked. We'll be going through it."

Longarm obeyed the pressure of Ferguson's gun. He opened the outer door and entered the narrow corridor formed by the bars which separated the cell into which he'd been looking from its mate, which had not been visible through the window. The door at the end of the corridor was cracked open. He pushed it open and walked through it.

Ferguson maintained the pressure of the revolver in Longarm's ribs during the few moments required to enter the lighted room into which the door led. The room spanned the entire side of the building. It held two cots, one at each end, three or four chairs, a small monkey stove, and a battered rolltop desk that stood near a second door in the back wall. A steeple-cased clock stood on top of the desk and on its openwork surface there was a bottle of Tom Moore and several glasses.

Nudging Longarm toward one of the chairs, Ferguson ordered, "Sit down, Long. And you'll regret it if you move a finger without me saying you can."

Without protesting, Longarm sat down in the chair Ferguson had indicated. Keeping his eyes fixed on Longarm and the muzzle of his revolver covering him constantly, Ferguson moved to a chair near the desk and settled into it.

"I thought you'd be too smart to let an old fart like me get you the way you did," Ferguson said after he'd stared at Longarm in silence for a moment. "That's why I was ready for you."

"I guess I made a mistake, Ferguson," Longarm said in his mildest tone. "I oughta remembered you used to be a lawman."

"Used to be, hell!" Ferguson bristled. "I still am!"

Longarm shook his head. "No. You stopped being a lawman when you got mixed up in stealing that Army pay chest. Maybe you was crooked before that, maybe it was Colby talked you into going over to the wrong side of the law—"

Ferguson interrupted with a loud snort. "That shows how smart you are, Long! Colby never was smart enough to plan a big job! He was just the most merciless son of a bitch I ever ran into, and that's why I talked him into throwing in with me. I needed him to do the dirty work."

"Like backshooting them Army deserters?"

"That was his idea! I didn't plan that part of it!" Ferguson protested. "All I was after was the money. Killing like he did wasn't part of my scheme."

Longarm said thoughtfully, "You know, Ferguson, I never did hear anything bad about you until I was sent out here. I got a hunch this was the first time you moved to the wrong side of the law."

"It was."

"Why'd you do it, then?"

"Because some dirty snoop from Washington came out on one of those routine inspection trips they like to dream up back there. He found out I'd been going to a doctor about some pains I was having in my chest, and told headquarters they ought to make me retire. Damn it, Long, how can a man like me retire without any money to live on?"

"Well, some seem to manage it," Longarm said mildly.

"I couldn't," Ferguson snapped. "And let me tell you something else. I don't have one single regret about that Army money, especially the way it's all worked out."

"I take it that you're figuring now on cheating your partners down at the ordnance depot?"

"What're you talking about?" the renegade lawman bristled.

"Don't try to pull the wool over my eyes, Ferguson," Longarm said calmly. "Why, that robbery had the marks of an inside job from the start."

"I don't see how you figure that."

"It wasn't hard. I seen right off that somebody at the depot had to give you the word about when the chest was due, and what the easiest way was to go about stealing it."

"They must've said something to give themselves away, then," Ferguson frowned. "It'll serve them right not to get any of that money, if they were such big fools."

"Meaning that now the gang you hired for the job are all dead, you're going to deal your partners out and keep the whole kit and caboodle for yourself?"

"Meaning exactly that," Ferguson nodded. "Those fools down at the depot don't count any more. They didn't do a damn thing to help, just set back and let me and the men I picked up do all the work."

"Once they find out what you aim to do, they won't be likely to let you get away with it," Longarm pointed out.

"They won't find out," Ferguson snapped. "Not until I've dropped down into a hole and pulled it closed after me."

"It's a lot easier to say what you're fixing to do than it is to do it," Longarm said smoothly.

"Oh, I'll do it," Ferguson boasted. "I'll tell you something about that loot, Long. It's going to keep me comfortable for the rest of my life, and that's a lot more than I can say for what I've been able to put by on my miserable pay from the damned government."

"Even if you and Colby loaded that Army loot on the wagon, you ain't got it yet," Longarm said levelly. "For all you know, I drove the wagon in and put it where you can't get at it."

Ferguson lifted the muzzle of the revolver until Longarm found himself staring down its ominous black muzzle. "If I even thought you'd taken that wagon..." he began. Then he shook his head. "You didn't, though. You haven't had time, for one thing."

Longarm did not reply. He met Ferguson's stare without blinking, his face expressionless. Ferguson's eyes grew wide.

"Well, I'll find out pretty damn quick!" he told Longarm, his voice raised until he was almost shouting. "With you helping me, there's plenty of time before daylight to get that money to town here and hide it." He looked at the wooden-cased steeple clock on the desk. Its hands pointed to seven o'clock, but its pendulum hung motionless. "Damn!" Ferguson went on. "Colby forgot to wind it."

"It's real easy to lose track of the time," Longarm said consolingly. "Just about everybody does now and again."

162

Ferguson looked at Longarm's watch chain. He said, "You've got a watch on, Long. Take it out and hold it so I can see what time it is!"

Longarm did not move. His voice soothing, he asked, "Now, you don't really want to ride all that way out to the canyon, do you? Just think how disappointed you'll be if you find out I'm telling you the truth."

"You're lying, damn you!" Ferguson almost shouted. "Take out that watch and let me look at it!"

Without appearing to do so, Longarm had been watching Ferguson carefully, judging the effects of his carefully calculated ruse to distract him. He decided that any further effort would be self-defeating.

Moving slowly and deliberately, he slid his watch from his vest pocket with his left hand. Ferguson leaned forward, letting his gun hand sag in his eagerness to see the face of the watch.

Longarm moved quickly. Shooting his foot forward, he kicked Ferguson's gun out of his hand. At the same time he lifted the watch just high enough to pull out the derringer attached to the other end of its chain. He grasped the stubby little weapon in his ready right hand and covered Ferguson.

For a moment Ferguson did not grasp the speed with which Longarm had reversed their positions. His jaw dropped when he realized at last what had happened, and he raised his empty right hand. When he looked at the black muzzle of the derringer an apoplectic flush began to suffuse his face. He gasped for breath, his mouth gaping, his lips twisted. Words formed in his throat, but he could not articulate them. All that came from his lips was a confused babble of sound.

Longarm almost forgot the derringer as he stared uncomprehendingly at Ferguson's reaction, but his instinct kept his hand steady, the derringer pointing unwaveringly at the gaping, gasping man.

Suddenly a convulsion seized Ferguson's body. He shuddered violently, his arms stiffened, and his head flew back as though some strong unseen hand had yanked him by the hair. He managed to straighten his arms and extend them in front of him as though spastically.

For almost a full minute the strange tableau held Longarm frozen in place. Then Ferguson went limp, as though his bones had suddenly melted. The gurgling in his throat faded to a whistle of escaping breath, then he was silent. He slid slowly from his chair to the floor where he lay motionless in a huddled, shrunken heap.

"Godamighty!" Longarm gasped. The expression was neither an expletive nor a prayer, unless an expression of solemn wonder could be considered praying. Still staring at the motionless form, he added, as though to convince himself, "He's dead!"

Longarm was no stranger to death. He had seen it in most forms, usually violent. Somehow he had never thought of natural death as being violent. He stared at Ferguson's crumpled body for a moment, then bent down and felt his throat, seeking the pulse of his carotid artery. There was no pulse.

He straightened up, his hands moving mechanically, automatically, as he replaced his watch and derringer in his pockets. Still looking at Ferguson's body, Longarm slid a cigar out of his vest pocket and lighted it. The routine act seemed to break the partial daze that had gripped him. His Colt lay on the floor where it had fallen when Ferguson collapsed. He picked it up and holstered it automatically. Only then did he look around the silent room.

Tom Moore's smiling face on the label of the whiskey bottle caught Longarm's eye. He stepped across to the desk, pulled the cork, and without waiting to fill one of the glasses, swallowed a healthy slug from the bottle.

Old son, he told himself, *having something like that happen is enough to give a man the blind shivers. This ain't no place for you to stay around. You better hightail it outa here. Anyways, you still got a job of work that needs to be finished before you knock off for the night.*

Heading for the horse he'd left standing, Longarm mounted and rode down the street to the Ritz. Scanlon was in his usual place behind the bar, and there were three or four customers lined up along it. Scanlon set a bottle of Tom Moore on the end of the bar. Longarm shook his head and motioned to the table by the door, where Colby and Joe had sat while he listened to their conversation. It seemed to him as though that had happened a long time ago instead of just that afternoon. When Scanlon brought the bottle of Maryland rye to the table, Longarm motioned for him to sit down.

"I'd better not," the barkeep said, indicating the men at the bar. Filling a glass from the bottle, he went on, "I've been wondering where the devil you were. I suppose you caught up with the men you were after? From the looks of your clothes, you had a little bit of trouble."

"I got sorta dirty because I didn't look where I was going and fell down. The rest of it wasn't all that much trouble. The main thing is, my case is closed."

Scanlon's jaw dropped. "Closed? What about Ferguson? And Colby? And the fat one who was in here today?"

"Dead," Longarm said succinctly, before draining his glass.

"Hold on," Scanlon frowned. "You're talking about half a dozen men! You mean—"

"Seven," Longarm said. "And they're all dead."

"Including Colby and Ferguson?"

Longarm nodded. "Colby and Ferguson shot the men in their gang. Then Colby got shot. Ferguson died a while later, but he didn't get shot. Heart failure killed him, I think."

Scanlon went over to the bar and got himself a glass, then returned to the table and filled it. "Go on, Long," he said. "Tell me what the hell happened after you left here."

"I just did," Longarm said. "Oh, there's more to it, but I haven't got time to tell you the whole story right now. There's a wagonload of U. S. government money in that canyon where the gang was camped, and I got to go out and get it."

"Tonight? But you're bound to be tired."

"Well, I ain't what you'd call fresh as a daisy, but if I don't get that money to town somebody might steal it again, and I'd just about as soon turn in my badge as have to get that damn money back a second time."

Chapter 19

A light tapping at the door roused Longarm. He stirred, but did not bounce out of bed as he usually did of a morning. The rapping was repeated, a bit louder. This time Longarm opened his eyes. There seemed to be a blanket of fog surrounding his brain, and the bright sunlight that trickled into the bare little room around the edges of the window shade stabbed at his eyes.

When the knocks on the door sounded for the third time, Longarm started to sit up. As he raised his head and shoulders, the muscles of his neck and back sent out signals of protest. He could almost hear them groaning at being stretched. He changed his mind about sitting up, and propped himself up on an elbow.

"Who is it?" he called.

"It's Mrs. O'Reilley, Mr. Long."

"What's wrong?"

"Nothing's wrong, except that it's almost noon, and the rubberneck stages will be getting here in a little while. If you don't intend to stay another night, I need to redd up your room."

"You did say it's noon?" Longarm asked, wondering what had happened to his usual early morning briskness.

"Yes," Mrs. O'Reilley replied. "Will you be staying, then?"

"If I don't, I'll still pay for the room, Mrs. O'Reilley."

"That's all I need to know. Thank you, Mr. Long."

When he heard the retreating footsteps of the landlady, Longarm swung his legs over the side of the bed and sat erect in spite of renewed complaints from his back and thighs. Blinking his eyes was like rubbing them with sandpaper as he looked around the room. His gunbelt was hanging as usual over the back of a chair beside the bed, and his clothing was arranged

166

in its customary neat style, though it was dirt-stained and rumpled.

You sure must've had more'n was good for you last night, old son, Longarm told himself as he straightened his back, disregarding its almost audible creaks of protest. *Hell, you ain't felt this way in the morning for going on twenty years!*

Still sitting on the side of the bed, flexing his muscles to ease their stiffness, Longarm lighted a cigar as his thoughts went back to the night.

When he'd started out of the saloon, Scanlon had handed him the half-full bottle of Tom Moore, remarking, "Here, take this with you. Maybe it'll help you get your job finished, if you're so damn set on doing it tonight."

While riding back to the outlaw hideout, the newly risen moon flooding the landscape with its rays and making the night almost as bright as day, Longarm had suddenly remembered leaving the filly tethered on the mesaland above the canyon. Cutting away from the road, he'd found the horse and switched to his own familiar saddle. Leading the outlaw's horse, he'd ridden around the canyon rim and along the trail to its floor.

Somehow, the blue hue of the bright moonlight had given the scene a macabre quality that might not have been evident in daylight. After his first glimpse, Longarm had reined in and taken one generous drink and almost immediately tilted the bottle for another swallow while he studied the silent tableau the canyon floor presented. He saw for the first time the contorted faces and twisted bodies of the men cut down by Colby's shotgun.

Sprawled on the bare ground, the corpses of the three who'd died first lay at the spot where the money bags had been stacked. A dozen yards apart from their fellows, the bodies of the two outlaws Colby had shot as they were leaving the canyon were stretched out on either side of a dead horse which had also been caught by the deadly buckshot. A bag of money was still clutched in the hand of one of the men, and the pistols of both were still holstered.

Colby's corpse was half a dozen yards from the bodies of the men he'd killed. The renegade lawman lay on his back, the shotgun beside him, his revolver still clutched in his rigid fingers. The purplish-pink neckerchief he'd sported looked black in the moonlight, and had draped itself under the dead man's chin to give Colby the appearance of being bearded.

Longarm's damaged Winchester lay by itself on the bare ground where the wagon had stood. At some time during the hours when the canyon had been deserted, the outlaws' saddle horses had moved to the spring, and the wagon horse had followed them. For a long while, Longarm did not go to the wagon, but sat on the filly's back, sipping from the bottle of Tom Moore.

I guess men generally get what's due 'em, old son, he'd thought as his eyes wandered over the grisly scene. *And I oughta feel sorry for them dead men, but I can't. They was a bunch of mean murdering thieves, and what they got was what they earned.*

Nudging the filly over to the wagon, Longarm had hitched the horse to the tailgate, tossed his Winchester into the wagon bed on top of the money bags, and, after retrieving the bag still held in the stiffened fingers of the dead outlaw, had climbed on the bullet-splintered seat of the wagon. During the slow ride back to town, he'd finished the Tom Moore and thrown the bottle away.

As the wagon jounced over the rough road, Longarm began to feel the effects of his fall down the canyon wall. He was aching all over by the time he pulled up in front of the Ritz and hobbled inside. The saloon was deserted except for Scanlon, who was stacking glasses on the backbar.

"I got to ask a favor of you," he told the barkeep. "I hope you got a place where I can lock up some money till I'm ready to start back to Flagstaff."

"There's a safe in the office," Scanlon said. "Will that do?"

"It'll have to be a damn big one. Take a look in the bed of that wagon outside."

Scanlon pushed through the batwings and came back shaking his head. "My safe won't hold all that, but I can put it in my liquor storeroom. It's got double-thick walls and a good padlock on the door."

"Let's put it in there, then," Longarm nodded. "But before I start lifting and hauling, I'm going to need a little sip of Tom Moore. You got a fresh bottle handy?"

"But I just—" Scanlon began, then stopped short and went through the door to the office, returning with an unopened bottle in his hand. Silently, he pulled the cork, set two glasses on the bar, and filled them. After he and Longarm had each swallowed a sip or two Scanlon went on quietly, "Your case is closed, I suppose?"

"Not all the way. But I can't wind it up here. All the loose ends is down at Flagstaff. Soon as I get the mess out in the canyon cleaned up and figure out what to do about Ferguson's body, I'll be heading back."

"You go upstairs and go to bed as soon as we've put that money away," Scanlon said. "I'll get old Belai from the livery stable to dig the graves and take care of the rest of it in the morning."

Now, with morning flooding the room with light, Longarm took the few puffs that finished his cigar and stood up, ignoring the protests of his aching muscles. His stomach was calling for breakfast. Pulling on his clothes despite the twinges that accompanied every move, he went downstairs and tapped at the office door. Mrs. O'Reilley opened it. When she saw Longarm her lips set in an angry line.

"I'm sorry if I wasn't real polite to you a while ago, Mrs. O'Reilley," Longarm apologized. "Fact is, I was still about half asleep. I had a right busy day yesterday."

Mollified, Mrs. O'Reilley nodded. "Of course. I didn't think about that when I knocked. But what about the room?"

"I'll be staying through tonight, and I'll pay you for it now, if you want me to. But I'd like to ask a favor. I'm going to get some breakfast, and I'd take it real kindly if you'd have a tub full of hot water waiting in the bathroom when I get back."

Surveying his clothes, she nodded. "I'd say you need it, Mr. Long. Don't worry. I'll fix your bath while you eat."

Leaving by the side door to avoid passing through the saloon, Longarm made his way to the restaurant. After a meal of fried eggs and bacon and several cups of hot black coffee he felt more like his usual self. Leaving the café, the red-and-white pole in front of the barbershop caught his eye, and the thought of getting rid of his stubble suddenly became so appealing that he walked on down to the shop. He was beginning to feel more like his usual self again when he returned to the Ritz.

A long, luxurious soaking in the tin bathtub completed his restoration. Though the tub was a size and a half too small,

Longarm lolled in the bath until the water cooled. He pulled on fresh balbriggans and stepped across the hall to his room to find that while he'd been bathing Mrs. O'Reilley had brushed and sponged his clothing into some semblance of freshness.

Puffing a freshly lighted cheroot, Longarm stepped into his pants and picked up his boots. Before he had time to put them on, the noise of rumbling wheels and the thumping of hoofbeats from the street drew him to the window.

He pulled aside an edge of the tattered shade just in time to see the first of a line of four crowded stagecoaches pull up in front of the building, and realized that the sightseers from the East had at last arrived. Longarm watched as the other three coaches halted behind the first, and the new arrivals began descending from the stages.

Longarm made no effort to count them accurately, but he guessed that forty-five or fifty people had gotten off the stage-coaches; there were half a dozen children and about equal numbers of men and women. They stood for a few minutes in a sort of pulsing knot around the vehicles, talking and laughing, as the drivers started unloading luggage from the boots. Soon they began to scatter. A number of the men had headed for the saloon the minute they stepped out of the coaches, and others soon followed. Some carried suitcases and portmanteaus into the side door that led to the Ritz's rooms. A few went into the café.

Three or four of the women had sketch pads, and these left the group quickly, walking along the street in search of subjects for their pencils to record. One woman carried an easel and paintbox; she walked across the street beyond the edges of the houses, set up the easel, put an artboard panel on it, and began a picture of the sun-drenched landscape to the east.

After he'd watched the new arrivals disperse, Longarm changed his mind about going down to the saloon for a drink. He dropped his boots beside the bed and stretched out on the bumpy mattress. He lay back and closed his eyes and, in spite of the strange thumps from the hallway as the new arrivals went into their rooms and the muffled hum of voices on the street outside, he was asleep in a few moments.

Voices raised in anger woke Longarm from a dreamless sleep. The room was dim, and he realized with a start that he'd slept through the afternoon. For a moment he did not realize what

170

had roused him, then realized why he'd been awakened when voices reached his ears, carrying easily through the thin partition separating his room from the one adjoining. As he listened, no great deductive effort was needed to tell Longarm that a man and a woman were in the middle of a quarrel.

"Now, damn it, Beth! It's not my fault you don't like this trip!" a man's voice said. "You told me you've always wanted to see the Grand Canyon. I thought you'd enjoy it."

"To be truthful, Albert, I was enjoying the trip very much until I realized how much it's costing me." The woman named Beth was bitingly sarcastic. "I've always understood that the bridegroom pays for the honeymoon."

"I just made a mistake when I figured how much money we were going to need."

Beth's voice was cold as she replied. "That's what you said in Chicago, when you asked me to lend you that ten thousand dollars. And you promised you'd wire your bank for more money before we left there."

"I did, but there must've been some kind of mixup. If they wired me the money, I didn't get it before we left."

"Then why didn't you wire again in Denver? We were there for three days. You certainly had plenty of time."

"We were doing so many things that I—I just forgot."

"You certainly knew you'd need more money. It would have been easy to wire your bank again."

"Well, we'd've had enough, but I got unlucky in that poker game on the train. Anyhow, I don't see what you're making such a fuss about," he said sullenly. "Don't forget, Beth, the minute you became Mrs. Albert Beasley, what was yours became mine."

"This is the second time you've said that, Albert." Beth's voice was thoughtful. "And it doesn't happen to be the case."

"What d'you mean?"

"Have you forgotten the marriage agreement you signed?"

"Oh, that thing! Now, you know that was just something your old man had his fancy lawyers fix up to try to scare me off. It didn't work, because here we are, married. We don't have to pay any attention to it."

"I'm afraid we do, Albert," Beth said coldly. "And I just hope you understood the terms."

"Now, Beth, you know your father never did like me! If his damn lawyers saw a way to trick me, he'd tell 'em to go ahead and do it. But what's that got to do with anything?"

"Because under Clause Three of that agreement, if you've misrepresented your financial condition and can't support me, or if you try to get me to give you my money, our marriage can be annulled."

"Oh, don't talk that way, Beth!" Albert wheedled. "That's no way for a brand-new wife to feel! There's no way to send a wire from here, but I'll take care of it as soon as we get back to Denver. Now, come on over here and lay down with me, and let's cuddle a while before supper."

"I'm not interested, thank you."

"Getting high and mighty, aren't you?" Albert sneered. "I haven't mentioned it before, but you were a long way from being a virgin on our wedding night."

"I never pretended I was. Yes, there were men before you, Albert, and there'll be men after you! Now, this conversation bores me. I'm going out to look at this funny little town. As long as I'm here, I might as well see what there is to see."

Longarm heard the sharp bang of a door being slammed and the tapping of footsteps going down the hall. Fully awake now and thinking of the final steps that were ahead in closing his case, he pulled on his boots, finished dressing, and went downstairs to the saloon.

Passengers from the stagecoaches were lined up three deep at the bar. Scanlon and another man, whom Longarm had not seen before, were busy serving drinks. Scanlon saw Longarm enter and gestured for him to step down to the end of the bar. Longarm did so, and after a few moments the salonkeeper joined him.

"I've been wondering where you were," Scanlon said, taking a bottle of Tom Moore from beneath the bar and setting it in front of Longarm.

"Catching up on some of the shuteye I lost lately. I guess I'd still be sleeping if a couple of your rubbernecks in the room next to me hadn't started fussing and woke me up."

"Nobody in Tuba City gets much sleep while the stages are in town," Scanlon said. "They'll be leaving at daybreak, and things will settle down."

Frowning thoughtfully, Longarm said, "I guess I better wait till they pull out tomorrow before I bother you about getting them money bags you got locked up."

"It'd be better if you don't try to leave before the stages

172

do," Scanlon agreed. "The livery stable's busy, so is the café. Why don't I knock on your door in the morning as soon as things get quiet? Then I'll give you a hand loading your sacks and we'll have a drink together before you pull out."

"That'll suit me just fine," Longarm agreed. He put a cart-wheel on the bar. "I owe you more'n this for that bottle of whiskey I had last night, but it'll pay for the drink I just had and we'll square up for the rest tomorrow."

"Don't worry about it," the saloonkeeper said. "I'm not."

Outside, the night air was cool, but Tuba City was like an anthill that had been disturbed. The stagecoach passengers were rested now, and exploring what few places there were in town to see. Lights glowed from the few businesses and, peering down the street, Longarm could see a crowd of customers waiting to get into the general store.

Looking in the other direction, he could see that the café was full, but not overcrowded. Having missed one meal that day, Longarm was not of a mind to miss another. He strolled down and went in, and stood just inside the door waiting for a seat at either the counter or a table. One of the men sitting at the counter got up and Longarm stepped over to take the place he'd vacated.

Sitting down, Longarm idly scanned the faces at the tables while he waited for service. The man whose place he'd taken was paying the proprietor, and a warning bell chimed in Longarm's mind. There was something familiar about the way the man moved when he left the café. Longarm began searching his memory, but the stranger's face did not register on it. Longarm was about to dismiss the feeling that he should recognize the man when he remembered the conversation he'd overheard in the next room. His sudden recall sent him jumping to his feet out of the crowded restaurant.

When he got outside, he saw the man trying to push through the crowd in front of the Ritz. The man looked back, and when he saw Longarm following him, redoubled his efforts to break through the group. Speeding up, Longarm hurried after him, but the clots of rubberneckers on the street delayed his progress. By the time he'd gotten through the group around the doors of the Ritz Saloon, the fugitive was pushing through a similar crowd in front of the store. Longarm lost sight of him momentarily, then saw him break away from the crowd and continue down the street.

A saddled horse was tethered at the hitch rail in front of the Deluxe Saloon. Over the heads of the crowd, Longarm saw his quarry heading for the animal. There was no way for Longarm to reach him. He started to draw his Colt, but the crowd pressing around him delayed his draw. Before he could reach the cleared area beyond the crowd, where he could shoot safely, the fugitive had mounted the horse and galloped off into the darkness.

Reluctantly, Longarm gave up. He knew that by the time he'd gotten to the livery stable and saddled his filly, the fugitive would be lost to the night and to distance. Holstering his Colt, not relishing the job he faced, he returned to the Ritz, went upstairs, and rapped at the door of the room adjoining his.

He heard the room's occupant stirring. Then the door was flung open. Longarm faced a very pretty young woman. Mrs. Beasley's face was square, with high cheeks and a firm chin. Her eyes were blue and shadowed by long lashes. Her lips were full, her teeth white and even.

"If you've come back here to try to explain—" she began angrily. Then she stopped short and brought a hand up to her mouth. She said, "I'm sorry. I thought you were someone else."

"I sorta figured you did, ma'am. My name's Custis Long, and I'm a deputy U. S. marshal." Longarm displayed his badge as he spoke. "I'm afraid I got some bad news for you, Mrs. Beasley."

"How did you know my name?" she frowned. "And how did you know where to find me?"

"Well, if you don't mind me stepping inside for a minute, I can tell you everything about that, but you wouldn't want me to talk here in the hall where folks passing by might hear."

After a moment's hesitation, Beth Beasley moved to one side and motioned for Longarm to come in. Closing the door, she faced him and asked, "Now, what's this bad news you have?"

"I'm afraid your husband won't be coming back tonight," Longarm told her.

"I really don't care if he never comes back, Marshal, but I don't see how you got involved in what should be a private matter between Albert and me."

"His name's not Albert Beasley, ma'am. It's Cooter Howard, and I taken a hand because he's a wanted killer. He's married three nice young ladies like you, and killed 'em soon as he got all their money away from 'em."

Beth stared open-mouthed for a moment. Recovering her composure, she asked, "You're sure of this?"

"I'm sure, ma'am. He won't be coming back, and he'll be too busy running to bother you again." Watching closely as Beth quickly recovered her composure, Longarm decided she'd be quite competent to make her own decision as to the course she should follow. He went on, "Now, maybe the best thing you can do is go on with the stages down to the Grand Canyon, and when you get home, talk to a lawyer and see what's the quickest way to get free."

"Yes. Yes, of course. Well, thank you for telling me what happened, Marshal Long. I'll make up my mind what to do now."

Relieved that he wouldn't be called on to wet-nurse an hysterical woman, Longarm walked slowly back to the café. He ate a long-delayed supper, decided he had no wish to return to the crowded saloon, and went up to his room.

Guess you can't win 'em all, old son, Longarm told himself philosophically a half-hour later. He was lying stretched out on the bed, finishing his cigar. *At least you saved that young lady a lot of trouble, and maybe her life, too. Anyhow, you done your best. And you better be getting your shuteye now, because Scanlon's going to be knocking at the door sooner than you want him to.*

Chapter 20

When Longarm opened the door of his room to Scanlon's knock the following morning, the saloonkeeper greeted him with a mock-serious grimace and shook his head. He said, "You don't know when to stop, do you, Longarm? I hear you just missed catching another crook of some kind last night."

"He got too much of a head start," Longarm replied. "He's grown a moustache and side whiskers since I seen him last. If I'd recognized him sooner, I'd've had him."

"Was he as bad as the ones you just wiped out?"

"Well, he was a killer, and a sneaky one."

"Murder's not a federal crime, though," Scanlon frowned. "How'd he happen to get crossways of a federal marshal?"

"Oh, he married a rich Chippewa squaw over in the Indian Nation and done her in. The Indian police couldn't do anything outside the reservation, so we got the case."

"Too bad you didn't catch him," Scanlon said. "Well, if you're ready, let's go. The rubberneck stages pulled out a half-hour ago, so there won't be anybody to bother us."

"We'll walk down to the livery stable and get the wagon then," Longarm said.

"No need. Old Belai's driving it up here. Sam Church saw there wasn't a water keg in it, so he fixed one up and put in a bucket. I figured you'd want to ride the wagon seat, so I had them hitch your filly to the tailgate. We can load right away, unless you'd rather eat breakfast first."

"If it's all the same to you, let's load first and then eat. I had supper late last night, so I need to work up an appetite."

With both Longarm and Scanlon working, loading the bags of money into the wagon was the work of only a few minutes. After sliding a sack of soda crackers and cheese under the seat to augment his depleted rations, Longarm tossed his bedroll and saddle gear into the wagon bed. The tarpaulin that had sheltered the money bags in the canyon had somehow been placed in the wagon, and Longarm lashed it over the load before he and Scanlon went to the café for breakfast.

During the meal, the two men were almost completely silent. They finished their coffee and walked back to the wagon. As they drew close to it, Longarm said, "Getting that wagon loaded is another job I got to thank you for helping me with. You been a real big help on this case, and I sure do appreciate it."

"I'm glad I was around to do it. I've learned a lot of things that people in a town like this need to do, and some that they ought not to do," Scanlon replied. "It was a dirty mess, but it could've been a lot worse."

"Sure, but thanks anyhow. Now, you figure up how much I owe you for what you're outa pocket. I pay for my own whiskey, so I'll settle for the drinks you've stood me, and I'll see you get a voucher for jobs like burying them outlaws and all."

Scanlon shook his head. "You and the government don't owe me or anybody else here a penny. I'm inclined to think that some of us in Tuba City are to blame for most of your trouble."

"How's that?"

"Why, if we hadn't brought Colby in, or if we'd kept an eye on him, Ferguson wouldn't have been able to use him to do the real dirty work, and this mess never would've gotten started."

Longarm shook his head. "If a man's going wrong, he'll go, even if he's got to climb over a ten-foot wall or bust through an iron door. Nobody's to blame for what happened but Ferguson and Colby and the others in it with 'em."

"You're probably right. Anyhow, you don't owe anybody anything. And I wish you good luck in closing your case."

After a final handshake, Longarm climbed up to the bullet-riddled wagon seat and pulled the team around. He headed down the trail, looking back and waving just before it curved south toward Flagstaff. Through the morning he let the horses work off their friskiness, then held them in to a steady pace that would put the miles behind without straining them.

He rested the team at noon, and in the late afternoon passed Cameron without stopping, intent on making as many miles as possible before dark. When the colors of the Painted Desert to the east began to change their hues in the reddening light of the setting sun, he started looking for a place to stop for the night. He had not yet reached the point where the steep cliffs that rose on both sides of the Little Colorado gave way to gentle banks, and in spite of its glowing colors the Painted Desert offered few spots where a wagon and team could shelter.

Just before dark, Longarm found the kind of place he'd been looking for, a low rock outcrop with a vee formation big enough to pen the horses into but small enough for the wagon to be used to block the mouth of the vee. Unhitching, he led the team and the filly into the vee and dropped the wagon tongue to close its front opening. Going back to the tailgate, he untied the rope to free a corner of the tarpaulin. He flipped the canvas back, and then jumped away from the wagon, his hand dropping to the butt of his Colt, as Beth Beasley sat up and gazed at him.

"I'm sorry I surprised you, Marshal Long," she smiled.

"You're just lucky you didn't get shot!" Longarm scolded. "Will you tell me just exactly what you're doing here?"

"I just couldn't stay in Tuba City and face those people when they got back from the Grand Canyon and found out what a fool I'd made of myself. So, when I overheard you and the barkeep talking about you going down to Flagstaff in a wagon, I just watched for my chance and stowed away in it."

"Well, why in the—" Longarm began, then went on, "Why in tunket didn't you just come ask me for a ride down to Flagstaff?"

"Because I was sure if I did you'd say no," she told him, holding out a hand for him to help her to the ground. "And you would have, wouldn't you?"

Beth's head barely reached Longarm's shoulder. He stared down at her for a moment before replying truthfully, "I guess I would. But you didn't have to stay hid under that tarpaulin all day."

"I wasn't going to. I planned to come out about noon, but when I found out you had a spare horse, I thought you might make me ride back by myself unless we'd come a long way."

Longarm grunted. "You're pretty smart at figuring, Mrs. Beasley. But it's been a real hot day. You must've just about smothered."

"I did," she admitted. "But it was better than riding all the way back to Denver with that bunch of gossipy sightseers.

And, if you don't mind, please call me Beth. I don't want to hear the name Beasley again as long as I live."

"You're lucky you're still alive to hear it now."

Beth nodded. "I overheard you and Mr. Scanlon talking this morning. That's one readon I decided to hide in the wagon. Albert might've laid in wait for me on the road back to Grand Junction, or even followed me in Denver."

"Well, I don't think you got much to worry about, going with me to Flagstaff. And you can catch a Santa Fe train there that makes connections to the East."

"That's what I plan to do, if you don't mind my company."

"Tell you the truth, I'm glad you're along, Beth. A man gets tired of talking to horses," Longarm smiled. "Now, let's rustle up some supper. I bet you're as hungry as I am."

"I'll bet I'm hungrier, Marshal Long. While you were eating this morning, I was crawling intc this wagon. I'm starving!"

"Well, when you're hungry anything tastes good, so let's get started, Beth. And while it's on my mind, if I'm going to call you by your first name, you might as well stop being so formal with me. I got a sorta nickname my friends call me—"

"Longarm," Beth broke in. "I heard the barkeep call you that, but I didn't know how you'd feel about me using it."

"I'd like it better'n Marshal Long. Now, let's eat. It'll be dark in a few minutes, and we'll want to fix our bunks while we can still see what we're doing."

In spite of Longarm's intention to hurry through supper, he recognized Beth's need to talk out her troubles. She told him of a whirlwind courtship and hasty marriage, in spite of the warning of her wealthy father that the man who called himself Beasley was a fortune hunter.

"But I guess I didn't really admit to myself what a fool I'd been until you recognized him back there in Tuba City," she concluded. "And I guess you saved me from getting killed sooner or later, like that wife he had in the Indian Nation."

"Oh, you'd've caught onto him before then, Beth," Longarm told her. "But we've set here jawing a long time, and daybreak's going to come mighty early. We better get to bed. Now, I'll fix a bedroll for you under the wagon, and take my saddle blanket and spread it out—"

Beth interrupted him. "Longarm, don't you think we're both old enough to make playing games a waste of time? I quit being a starry-eyed little girl more than ten years ago, and in those

179

ten years I've gotten to be a pretty good judge of men. I'll admit I was wrong about Albert, but I'm sure I'm not mistaken about you."

"Well, I hope you ain't. As long as both of us know that when we get to Flagstaff—"

"We'll say goodbye with a smile and walk away with happy memories," she broke in. "Now, spread the blankets and let's go to bed. Like you said, daybreak's going to come early."

Standing beside the wagon, they began undressing, both a bit self-conscious, aware of the blankets spread at their feet. Beth moved more quickly than Longarm. She stood waiting while he shed his balbriggans, a pale wraith in the dim star-shine. Longarm could see her high swelling breasts upthrust against the shadows that veiled her waist, their rosettes pale and almost invisible. Beth waited until he'd dropped his bal-briggans to the ground and then stepped up to him, her hands seeking his upthrust shaft.

"Oh, how nice!" she exclaimed. "I'm glad now that I spoke up, Longarm. You've really got a lot to give a woman!"

Longarm did not answer. His face was buried in Beth's full breasts, inhaling the woman-scent that flowed warmly from the deep cleft between them. He brushed his lips over the smooth globes, feeling their tips pebble and grow firm under the softly insistent pressures of his lips and tongue.

Beth's body was vibrating now, small shivers of delight rippling through her. She pushed Longarm's rigid erection between her thighs and began moving her hips in a slow, easy rhythm.

Longarm's lips sought hers, and they clung together in a long kiss that Beth broke at last to gasp, "I don't want to wait any longer, Longarm! I want you in me! Now!"

She sank down to the blankets, pulling Longarm with her. He leaned above her, Beth guided him, and he sank into her moist warmth while she trembled and sighed with little throaty cries of delight. She stirred, and he began thrusting in a slow measured rhythm. Beth's sighs grew into gasping moans as Longarm speeded up the tempo of his thrusts.

Beth's moans became cries and her body writhed beneath him as he sank into her again and again, driving harder and faster until her body began trembling and her response to his thrusts lifted her hips in a frantic rhythm that continued long after her climactic cry rose in the still night air. Longarm continued his stroking, but at a gentler pace, until Beth's trembling ended. He stopped then and lay quietly as she relaxed beneath him.

After a long silence, Beth said, "You're still filling me, Longarm. Was I too quick for you?"

"Don't worry about it, Beth. It'll take me a little while longer, is all."

"You mean you're ready to start again?"

"Whenever you are."

"I'm always ready," she smiled. "So what're we waiting for? When I'm with a man like you, the night's always too short, and I don't want to waste a minute of this one!"

Longarm waved for the last time as the observation car of the eastbound Santa Fe Limited dropped down the Walnut Canyon grade and Beth was hidden from sight. He went into the depot and up to the window where the telegrapher sat in front of his silent key. Opening his wallet, he showed the brass-pounder his badge.

"I got to send a private message to my chief in Denver," he said. "There's a key in the federal building there, and you can tap into it through your Denver station circuit."

"Well, I never have tried it before, but you seem to know what you're talking about," the operator said. "Let's see what I can set up."

Within a quarter of an hour Longarm was dictating to the telegrapher a message that went direct to Billy Vail, who was standing by the key in the basement of the federal building in Denver. As briefly as possible, he informed the chief marshal of Ferguson's death, and of the moves he needed to make to close the case.

Vail's answer was brief and to the point:

WIRING HQ TO SEND NEW MARSHAL TO FLAGSTAFF STOP WIRING ARMY HQ TO SEND PROVOST MARSHAL ON NEXT TRAIN FROM FORT WINGATE WITH INSTRUCTIONS YOU ARE TO HAVE FULL CHARGE IN CLOSING CASE STOP DO IT AND GET BACK HERE

After he'd thought over Vail's message for a moment, Longarm asked the telegrapher, "That westbound passenger that pulls in here about dark, what time does it leave from Gallup?"

"Three-ten," the brass-pounder replied promptly. "Gets in here at seven-twenty."

Longarm glanced at the railroad clock on the station wall. It's hands stood at high noon. Nodding thoughtfully, he thanked the telegrapher. Then, since he and Beth had pulled into town that morning with barely enough time to get her a ticket on the eastbound train, he left the wagon in care of the baggagemaster and walked the short distance to the Harvey House.

After he'd registered and eaten the best meal he'd had since leaving on his trip north, Longarm went up to his room. For an hour he soaked in a tub of hot water, and for another hour or so he napped. Toward five o'clock, Longarm left the hotel and took his time finding a saloon whose looks he liked. He sipped Tom Moore while enjoying a cigar, and returned to the Harvey House for a light supper before going back to the depot.

At a quarter past seven, Longarm was standing on the station platform, waiting for the westbound train. It huffed in and came to a halt with a final squeal of brakes. Longarm's jaw dropped when Beth was the first passenger to alight.

"Longarm!" she called, running to him and wrapping her arms around him. Longarm was so lost in her kiss that he almost missed seeing the Army officer who had followed her off the train. Beth released him at last and said, "I'm such a fool! I didn't think until the train was halfway to Gallup that we could go on to Denver together."

Longarm saw the officer scanning the platform with a puzzled frown. He told Beth, "You just stay right here for a minute. I got some business that's got to be tended to first." Walking over to the officer, he said, "Sorry I kept you waiting, Colonel, but the young lady—"

"Yes, so I noticed. You're Marshal Long, I assume. I'm James Sexton. I hope you can explain the orders I got at Fort Wingate, because I certainly don't understand them."

"Colonel, if you'll just be kind enough to wait for me while I take that young lady over to the Harvey House, I'll be back here in about two minutes," Longarm promised.

"Since my orders are to place myself under your command until you release me, I don't have much choice," Sexton replied. Then he added quickly, "Of course I don't mind waiting, Marshal. I think I'd want to see that she was safe, if she'd greeted me the way she did you."

Longarm's two minutes stretched to ten, and he was smiling when he returned to the depot. He said, "I don't know if you're a drinking man, Colonel, but explaining them orders to you is going to take a little time. I figure we might as well enjoy it as sit here and talk in the depot."

"At least we'll start out by agreeing about something," Sexton said. "Lead the way, Marshal. I'm right with you."

Almost two hours later, Longarm pulled up the wagon in front of the sentry box at the Navajo Ordnance depot.

"I got some stuff to deliver to Colonel Brady," he told the sentry. "I know where his quarters is. I been there before."

Waved on by the sentry, Longarm wheeled the wagon to the depot commander's quarters at the side of the drill ground. He swung to the ground and tapped at the door. Halloran opened it and recognized Longarm at once.

"Is the colonel expecting you, Marshal?" the orderly asked.

"He ain't exactly expecting me, but I'd imagine he'll be right glad to see me," Longarm told the soldier.

"You'd better come in, then. I'll tell him you're here."

Brady came down the hallway a few minutes later. He was in officers' fatigues, and looked as bandbox-fresh as he would have in dress uniform. He did not appear to be happy, however. His brow was furrowed into a frown and his lips were compressed as he looked at Longarm. "What brings you here at this hour, Marshal Long? I hope you haven't run into trouble."

"Well, I ain't had what you'd call an easy trip," Longarm replied. "But you'll be glad to know I got the money back."

His frown deepening, Brady exclaimed, "The hell you say!"

"I sure wouldn't be here if I didn't have it to show you, Colonel," Longarm said calmly. "It's in a wagon right outside, still in the bags it was put in at the mint."

"Did you get back *all* of it?" Brady asked.

"I hope so. But I can't let go of it till you and Major Craven count the bags. They're still all sealed up, so there ain't no question but what it's all there. Soon as you finish counting and give me a receipt, I can turn it over to you and be on my way back to Denver."

"Well..." Brady hesitated. "I suppose if we went by the book, I'd have you pull the wagon over to Major Craven's office. However, it's late, and I'm sure you're in a hurry to get this over with. Suppose I just ask the major to step over here, and we'll unload the money in my quarters long enough to count it."

"That'll be fine with me," Longarm agreed. "It'll save us time all the way around."

"Halloran, inform Major Craven and tell him to report here with his sidearm on," Brady said. "And just so we can't be accused of being careless, put on your own weapon and join us."

When Craven arrived, Longarm led the three Army men out to the wagon. As they approached it he said, "You ain't asked, but there was some shooting when I tangled with the gang. They're all dead now."

"You mean you killed them all singlehanded?" Craven asked.

"Oh, I had some help from Marshal Ferguson and the Tuba City marshal, fellow named Colby," Longarm replied quite truthfully. "I couldn't've broke this case without them two."

"Then you'll be seeing Ferguson when you leave here?" Brady asked.

"No, I don't guess I will. My job's finished when I turn this money over to you," Longarm answered. He turned to the wagon and began working at the knot holding the tarpaulin. "I'll just loosen this and—" He stopped short as he felt the cold muzzle of a gun jammed into his neck.

Craven said harshly, "You don't have to untie the tarp, Long. In fact, if you move, you're a dead man."

"I don't—" Longarm began.

"Of course you don't understand. Ferguson did his job very well," Brady said. He turned to his orderly. "Halloran, get a horse from the stables and take Long into town. Turn him over to Ferguson." When the orderly had gone, Brady told Craven, "We'll let Ferguson do the dirty work of getting rid of Long."

"Now, wait a minute!" Longarm protested. "I didn't—"

"Shut up!" Brady snapped. "You're a damn fool, Long! I was afraid you'd suspect the major and me, but it seems you're not as smart as your reputation makes you."

"You mean you and the major was in on this all along?" Longarm asked.

"It won't do any harm to tell you now," Craven replied. "We're the ones who planned the whole thing. Ferguson did his part, of course, and he brought Colby into it."

"I guess I don't see—" Longarm began.

"Of course you don't!" Brady broke in. "Damn it, we're

all due to retire soon—Craven and me, and Ferguson, too! We need this money to keep from starving on our pensions."

In that instant the tarpaulin was thrown aside and Colonel Sexton rose from the wagonbed, a Colt in his hand, covering Craven. Craven turned in surprise and, with a lightning-like move, Longarm twisted away from the muzzle of the threatening pistol. He swept out his own Colt and joined Sexton in covering the two officers.

"I've heard all I need, Long," Sexton said. "Drop your gun, Craven! Brady, you stand still! You're both under arrest, and I don't have to tell you where you'll wind up, with Halloran to keep you company."

Longarm said, "You can go rouse the other officers, Colonel Sexton. I'll guarantee that if these two move it'll be the last thing they do."

After Sexton had left, Brady asked, "But what about Ferguson, Long? He's not going to go free, is he?"

"Ferguson's dead," Longarm said curtly. "So's Colby."

"Did those bastards give us away?" Craven asked.

"They didn't need to," Longarm said. "Right from the start, this smelled like an inside job, and you two men were the only ones who could've planned it. You needed the others to help, but then you wanted to get rid of 'em to keep from splitting the money so many ways, so you brought in Ferguson and Colby to do the dirty work. But with everybody else dead, the only way I could get you cold was to make you confess, so I planned this little surprise party."

Before the two could find their voices, Sexton returned with the military police squad. As Brady and Craven were being led away, Longarm turned to Sexton and said, "Colonel, I got one little favor to ask of you. Lend me a horse to ride back to town on. You don't need me here, but I know somebody who does."

Five minutes later, Longarm was riding toward Flagstaff and the Harvey House, where Beth awaited him.

Watch for

Longarm on the Ogallala Trail

seventieth novel in the bold
LONGARM series from Jove

coming in October!

LONGARM

Explore the exciting Old West with
one of the men who made it wild!

__07524-8	LONGARM #1	$2.50
__07142-0	LONGARM AND THE TOWN TAMER #23	$2.25
__07363-6	LONGARM AND THE RAILROADERS #24	$2.25
__06952-3	LONGARM AND THE DRAGON HUNTERS #26	$2.25
__07265-6	LONGARM AND THE RURALES #27	$2.25
__06629-X	LONGARM ON THE HUMBOLDT #28	$2.25
__07067-X	LONGARM ON THE BIG MUDDY #29	$2.25
__06581-1	LONGARM SOUTH OF THE GILA #30	$2.25
__06580-3	LONGARM IN NORTHFIELD #31	$2.25
__06582-X	LONGARM AND THE GOLDEN LADY #32	$2.25
__08062-4	LONGARM AND THE LAREDO LOOP #33	$2.50
__08059-4	LONGARM AND THE BOOT HILLERS #34	$2.50
__07727-5	LONGARM AND THE BLUE NORTHER #35	$2.50
__08063-2	LONGARM ON THE SANTA FE #36	$2.50
__08060-8	LONGARM AND THE STALKING CORPSE #37	$2.50
__08064-0	LONGARM AND THE COMANCHEROS #38	$2.50
__07412-8	LONGARM AND THE DEVIL'S RAILROAD #39	$2.50
__07413-6	LONGARM IN SILVER CITY #40	$2.50
__07070-X	LONGARM ON THE BARBARY COAST #41	$2.25
__07538-8	LONGARM AND THE MOONSHINERS #42	$2.50
__07525-6	LONGARM IN YUMA #43	$2.50
__07431-4	LONGARM IN BOULDER CANYON #44	$2.50
__07543-4	LONGARM IN DEADWOOD #45	$2.50
__07425-X	LONGARM AND THE GREAT TRAIN ROBBERY #46	$2.50

Prices may be slightly higher in Canada.

Available at your local bookstore or return this form to:

JOVE
Book Mailing Service
P.O. Box 690, Rockville Centre, NY 11571

Please send me the titles checked above. I enclose _____ Include 75¢ for postage
and handling if one book is ordered; 25¢ per book for two or more not to exceed
$1.75. California, Illinois, New York and Tennessee residents please add sales tax.

NAME _____

ADDRESS _____

CITY _____ STATE/ZIP_____
(allow six weeks for delivery.)

5